Rachel SINCLAIR
THE HATE CRIME

vinci
BOOKS

By Rachel Sinclair

Kansas City Legal Thrillers

Bad Faith

Justice Denied

Hidden Defendant

Injustice for All

L.A. Defense

The Associate

The Alibi

Reasonable Doubt

The Accused

The Hate Crime

Secrets and Lies

Until Proven Guilty

Vinci Books

vinci-books.com

Published by Vinci Books Ltd in 2026

1

Copyright © Rachel Sinclair 2018

The author has asserted their moral right to be identified as the author of this work in accordance with the Copyright, Designs and Patents Act 1988. This work is a work of fiction. Names, characters, places and incidents are the product of the author's imagination or are used fictitiously. Any resemblance to actual persons, living or dead, places and incidents is entirely coincidental.
All rights reserved. No part of this publication may be copied, reproduced, distributed, stored in any retrieval system, or transmitted in any form or by any means, including photocopying, recording, or other electronic or mechanical methods, nor used as a source for any form of machine learning including AI datasets, without the prior written permission of the publisher.
The publisher and the author have made every effort to obtain permissions for any third party material used in this book and to comply with copyright law. Any queries in this respect should be brought to the attention of the publisher and any omissions will be corrected in future editions.
A CIP catalogue record for this book is available from the British Library.
Paperback ISBN: 9781036703240

The EU GPSR authorised representative is Logos Europe, 9 rue Nicolas Poussion, 17000 La Rochelle, France
contact@logoseurope.eu

Chapter One

GOD, it was good to be back. There was a time when I thought I would never be free again. It wasn't looking good for my murder case there for awhile. Harper pulled it off at the last moment, however, and I was a free man. I couldn't thank her enough.

I got into my office, singing a song and carrying a cup of coffee. I immediately saw Heather was there, waiting for me. She'd been crying.

"Hey," I said to her. "Heather, what's going on?"

She just shook her head. "It's my boyfriend, Beck. He's been accused of something terrible. I don't know what to think. He says he didn't do it, and I think I believe him. I don't know." She looked up at me. "I want you to represent him."

I rubbed my hands together. It was time to get back into the game, and representing Heather's boyfriend would be a way of getting back into it.

"What about Harper? How come you don't want her to represent him?"

Heather rolled her eyes. "Beck don't like women representing him. He thinks women aren't aggressive enough. Shhh, don't tell Harper that, though. She'd be pissed."

I had to smile. I guessed Beck was just a little bit…old-fashioned? Whatever, a lot of men felt that way about women lawyers. For my money, nobody could match Harper in the courtroom, but you can't change attitudes, no matter how hard you try.

"Come on in my office," I said. "Let's get some facts together, and I can visit Beck. I'm assuming he's in jail?"

Heather nodded. "He is. God, he couldn't have done this. I just know he didn't do this."

I sat down at my desk and got out a yellow pad of paper. "What is he accused of doing?"

"He's accused of killing one of my sisters. By sister, I mean not an actual sister, but another transgendered woman. They're charging it as a hate crime."

To me, this seemed almost like an open and shut case. The guy was dating Heather, so that had to mean he was open to transgendered people, so it followed that Beck probably wasn't prejudiced against them, nor did he hate them. This couldn't be a hate crime.

"I don't see this being a problem. I can get the prosecutors off the hate crime issue. And if I can get them to drop the hate crime designation, that's the first step."

"That's not good enough," Heather said. "I need for you to try to get him off, period. I don't want him going to prison at all."

"Well, of course you don't want him going to prison. Who wants to see someone they love or like going to prison? It's not always realistic, however."

Heather crossed her arms in front of her. She tapped her foot. "I need for you to approach this case like you can win it. It doesn't sound like you're that confident about it."

"I'm *not* confident about it. I never am when I first get a case. Let me get into it. Let me talk to Beck and do my investigation. I'll find out if he's good for the crime. Just like any other case."

"Go and talk to him. He's in the Jackson County jail. He can't make bond. I'm going to have to pay your fee. I was hoping maybe I could do work for you, in lieu of the fee. Would that be possible?"

"How well do you know this guy?" I had the feeling Heather didn't really know this Beck person that well. I got that impression because she'd been working for Harper and me for awhile and I never heard her talk about this guy. Heather was an open book. If she'd been dating this guy for awhile, I would've heard about it.

"I know him well enough." Heather was getting defensive.

"Meaning?"

"Meaning I know him well enough. That's all you need to know."

"No, I need to know more than that. Listen, I consider you a friend, as well as being a very good employee. That means I care about you. I want to make sure he's really worth it if you're going to pay his way. I'm going to have to charge my usual $400 per hour fee for him. If you're paying for him, and going to be working it off, you'll be working for me for free for quite a while. So I just need to know he's worth it."

She looked down and crossed her arms in front of her. "I-"

"I need to know one thing. Do you have sex with this guy?"

"What does that have to do with anything?" She was becoming evermore defensive, not that I blamed her.

"Does he know you're a transgendered woman? Or does he think you're just a woman? Does he know you still have male parts?"

She looked embarrassed. "No. He thinks I'm a woman. No, we've never had sex. I mean, I've blown him, but that's as far as its gone. He's asked to have sex with me but I won't do it. I haven't found a way to tell him I'm biologically a male."

That did it. I didn't trust this guy. Just from what she told me, I didn't trust him. "How long have you been seeing him?"

"For a couple of weeks."

"Why does it mean so much that he not know the truth about your biology?"

"Because I don't think he'd accept it."

"That makes no sense to me. After all, if you guys will keep dating, doesn't that mean he'll have to eventually find out about it? And when he does, he'll be really upset, don't you think? Even if he's not prejudiced against LGBT, he'll still be angry with you because you've hidden this from him. You're just digging a hole."

"Why is it your business if I'm digging a hole with him or not?"

"I told you, I'm looking out for you. Listen, I'm sure there are men out there who are okay with dating a transgendered person."

"Oh yeah? How do you know so much about it?"

"I guess I don't. At least not first-hand. Obviously. I just think there's a lid for every pot out there. There's no need for you to settle for somebody who might not like the real you. That's all I'm saying."

The Hate Crime

I also was concerned that my initial hunch might not have been true - that Beck couldn't possibly be prejudiced against transgendered people if he was dating one. If he didn't know Heather was transgendered, that theory went out the window.

She looked ashamed. "Well, here's the thing. It's not as easy as you might think to find somebody to date me with my male parts still intact. How many men do you know who would date a chick with a dick? They either want a woman or they want a man. They don't want people like me."

"Well, it's true enough that it's hard for anybody to find a lasting relationship. I can see your dilemma. I just think it's better for you to keep on looking for somebody who would want to date a transgendered woman."

"Okay, I get the lecture. I understand what you're saying. Are you going to take his case or not?" She obviously wasn't having any of my advice. Her loss.

"I don't know. I still think you'll end up owing me thousands of dollars, I'll get him off, and then he'll dump you. You'll be left holding the bag. That's what I'm worried about."

She sighed. "I'll go ahead and risk that. You know I'm good for his lawyer fee. You know I won't cheat you. So what's the problem?"

"Nothing, nothing. I just hope you know what you're doing. And if he really doesn't know you're a transgendered woman, there's still a possibility this might be a hate crime. If I thought he was dating you while knowing you're transgendered, then that would make me feel more comfortable in taking this case, because it would make it less likely this actually was a hate crime. Not saying it's totally impossible this was a hate crime if he was dating you while knowing you're transgendered, but it would make it less likely.

However, I'll be starting from the ground floor, trying to figure out if this was a hate crime or not."

"I'm telling you, it wasn't a hate crime. And he didn't do it."

"Whatever. Okay, let me go down and talk to him. Just talk to him. I won't make any kind of promises to you. I'll just visit him and talk."

She nodded her head. "That's all I can ask for at this point."

"Well, worst case, he gets a Public Defender. There are worse things in the world than that. I know that for fact. I was a PD and I can tell you that the people in that office are among the most dedicated and intelligent people I know. He could definitely do a lot worse."

"I know that. But I don't want him to have a Public Defender. I want him to have you. I trust you. I mean, what if he gets a Public Defender who's prejudiced against him? You never know. He looks a little rough. And I want to work on his case too. I want to get involved."

"I understand that. Okay, I'll see him and let you know. That's all I can promise for now."

She nodded her head. "That's all I ask." Then she smiled. "You'll take his case. I know it."

I certainly wasn't as sure as she was.

I hoped she realized that.

Chapter Two

THAT NIGHT, I went to see the guys. They were doing pretty well. Actually, they were doing *very* well. Connor, in particular, was doing something near and dear to his heart. He knew how lucky he was to be on the outside. He assumed he would be in prison for the rest of his life and there was no hope for him. When he was given a second lease on life, he decided to do something to make himself proud. So, he'd already enrolled in the University of Missouri-Kansas City program for social work. As he told me, he wanted to help people who were on his same path so they could possibly avoid it.

On the weekends, he volunteered at a sober living facility. At the moment, he was more or less doing dishes, laundry and things like that. He didn't know enough to really get into counseling, but he wanted to help out as much as he could.

Tommy was working construction. Nick, who had been caught up in the whole Josh drama, had been looking for a job, but I managed to talk Tom Garrett into hiring him as an assistant. Tom had already hired Jack O'Brien, Connor's older brother. Then he hired Nick, so the three of them were doing investigations for Harper and me, as well as several of Tom's other private clients.

I knew Nick and Jack, the same as Tom Garrett, would do well with this job. After all, they were from the streets. They spoke the language. They knew the guys they were dealing with. They also did well with the psychology of it all. The three of them could do a good job of investigating all types of crimes.

I was proud of my boys. I was proud they landed on their feet so quickly. Granted, I helped them out by buying them all cars. It seemed like that the least I could do for them. Other than that, they did everything on their own.

That night, we got together at a bar. I tried to see them at least once a week.

"Hey!" Connor spotted me first. He waved his bottle of beer into the air as I approached the table. They had already ordered nachos. Connor handed me a menu as I sat down. "Look at this and see what else you'd like to have."

"I'll just have nachos with you guys."

"Then I guess we'll have to order another one."

I found the waitress and ordered a whiskey and seven and another order of nachos. Then I went to the table and joined the guys.

We chatted for a while, and then Connor asked me if I could take a case for him.

"As you know, I'm working at that sober living facility, and there's a girl there whose name is Tina. She's been in and out of jail for drug possession for most of her life. And she got caught again, this time for distribution. They caught her with 5 kilos of coke and are offering her 5 years in prison."

The Hate Crime

"Sucks to be her." I shook my head. "I suppose you want me to represent her? Is that why you're telling me about her?"

"Yeah. That's what I was hoping. Listen, she told me she distributed drugs because she had to. She's scared to death of her boyfriend, who is also her pimp, and he's been using her as his mule. He's been sending her over the border to pick up drugs and said if she doesn't do that for him, he'll kill her. So that's the reason she was caught distributing drugs. I'd like for you to fight for her."

I shook my head. "Okay, here's the thing. As long as the boyfriend's in the picture, she'll keep on doing this. Isn't that right?"

Connor shook his head. "Well, no. Actually that's not the truth."

"And why is that? Why won't this keep happening again and again, as long as this guy's in the picture? If something happens, and I talk to the prosecutor and get some kind of a deal for her, probation or Drug Court or something like that, she'll be right back on the streets again. And she'll be dealing again. What am I missing here?"

"Well, here's the thing. The guy forcing her into this, his name is Larry Rodriguez, got caught himself. And he's in jail. He got caught with a firearm and he's a felon, so he's being tried in federal court. So he's out of the picture."

I nodded. "So basically I have to show this was an extortion thing. A coercion thing. And what do I tell the prosecutor, when she asks, if this Tina person will get involved with the same kind of person? Who will force her into dealing some more drugs? And how do I find out if it's true what she's saying? How can I take her at her word that the only reason she was dealing was because she was forced into it?"

Connor was getting annoyed. "Just please, see what you can do about it."

I put my hand on his shoulder. "Connor, believe me, I know what you're doing. You know what prison is like. You're gonna try to save as many people you can from making the same mistakes you made. But you can't get so emotionally involved with the people you meet, especially your clients. That's the most important thing. Because when you do, trust me on this, you end up getting involved in bad situations. You have to look out for yourself. That's really the most important thing. And I know where you're coming from. I represent criminals and I'm the same way. I get emotionally involved, too. That's the worst thing you can do. Just stay detached."

Connor shook his head and looked at his beer. "I know. I know what you're saying. But this is different. I really feel bad for this person. I heard her story and what she's had to go through in her life. I just think she's worth a second chance. And you're right, if the person threatening her was still on the streets, it wouldn't do any good to actually try to get her off this charge. She would just be right back on the streets, dealing, if that were the case. But that's not the case. She has a chance to actually get out of the drug and prostitution life."

"Okay." I took a deep breath. "Why not? After all, I might be representing a Neo-Nazi. I don't know, however." I shook my head. "No, I shouldn't say that. I shouldn't jump to conclusions that Heather's boyfriend is a Neo-Nazi. I only know he's been accused of a hate crime. These are my first few cases after what happened with my dad. I'm getting my feet wet." I paused. "Alright, I'll take Tina's case. For you, buddy. Only for you."

"Thanks, buddy." He clinked his glass with mine.

I started to feel a bit of a scold with everybody. Like I was trying to tell them how to live their lives. That was never my intention. I just hated when people did stupid things. Like Heather. She didn't know this guy from Adam. Yet she was willing to hire me to represent him, which would cost her a lot of money. If it was Heather herself charged with a crime, I would've given her a break on my rates. But it wasn't Heather. It was her boyfriend. And not even that. I wouldn't give him a cut at all.

"Nick, Jack, I think I have something for the two of you. I don't know yet, though. I don't know if I'm taking this case. But stay tuned."

"Why?" Nick asked. "What kind of case you looking at?"

"A guy in jail right now, his name is Beck Harrison. He's been charged with killing a transgendered woman. I'm guessing this transgendered woman is a friend of Heather's. Anyhow, once I figure out if I'll take this case or not, I'll give you the information and you could maybe look at his background for me."

"You got it buddy," Nick said. "Just let us know."

"I will."

Chapter Three

"OKAY," Heather said to me when she came back into my office the next day. She had an envelope of money in her hand. "Here's a down payment. I've been saving money, as much as I can. I wanted to use this money to get my paralegal certificate but I need to do this."

I looked in the envelope of money, counted up the money inside, and saw it totaled $5,000 in hundred-dollar bills. I looked up at Heather.

"Okay, I really don't understand this. Seriously. Now you're giving me your schooling money, all to represent this guy you don't really know? You need to come clean with me about this. Who is this guy to you, really?"

"I'm telling you, he's just a guy I like. I'm digging him. That's it."

I pushed the envelope back to her. "You're not gonna give me your school money. I told you, you can work off my fee."

"But that's gonna take me years." She twirled her long black hair around one finger and pursed her lips.

I finally just sighed. "Okay. There's something you're not telling me. You don't have to tell me right now, but you'll have to tell me sooner or later, because I need to know. In the meantime, I'll talk to him and see what he has to say. If I think he's worthy of my representing him, I'll represent him. And I'll do it *pro bono*. I won't have you sacrificing your future to pay my legal fee. Harper requires me to do so many *pro bono* hours a year anyway. I might as well knock them out with this case." I didn't tell Heather I'd planned to get my *pro bono* hours with minor cases, not a murder case. What she didn't know wouldn't hurt her.

She looked down at the floor. "You don't have to do that."

"Of course I do. Listen, this obviously means a lot to you. I don't know why, but it does. And I'm not exactly hurting for money. I settled that wrongful death case a few years back, so I still have millions of dollars in the bank. I can afford to take a *pro bono* case here and there if I believe in it. That's the big caveat here. I have to believe in it."

Heather sighed. "Okay. I'll tell you the truth. But, I'll have to hire you for my own lawyer. Otherwise, I won't tell you a thing."

I knew it. I knew there was more to the story. "Okay. Out with it. You have to tell me why it's so important I represent this guy. There's obviously something you need to tell me, so go ahead. Once I get the whole story, I'll piece everything together and can tell you how I plan to proceed on this. So go ahead."

Heather took a deep breath. "You won't tell Harper about this, right? She'll kill me if she finds out."

This wasn't sounding so good. To say the least. "Go ahead, tell me what happened. Why do I have a feeling this guy, this Beck person, has something on you?"

Heather paused, looking ashamed. "He does. Harper knows a few years back, when I first got put into jail for killing my mother, I was dating this guy named Charlie. Charlie was a drug dealer. And he paid my lawyer fee back then. She knows I had to pay him back. And the way I paid him back was by bringing drugs from over the border to him. I never got caught doing that, either."

"Okay. Go ahead. What does Beck has to do with any of this?"

"Well, he has nothing to do with that. He wasn't involved in the drug mule issues. I didn't want to be involved with that either, but I had to do it for Charlie. I owed him all that money. I ended up paying Harper $20,000 for my murder case and didn't have that. No way could I have gotten that money. So I had to pay him back by carrying drugs for him over the border. I told Harper about this. She gave me a lecture, but I think she understood. She knew there was no other way I could pay that back."

I sat there, looking at her. I was trying to figure out what this whole Beck thing had to do with the Charlie thing.

"Okay," Heather finally said. "Listen, I want you to know one thing. I have a mother. A birth mother. I didn't even know about her until just recently. In fact, it was just a couple of years ago that I found I was adopted. Well, I found out about it, because my birth mother was the key witness in my case. If not for her testifying, I'd be in prison right now. What she did was very brave. I actually love her. I didn't love my adoptive mom, because she was one cray bitch. But this one's pretty cool."

"Okay. Go on and tell me what you need to tell me." I found myself holding my breath, because I had a feeling that what she would tell me was bad. Very bad.

The Hate Crime

Heather shook her head and looked down at the floor. "Well, she got sick. Very sick. I thought she was gonna die. They didn't know what was wrong with her, but they weren't doing much at the hospital because she didn't have insurance. They didn't run tests and all that. She was just really tired all the time, had very bad headaches and her joints were aching really bad, to the point where she couldn't even walk. She needed money and needed it fast. She needed cash for all the tests that had to be run to find out what was wrong with her."

"Okay. Go ahead."

Heather was quiet for a few minutes. "I didn't really know what to do, so I asked Charlie to help me out. He said he couldn't help. He was done with me. He was done with me romantically and done with giving me money, too. But he gave me Beck's name."

"So Beck is a friend of Charlie's, then? Is that what you're telling me?"

"Yeah, that's what I'm telling you. He was a friend of Charlie's. I don't know what he did for Charlie, or if he did anything at all for him, but somehow the two of them knew each other. And I needed money fast. I needed about $50,000, so my mom could get testing done. I'm glad I got that money for her. They found out she has Lyme disease. That's something that can kill you. She had to get treatment and that cost even more money."

I didn't know if I wanted to hear what Heather did for that money. But yet, I knew I was going to have to. "And what did you do for that money?"

"A job for Beck."

"And what was this job?" I didn't want to hear her answer. I knew it was illegal, to say the very least. How else would she get that kind of money in a short period of time?"

She took a deep breath. "I helped him burglarize a jewelry store. In fact, Beck and a friend planned it all out and I actually did the deed. I stole a bunch of jewelry." She looked down at the floor. "$750,000 worth of jewelry. I got 10%. That was enough money to make sure my mom got the testing and the treatment she needed. She's alive now, but only because of that money."

That was disgusting to me, at least the part about her mother, who would've died if Heather didn't knock off this jewelry store. What kind of a country allowed something like that - if you don't have money, you die? If you get sick, you get desperate enough to commit a crime to pay the medical bills? But that was neither here nor there.

"So, let me guess - Beck is threatening to turn you in. Is that what's going on? If so, I don't understand. He was the mastermind behind it. If he turns you in, you'll turn him in, and you both will go down."

"Yeah. But here's the thing. Beck and his friend, I'll say his name is Fred Johnson. That's not really his name but that's the name I want to give you - Fred and Beck have each other's backs. They're in it together. They're tight. Nobody caught us. But the two of them will hang me out to dry. That's what the problem is – I'm an outsider with them. Beck has already threatened me, telling me he'll tell the authorities I knocked off the jewelry store. So, yes, he has something on me. He told me if I can find him an attorney and pay for it, he'll leave me alone. So that brings me to you."

I rolled my eyes. "So that's the real reason you don't want Harper involved with this - because you know she's gonna smack you upside the head?"

The Hate Crime

"Yeah. That's why I don't want Harper involved. Although I think she'll understand. At least more than you apparently do. I told you, I did this for my mother. I saved her life. Doesn't that mean nothing to you?"

"Of course it does. But it doesn't negate that what you did was stupid. And now, here you are, being raked over the coals. And I'm frankly sick of taking these dog cases just because people are getting threatened. You're not the first person who has come in here, asking me to represent them, just because they're being blackmailed. I don't like it."

Heather crossed her arms in front of her. "So does that mean you won't take the case?"

"What'll happen if I don't?" I was inclined to turn her down.

"If you don't, Beck's gonna roll on me. And you're right, he's more liable than me, but with Beck and Fred backing each other up and hanging me out to dry, I'll probably be the one paying for this crime. That's what's gonna happen. I'll go to prison. And I'll have to pay back all that money I got from the jewelry store."

I sighed and shook my head. "No promises. I know, I know, you can be in big trouble if I don't do this for you. Here's the thing, though - if this guy is good for it, there's little I can do for him but plead him out. I mean, I can try it, but if I do, chances are he'll go down. Then he'll hate me and also hate you, and guess what? He'll roll on you to get his revenge, because criminals are irrational like that, and they also look for ways to get back at us defense attorneys when things go south. Even if he's *not* good for it, there are no guarantees. We could still lose at trial, and, once again, you're back to square one. Either way, you're going down. So-"

"Just try, alright? Just go see him. See what he has to say.

Then get back to me. In the meantime, I have some research projects due for Harper." At that, she got up and walked away.

Whatever. I would have to see this Beck person and see what he had to say. This wasn't exactly the way I envisioned coming back to my practice after being threatened with life in prison for the death of my father, but it was what it was.

Chapter Four

I GOT down to the Jackson County Jail to see Beck. I reviewed his file a little bit before I got there.

From the Statement of Information, I understood Beck apparently picked up a woman in a bar. This woman's name was Adele Whittier, who was transgendered and working as a nurse at Truman Med. Apparently, Adele and Beck met at a downtown bar called Zoo Bar, and the bartender, Quince Newton, told police they left together that night. Apparently, Adele was a regular at the bar, so that was how Quince knew who she was. She was the kind of person who would come to the bar early, sit at the bar and talk to the bartenders before the place got really crowded. Quince told the questioning officer that Beck and Adele had been talking and flirting all night. They left the bar around midnight, and the next day, Adele's body was found next to a dumpster in an alleyway by Beck's apartment. She'd been strangled and the time of death was calculated to be between 1 AM and 1:15 AM on the morning of June 6. Because Beck was the last person to see her alive, and because Adele's body was found in an alleyway by his apartment, he was charged with her murder.

Things didn't look too good. He was the last one to see her alive and her body was found by his apartment. At the same time, I knew this was all circumstantial evidence. There apparently was not an eyewitness and no murder weapon was found. I was encouraged there was a good possibility I could probably convince the jury he didn't kill her.

I had also looked through the statement that Beck had given to the police. Unfortunately, this was a hurdle I had to overcome. Beck had apparently signed a confession to the police stating he killed Adele. Not that this was fatal. People signed confessions all the time when they didn't really do it. There were many reasons why they would do something like that. I had to find out what kind of tactics were used - did the cops threaten or bribe him somehow? I could show the confession was somehow involuntary and get that thrown out of court. That was a heavy lift, however - police were allowed to use all kinds of tactics that skirted the line. They could lie to the suspect and leave him in a room without food or heat for 24 hours, and, still, the confession would be considered valid.

But I wouldn't give up, not until I spoke with Beck and got his side of the story.

I was a pro at these visits. From my years at the Public Defender's office, combined with my years in private practice, I had done hundreds of jail visits. Maybe thousands. I had to admit, however, I'd done quite a few less visits in my private practice than when I was a public defender. Generally, people in jail cannot afford a private attorney. That was why my usual clients weren't in jail awaiting trial - they generally were out on bail. I took quite a few drug dealers and white-collar and organized criminals, because these were all people who could afford a private attorney at $400 an hour.

Looking at Beck's background, it seemed he probably couldn't afford my fee. He was working at a sanitation plant, which paid well enough, but not enough to afford an attorney, any attorney, for a murder trial.

So if I liked the way this person talked, I'd take his case on a *pro bono* basis. I would do that for Heather.

But if I didn't like the way he talked, I probably would walk away. As I told Heather, dog cases are bad for everybody involved. They were bad for the client, because they ended up going to prison. They were bad for the attorney because the client usually blamed the attorney for losing the case. And they were bad for the court system because dog cases end up clogging dockets needlessly.

I waited to see Beck for about 20 minutes before he finally appeared. He was about 6 foot tall, extremely muscular, with tattoos all up and down both of his arms. His head was bald and his eyes were light-colored. Several of those tattoos were Swastikas and other symbols I knew were used by Neo-Nazis and white supremacists. I also noticed quite a few symbols used by the Aryan nation. I was something of an expert on symbols because I'd represented Neo-Nazis in the past.

I had to admit that seeing him with all those tattoos made me immediately pre-judge him. This man was being charged with a hate crime. His background apparently was grounded in hate. That was something Heather neglected to mention.

It would've been nice to have known that coming in.

He swaggered over to me. "S'up, dog?" he asked. His

wrists were shackled, as were his ankles. "Guess Heather sent you here, huh?"

"She did. I wanted to see you and get your story. I won't promise to represent you. But I guess Heather feels threatened by you. She asked me to represent you because she's afraid you'll roll on her for something. I have to admit that if Heather's story is true, it doesn't exactly endear you to me. I want to make sure you know where I stand."

Beck immediately affected a defensive posture. He stood up. "Guess you're gonna judge me too, aren't you? Don't give me this bullshit about wanting to represent me because I threatened Heather. Number one, I didn't threaten her, or should I say him? I didn't threaten nobody. And I certainly didn't threaten that tranny bitch. I don't know what Heather told you, but whatever it is, she's lying. That bitch is always lying. Her lips move, she lies. So let's just get that out of the way."

I didn't know what to believe. Who to believe. I knew this guy Beck was a character, and I wasn't sure I wanted to still be in that jail talking to him. "Okay, so you say Heather's lying about you threatening her to get me to take your case. Do you mind telling me, then, why Heather's so desperate for me to take you on as a client? She's willing to pay my fee out of the money she saved up for her paralegal school. She's willing to work for me for free as long as it takes to work off my $400 an hour fee. I'd like to know your story, starting with why Heather wants me to take this case so badly."

"$400 an hour? Are you fucking kidding me?" He shook his head. "Goddammit, where can I get a job like that? If I could make that much money, no fucking way would I be doing shit work. Literally." Then he laughed. "Literally. You know I fucking work at a sanitation plant don't you? Talk about a shitty job." Then he laughed again. "I'm cracking myself up here."

I sat with my pen in my hand and my pad of paper at the ready. I didn't smile. I had to show this guy I was there for business, not to be one of his glad-handing buddies behind bars.

"Yes, that's my fee. Now you have to answer my question. Why would Heather be willing to pay that fee, going so far as giving me her school money and working for free, just so you can get your sorry ass out of jail? There's something you're not telling me or something she's not telling me. Either way, I'm not getting the whole story. Now, why don't you tell me the whole story? Starting why Heather wants you out of prison so badly."

"Eh, I don't know why Heather wants me out of jail right now. I hardly know that tranny bitch."

"How do you know her?"

He shrugged. "She knows my homey, Charlie. Charlie's a good dude."

"I understand that." I wondered what his game was. Why was he being so evasive about how he knew Heather? "Listen, when I first talked to her about this case, she told me you were her boyfriend. Did you and Heather have a relationship like that?"

"No, man. What kind of a person do you think I am? Do I look like somebody who'd be messing with a chick with a dick?" He shook his head. "No, man. That's not my game. I like chicks that don't have dicks."

"What about Adele? She was a chick with a dick, wasn't she?"

"Yeah. I guess it turned out she was. She didn't tell me that though when I was talking to her at the bar. That was something she didn't say." Then he put his finger in his mouth like he was gagging himself. "Thank God I didn't end up going home with her. That would've been sick, man. Disgusting."

"So you didn't go home with her, then? Is that what you're saying?"

"Fuck no. Listen, I thought she was a hot bitch. She looked like a chick. If you saw her, you wouldn't have known either."

I had seen the picture of Adele. Beck was right about that. She very much looked like a woman. From the photos, I had to agree I probably wouldn't have known she was biologically a man if I saw her in the bar. "Okay, at what point did you find out she was a man? Biologically, at least?"

"Shit. We went out to my car, we started to mess around, I put my hand on her junk and felt a lump there."

"Did you not notice an Adam's Apple?"

"No, man. Bitch was wearing a scarf around her neck. So I didn't know until we got out to the car she had guy's parts down there."

"And what happened when you found out she had a penis?"

He shrugged his shoulders. "Nothing, man. I told her to get out of the car. I told her I don't play that. I don't get with men even if they look just like a chick."

I leaned back in my chair. I examined his tattoos a little bit further. In addition to the Swastika, there were other symbols associated with white supremacy, such as a tattoo of a WWII German soldier and a skull and cross-bones with the letters *WAR* above it, which was the initials for "White Aryan Resistance."

He noticed me looking at his tattoos. "Dog, I see you looking at me like that. I see you looking at my tattoos."

I nodded my head. "Do you mind explaining them to me?"

"Yeah, man. I was in the joint when I was 21 years old. Rob One. 5 fucking years I was in there. It was join a goddamn white supremacist gang or die. Man, I had black dudes jumping my ass every fucking day in there. Every fucking day. My old man's reputation preceded me and he was in that joint, too, stirring shit with every black guy in there, so the black dudes be coming after me too. I met this dude in there, name's Clinton Todd, he was a skinhead. He became my cellmate and told me if I join with the white supremacist dudes they'd protect me. So I did. That's what I did. I got these tattoos and now I wish I didn't. Because here I am on the outside, nobody wants to hire me and I get black dudes jumping me out here all the time. Not to mention the Jews." And then he laughed. "Some of the little guys can beat your ass."

"So you're not a white supremacist? You only joined that gang in prison to protect yourself?" I didn't really believe him. Sure, maybe he joined the white supremacists in prison for protection, but there was no way that he could hang out with those guys and not be influenced by them. If I were to guess, he probably harbored white supremacist feelings. And if he had hate for other ethnicities and races, he probably had hate for transgendered people such as Adele.

Hate was hate.

At any rate, his white supremacist past was something the prosecutor could definitely use against him. They could use it to give him motive for killing Adele.

"Yeah, man. That's right. Listen, I ain't got no hate in my heart for nobody. I went to a school that was almost all black. Black, Mexicans, and boat people. I had better black friends growing up than white friends. Anyhow, what does any of that have to do with my being accused of killing a tranny?"

"I'll tell you what that has to do with you killing a transgendered woman. Because of your background, the prosecutors could enhance the charges and claim this is a hate crime. Which means little in the State of Missouri. More importantly, the prosecutors can use your hateful past to give you motive to kill Adele. In the process, that prosecutor can use your prejudices to make the jury hate you. People are becoming more aware of hate crimes. Our society is gradually moving in the direction of protections for people like Adele. It's a bad atmosphere right now for doing something like this. I can try to keep your white supremacist past out of court. I can try to claim it's not relevant, because there's nothing in your past that shows you're prejudiced against transgendered people. But I have a feeling the prosecutor can make a creative argument to bring your white supremacist past into the court, which means we'll be starting at a disadvantage."

"They can't bring that in. I didn't do it. Why will it be brought in if I didn't do it?"

"I'll tell you why it can be brought in. The prosecutors will use it to show you did this. Right now, we have circumstantial evidence that points to you as being Adele's killer. We have an eyewitness, a bartender, who saw the two of you leave the bar that night together. And, somehow, we also have a confession. I need to ask you about that too. Why did you confess to killing Adele?"

Beck shook his head. "Dog, that was bullshit right there. They had me in that goddamn interrogation room for hours. They had me drink a bunch of pops and didn't let me go to the bathroom. They had that fucking room so cold my nuts were freezing off. That didn't matter much to them. Those pigs were wearing their uniforms and I had on a short-sleeve shirt."

"Okay, so they made you feel uncomfortable. What else did they do to make you confess to killing her?"

"Goddammit. Listen, I got a little brother. Name's Matt. Only 15. Thinks I walk on water. Wants to be just like me. I keep telling him that he don't want to be like me. He don't need to be going to the joint."

"Okay. Go on."

"Those pigs told me they picked up Matt for drug dealing. They told me that if I signed this confession, they'd let Matt go. I didn't believe them. I told them I wanted an attorney. They told me they would let me get an attorney and then started to talk me out of it. They tell me I could just trust them. Trust them that they would drop the charges against Matt if I signed a confession. So I did."

I made some notes. "Okay, so you're telling me that after you asked for an attorney they kept talking to you and tried to talk you out of getting an attorney? And they promised that they'd drop the charges against your little brother if you signed this confession?" I shook my head. "I guess I don't really understand. This confession will be something that could nail you. Was it really worth it to you to sign a confession like that?"

"Shit. It sure as hell was. Listen, I know the game. I know because I signed this confession after I asked for an attorney that this confession ain't worth the paper it's signed on. I don't even have to talk about how those pigs bribed me into doing it. Held my brother's life over my head. I figured it was worth a shot."

"And what happened with Matt?"

Beck shook his head. "Turns out those fucking pigs were

lying to me anyway. Matt hadn't been arrested for drug dealing."

"Has he been drug dealing?" It was possible the cops were looking at Beck's brother for drug dealing and maybe would drop the investigation against him if he signed this confession.

"Matt be dealing." Beck shook his head in disgust. "I told him not to be dealing. I told him not to be hanging around with dudes who'll get him into trouble. No way did I want him going to the joint like I did. So yeah, he's been dealing, but hasn't been arrested for it."

"Is it possible he hasn't been arrested because you signed a confession and the cops were as good as their word?"

"No, man. I don't think so, man. I think those pigs tricked me. But I know you can get me out of that confession, right?"

I sighed. "Yeah. I guess I can. I can show the court you signed the confession after you asked for an attorney and weren't given one. And the cops tricked you into signing it. But your confession makes your case that much more of an uphill battle. It's bad enough that you were apparently the last person to see her alive. It's bad enough that Adele's body was found outside your apartment building in the alleyway. Add in a signed confession and you can see the problem. I don't think this case is winnable at this point."

I knew that wasn't the truth. It *was* winnable. Every case was winnable until it wasn't. I hadn't yet done any investigation on this case. It was entirely possible that once Garrett, Nick, and Jack started to investigate this case, they could find something exonerating. At the moment, however, this case was as much of a dog as any case I'd seen in a while.

"Are you telling me you won't take my case?"

The Hate Crime

"I think so. I don't think this case is worth my time. Nothing you told me makes me think this will be a successful case. I have a feeling I'll end up pleading you out and I also have a feeling you'll blame me for going to prison. So, at the moment, it looks like I won't take you on as a client."

Beck looked at me and shook his head. "You'll have to take my case. If you don't take my case, then you'll see what happens. I can almost guarantee you it won't be pretty for Heather."

I crossed my arms in front of me. "Okay, what do you have on Heather?"

"That bitch's life ain't gonna be worth nothing if I go down for this bullshit. She told me she'd get me a real attorney and that attorney is you. If I have to get myself a Public Defender, I ain't gonna be happy. And if I ain't happy, then, trust me, Heather the tranny bitch is going down."

"Okay, you're going to have to come clean with me. Tell me the truth about Heather and your relationship to her. She told me she burglarized a jewelry store and got some money for her sick mother. And you gave her that job. You planned it all. And she said you'd roll on her if I didn't take this job. Is that the truth?"

"Shit no." Then he snorted. "You hear anything about a jewelry store getting knocked off? You read anything about that in the paper?"

"No. I admit I haven't read a thing about that. I'm just going by her story. I haven't checked it out yet. I wanted to ask you about it first."

"Go ahead and see if a jewelry store has recently been knocked off. Go ahead. Do a Google search on it. I can guarantee you won't find nothing about no jewelry store getting knocked off."

I got out my cell phone and looked at it. A quick Google search confirmed there was not a report of a jewelry store being burglarized at any time in the past two years. At least no jewelry store in the area.

"So, what did you find out?" Beck was waiting for my answer with a death stare on his face.

"Doesn't look like there's been a jewelry store burglarized within the past few years. So what do you have over Heather?"

"Well, let's just say there's a bad dude who was alive a couple weeks ago and he ain't alive no more. That's all I'm going to say right now."

I stood up. "Listen, you're going to tell me what she did. You tell me what she did or I walk right now." I pointed to the door. "I swear to God, I'll walk, and then you'll have to find your own attorney."

"Easy, easy now. Listen, I can't tell you shit. I don't really care if you find out but it ain't coming from me. That's all I'm saying." He leaned back in the chair and gave me a smirk. It was a smirk I wanted to smack off his arrogant face. Then he leaned forward. "She killed a man. That's what I have on her."

"What do you mean?" Was he serious or playing a serious head game? I thought the latter but was scared that the former was true. I couldn't imagine Heather doing something like that. Then again, I killed a man - my stepfather, Stephen Harrington. Anybody was capable of murder under the right circumstances. Anybody.

He shrugged. "Talk to her. Ask her. I'm not telling you no more than that."

I stood up. "I'm not playing your games," I said. At that,

I took his file and put it back into my briefcase. I stood up and looked at the guards, who were behind a window. The guards were looking at me and I gave a motion I wanted to leave. I looked behind me at Beck, who was still looking at me with the same smug look on his face. *Talk to Heather and you'll be back*, his expression said.

"You want to come clean with me, and I'll come back," I said. "You still want to play your stupid games, then find your own attorney. You're due back in court in a couple of days. After all, you told the judge to continue your case while you looked for a private attorney. You better tell the judge you're going with the Public Defender's Office."

The guard behind the window buzzed me out. As I walked away from the door, I smiled as I thought about Beck getting an attorney who was Jewish or black or Mexican. He or she would take one look at his tattoos and hate him.

I don't know why that thought made me smile, but it did.

Chapter Five

AFTER I LEFT THE JAIL, I decided to meet with Tina. Tina was out on bail but was staying at a halfway house. Actually, she was back in the sober living facility she was in when Connor met her. As with Beck, I had no clue if I could take her case or not. Then again, it was Connor asking me to take her on. Connor was always a sensitive sort. That was what made it so ironic that he actually pulled the trigger on the security guard in that robbery. That's what made it so ironic that, up until my blackmailing the governor, Connor was going to serve the rest of his life in prison.

After I met with Tina, I'd have to meet with Tom Garrett. He called to tell me he had some news about Beck. There was obviously something Beck was hiding from me about Heather or that Heather was hiding from me about herself. Once I found out what was going on, I could make up my mind to decide if I would represent the guy.

I got to Tina's sober living house, which was a large house on the east side of Kansas City. It was at least three stories tall, with a large porch and heavy wooden door. I rang the doorbell, and a tall lady with short brown hair greeted me.

"Who are you here to see?" she asked me.

I showed her my Bar Card. That was important, because this was a private place, and not just anybody could come in and visit the people living there. "I'm here to see Tina Phillips."

The lady nodded. "I think Tina is expecting you, actually. She's been talking about you coming to visit her. But if you have a seat, she'll be here in a second." The lady motioned to the couch in a waiting room, which was right next to the hallway.

In a matter of minutes, Tina appeared. She was tiny. She couldn't have been more than 5 foot 2 and 110 pounds. She had jet black hair shaved on the side and long on the other side. She was wearing a concert T-shirt and tight jeans with bare feet. She was wearing a lot of makeup, including a lot of lipstick that made her extremely large lips look even bigger. Her eyes were as big as her lips, and she had a broad face and high cheekbones. She almost looked like she could be Eastern European, just by looking at her features.

She came up to me and wrapped her arms around me. "Oh my God, I can't tell you how glad I am to see you. I've been going crazy in this place. See, I got out of rehab and came here right away. I've been here for three months now. Three months. I want to go home. I thought I could go home but then I caught this charge. I'm stuck here now. The judge told me as a condition of my bond I had to stay here. I kicked the drugs. Now I just want to go home and stop being around all these other addicts and druggies. Man, they got some characters in here." She shook her head. "Some real Looney Tunes."

I motioned to a table in a small room that didn't have

much in it except for a table and chairs. It did have a window, though, so it wasn't entirely a depressing space.

When we sat down, she started talking again. "Connor was telling me that hopefully you can keep me out of the joint. No way I want to spend my life behind bars. I'll go crazy. Hell, I'm going crazy just being here, can you imagine if I had to spend time in prison?" She shook her head. "I can't even imagine it." She lowered her voice. "Trust me on this, I've been behind bars before and there are more drugs behind bars than on the street. How am I supposed to kick the dragon if I can't change my playmates and my playground? That's what they always tell us in rehab, change our playgrounds and our playmates."

Her tiny hands were shaking. She kept putting her fingers to her lips and to her hair and then onto her shoulders. She looked like she was trying to dust imaginary creatures off her.

As I watched her, I realized she was high. Her pupils were dilated and she was talking a mile a minute.

"Tina, are you high right now?"

She shook her head rapidly, but I knew the truth.

"Tina, I think you're high on meth or cocaine at the moment. Now there are a couple of things I can do for you. This is your first distribution charge, so I can try to get you a thing called Drug Court. If you get Drug Court, you have to agree to probation for two years, drug test when they ask you to, go through counseling and a 12-step program, maintain employment, and just do whatever it is the judge asks you to. If you get through all that, you'll have the case dismissed. It's a very good deal. I would like to get that for you - I'd like to try to get you a deal like that but I need to know you can walk it down. I need to know you can comply with the court requirements for two whole years."

She nodded and proceeded to avoid my question to her about taking Drug Court. "I know you think I'm high right now, but I'm really not. This is just how I am. I can't help it. I've always been ADHD. And I know you're looking at me scratching, but trust me on this, I don't feel bugs underneath the skin. Been there, done that, not doing it again. I'm really trying to be clean. It's hard in here, but I'm trying."

I was skeptical but decided to believe her. "Now here is what Connor told me about you. He told me your pimp, Larry Rodriguez, forced you to distribute these drugs. He told me that if you didn't distribute these drugs, you'd be in big trouble with Rodriguez. You owed him. Is that right? In fact, he told me Rodriguez would kill you if you didn't become his mule."

She nodded her head. "That's right. And Larry is in prison. I mean jail. The feds are gonna get his case because he was caught with a firearm and he's a felon. I'm glad he's behind bars. I didn't want to keep doing what he asked me to do. I need out of the game, man. I'm getting too old for this shit. I want to get clean, want to get off the streets, want to have a normal life. You know what I mean?"

I knew what she meant. More than she could possibly know. When I was getting in trouble when I was young, I was always desperate to start leading a different life. I was tired of looking over my shoulder all the time, tired of getting arrested all the time, tired of going to jail. My stint in prison straightened my ass up, so it was a blessing in disguise.

"I'll see what I can do about your drug charge. Not making any promises, of course. I can't possibly make you any promises." I paused. "Let's go over a few things. I need to know if there's anything in your background that might cause a prosecutor to go easy on you. Maybe there's something in your background that'll help you because maybe you know somebody you can roll on to get a better deal. I can even see if the prosecutors will offer you a better deal if you agreed to testify against Larry, if they need that to happen."

"Oh God, no. No fucking way will I narc on that guy. I rat on him and my life ain't worth nothing. I won't live long enough to enjoy my freedom." She shook her head adamantly. "No fucking way."

I sighed. I had no clue what kind of trump card we could really use for this woman. Coercion, unfortunately, was not a get-out-of-jail-free card. I could use Larry's coercion to get Tina a lesser sentence, but no way I could use it to get her completely off scot-free. The only thing that could possibly work in her case would be if she knew something that would bring down bigger fish.

The problem was, people were usually afraid to rat out bigger fishes. Just like what Tina was afraid of, it was my experience that my clients were hesitant to testify against higher-up people because those higher-ups usually had their fingers in a lot of pies. They could have anybody killed at any moment. That was why little guys usually ended up going to prison rather than avoid it in exchange for testimony.

She looked very nervous. Her legs were going up and down, up and down, up and down, and her hands were shaking. She looked at me. "So, what's your other idea? You must have something else up your sleeve to get me out of jail. Come on, Connor told me you're some kind of magician. You must have something that can help me out."

All I could think of was that this woman was stupid for getting involved with a guy like Larry. But, then again, people were stupid sometimes. People made bad decisions.

People like my mother. She made one bad decision after another. I mainly paid for her bad decisions, and I knew my life would've been different if I didn't have a mother like her. Whether or not I'd have chosen a different life was another story. I was a firm believer that everything that happened in my life up to this point, good and bad, brought me to where I was. If I would've changed just a few things in my life along the way, I wouldn't be here. And, since I was happy with my life, I also looked back on my experiences and realized everything happened for a reason.

"I don't know, Tina. I don't know if I can get you a decent deal. By decent, I mean probation or Drug Court. At the moment, the prosecutors are offering 5 years in prison. As you know. They consider this to be a pretty serious charge. You're lucky they're not trying to send your case to the Feds, however. That's one thing."

She chuckled ruefully, and shrugged her shoulders. "Guess I gotta take what I can get, huh?"

"I guess so. I guess so."

Chapter Six

THAT NIGHT, I got the shock of my life. Amelia was crying when I got home. Nate was nowhere to be found, but, when I asked Amelia where he was, she said he was up in his room, playing video games.

"What's going on?" I asked her.

She shook her head. "It's Sarah. Sarah's been calling me again. She's been saying all kinds of terrible things about you. Is it true, dad? Is it true you really aren't my father?"

My heart sunk into my shoes. Why was Sarah doing this? She had zero interest in Amelia when we were married. She made that abundantly clear. In fact, her behavior towards Amelia when she was sick was the reason why I divorced her. Yet, here she was, making trouble. Telling my daughter vile and untrue things.

At least, I hoped they were untrue. I had never taken a paternity test. There was never a reason to before. There was never a question in my mind that Amelia belonged to me. She was mine.

Granted, she didn't look like me. With her light blonde

hair, blue eyes and pale skin, she definitely favored Sarah over me, as far as looks went. There was nothing in her bone structure, height or features that told me she was my daughter. However, I always felt in my heart she was mine. There was never a doubt in my mind about her paternity.

Was it wishful thinking? Did I talk myself into not doubting she was mine? Did I not want to face the reality about the situation and that was why I was so sure? I didn't really know.

I wondered what Sarah's game was. We were divorced and she got a decent settlement out of me. Specifically, she got $2 million in cash and $200,000 worth of equity out of our home. She didn't try for maintenance, and I probably would've fought it if she tried. I knew the law in Missouri. Maintenance was hard to come by for spouses, especially spouses supplied with a large property settlement, as Sarah was, and who could work. Plus, Sarah was clearly at fault in the breakdown of our marriage, considering she abandoned Amelia and me at a critical time to take off with John Gibson. Because of all that, my lawyer told me the reason Sarah wasn't asking for maintenance was because she knew she wouldn't get it.

I wondered if she would try to shake me down by using Amelia to do it.

"Where is Nate?" I asked Amelia. "How is he taking this?" I knew Nate was unbelievably jealous of Amelia, considering Sarah refused even to talk to him. He loved her still while Amelia appeared to not be bothered by that Sarah was no longer in the kids' lives. It was really strange - even though Sarah's relationship with Amelia, such as it was, was clearly toxic, Nate was jealous of it anyway. I guess he figured a toxic relationship with Sarah was better than none at all.

"Dad, you're avoiding the question. I asked you a question. Are you really my father?"

"Of course I am. Why would you even ask that question?" My voice was shaking, which Amelia probably picked up on. She was too clever by half sometimes.

She crossed her arms in front of her. "Dad, I'm not talking about you saying I'm your daughter because you raised me. And you've always considered yourself to be my father. I'm talking about whether or not you gave me your DNA. That's what I'm talking about, dad."

I sighed. Amelia was seven years old going on 70. She was way too smart for me. Maybe she wasn't my daughter? I was never that smart at her age.

"Amelia…" I wanted to tell her the BS she wasn't in the mood to hear - she was my daughter, no matter what. But she wasn't having it. She wanted to know if I was her *biological* father. And I didn't know the answer to that question. There was no way I could know that for sure unless a DNA test was done. That would probably be next. Sarah was clearly angling for that.

Amelia was still watching me, looking at me suspiciously. "Come on, Dad, it's not that hard of a question. Are you or aren't you my father? If you were never in the picture, would I still have been born?" She tapped her little feet on the floor.

"Amelia, I don't know the answer to that question. I can't know the answer to that question unless I take a test. So that's what I'll do."

As soon as I said that though, I started to feel terrified. What if the test came out I wasn't her father? What could Sarah do? A judge would have to look at the best interest of the child in determining who got custody. So even if Sarah could prove I wasn't Amelia's biological father, I could still retain custody of her if the judge decided it was in her best interest to keep her with me. Then again, it would be up to the individual judge. There was always the chance a judge could decide to give Sarah custody.

"Okay, Dad. Thanks for being honest with me. I didn't think you would. I thought you would try to snow me and tell me some kind of nonsense about how your feelings for me make you my father and that's all that matters. That's not all that matters, at least according to Sarah. She's been talking to me and telling me that if she can prove you're not my father, I might have to go with her." Amelia hung her head. "That can't happen, Dad. I can't live with her. I don't like her and she doesn't like me either."

"Now, Amelia, that's not true. She loves you." My voice was weak when I said that, though. I knew it was a lie. Sarah didn't love Amelia nor did she love Nate. If she loved them, she wouldn't be treating them the way she did. Ignoring Nate and using Amelia as a pawn - that wasn't how a mother should treat her children. If she loved either one of them, she wouldn't be acting the way she was.

"Liar." Amelia's tone was accusing. "Don't lie to me Dad. You know as well as I do that Sarah wants nothing to do with me and Nate. So what's her game, dad? Why is she doing this?"

"I don't know." And that was the truth. I really had no clue what she was thinking.

"Dad, what happens if you take a test and it turns out you're not my father? What if my father is some kind of rando? What if he's somebody mean? What if he doesn't want me and Sarah doesn't either, but they make me go and stay with them anyway? What then, Dad?"

"Amelia, that's not going to happen."

"It might. It might happen if you take a test and find

out somebody else is my father. Dad, I don't want to go with Sarah. I want to stay here with you." At that, she threw her arms around my neck, and started to bawl. "Dad, don't make me go stay with that witch. Please, please don't make me stay with her. Please say I can stay with you always."

I hugged her tight. As much as I didn't want to make a promise I couldn't keep, I decided to anyway. "I promise you. I promise I will never let you stay with Sarah. Now you need to go upstairs and do your homework."

Amelia looked at me. "You're going to call Sarah aren't you? If you call her, tell her that no matter what happens, I won't stay with her. There's no way I would ever stay with her and whoever my father happens to be. No way."

"Yes, I'm going to call Sarah. And I'll tell her exactly what you told me to tell her. I'll tell her that, no matter what, I will fight her tooth and nail it she tries to take you away from me."

"Okay then, Dad," Amelia said. "I'll go upstairs and do my homework. I want you to tell me what she says though, when you call her." She wagged her finger at me. "And you better be firm with her, Dad. You better just tell her there's no way I'll move to Chicago and leave my school, you, Nate, and everything I know, just to be with her and some rando I don't even know."

At that, Amelia marched upstairs, and I called Sarah.

"I knew you would be calling me," Sarah said when she answered the phone. Her voice was slurred and I knew she'd been drinking.

"Yes, you had to know I would call you. What the hell are you thinking? What's your game? Do you want more money? Is that what this is?"

She laughed a little on the other side. "Damien, what kind of shrew do you think I am? Do you really think I'd do something like this just because I wanted to shake you down for some more money? You gave me enough. No, I don't want more money from you."

"Then what do you want from me?"

There was silence on the other end of the phone. It was a deafening silence. A pregnant silence. In that silence, I knew there would be a bombshell to be dropped on me, sooner rather than later.

"Damien, believe it or not, I don't want money from you, and I also don't want custody of Amelia. You always told me I was a terrible mother, and I guess I am. When Amelia was sick, I left her and you and took up with another man. I haven't been in contact with her, for quite some time, except to call her up and harass her. I know I wouldn't be a good mother to her. I'm more self-aware than you might think."

I took a deep breath and let it out. I didn't know whether to believe her when she told me she didn't want money and didn't want Amelia. She clearly wanted something. But what was it?

"Okay, you got me. What's your game?"

"Why do you think there's a game?"

My temper started to flare. "There's obviously some game you're playing. Why would you tell our daughter I'm not her father? And is that true? Is it possibly true?"

More silence. "Yes, it's quite possibly true. In fact, I can tell you it *is* true."

My heart started to race. "What do you mean, it's true? Are you trying to tell me you know for sure I'm not Amelia's father? Are you telling me you've already done DNA analysis and found this out?"

Sarah was very quiet. "Listen, Damien, it's better for Amelia to know her actual father. I've already told him and he wants to know her. He can give her anything she needs or wants. Can you say the same?"

My head was spinning. I had no idea what she was talking about. No clue. "Sarah, who is Amelia's father?"

"His name is Baron Wicker. He's one of the wealthiest men in the world."

Chapter Seven

BARON WICKER? Baron Wicker? I knew a little bit about him, only because I'd seen his name in *Forbes* magazine when they went through the rundown of the richest 50 people in the world. He apparently was an heir to an oil fortune. Other than that though, there wasn't much I knew about him.

"What are you doing, Sarah? Seriously? Amelia is seven years old, she's established in school here, she has her doctors here. Her whole life is here with Nate and me. I don't know why you'd tell her, without clearing it with me, about Baron Wicker being her father, unless you're up to no good. Why do I feel like Baron will try to get custody of her?"

"He doesn't want custody of Amelia. He simply wants to get to know her. That's all."

"No, that's not all." I felt my anger rising inside me. "That's not all, and you know it. You know it." I felt like throwing up. "Admit it, Sarah. You and Baron are working together to take Amelia away from me. Admit it."

"Damien, you're not her father. Baron is her father."

"You know as well as I do that because Amelia was born during our marriage, I'm the presumed father. She's lived with me all her life. There's not a judge in this circuit who'll allow you and Baron to take her away from me. There's a little thing called the best interest of the child, and that's the standard the judge has to use when deciding paternity cases. Any judge will decide it's in Amelia's best interest to stay with me. You hear that? She'll stay with me."

"Damien, you're being selfish. I know you make a good living and you still have millions from that wrongful death lawsuit, but you can't possibly give her the kind of life Baron can. Amelia is a very bright child. I wouldn't be surprised if she ends up at Harvard. Can you pay for that college? Not to mention Nate? Baron can give her the kind of advantages I could never give her and neither could you. Just think about that for a second."

"Listen, Sarah, my father was a rich man like this Baron person. He was a rich man and had no morals whatsoever. In fact, he was a sociopath. He hurt a lot of people, including you. Money doesn't buy sanity, it doesn't buy love, and it won't buy Amelia. Do you hear me? It won't buy Amelia."

By this time, I was screaming and shaking with rage.

"Damien," Sarah said sweetly. "Calm down."

"You tell me to calm down? You're gonna try to take my daughter away from me and you tell me to calm down? And, listen, I'm not going take your word for it. I won't believe you that this Baron asshole is Amelia's father. I'm doing a DNA test of my own."

I suddenly realized I would be in for the fight of my life. Baron Wicker had untold billions of dollars, which meant he could hire a team of lawyers to beat me down if he wanted to. I didn't know how I could fight that, but I knew I would have to try. Nobody would take Amelia, or Nate for that matter, away from me without a fight.

Sarah was quiet. "Damien, I never wanted to hurt you like this."

"Oh, you didn't? You didn't? You apparently had at least one affair while we were married, with this Baron Wicker person, and then you had an affair with John Gibson. And now you're trying to take Amelia from me. I won't let you do it. I won't let Amelia be raised by a rich bastard like Baron Wicker."

"Okay, okay, calm down. I want Amelia to meet her father. That's all. Just meet him. I haven't said anything at all about trying to take her away from you."

"Oh, but that's next. You know it's next. You hate me because I asked you to leave and will do anything to hurt me. You'll do anything to hurt me, and you know that taking Amelia away would be like ripping out my soul. After all I've gone through with her, thinking she would die, going through all those nights at the hospital and all those doctors' appointments. All those nights when I listened to her cry in pain and because she thought she would die soon – and now, after all that, you want to take her away from me."

"Damien–"

"And if you have the best of intentions, you wouldn't have said a word to her about this. You would've kept it to yourself. That is, if it *is* the truth this Baron Wicker is her father. There was no reason for Amelia to know the truth. That's why I think you and Baron are up to no good."

"Think what you want."

I hung up the phone. I had no desire to talk to her anymore. Plus, I had to talk to Amelia. I would have to be straight with her. There was no use in lying. She was too smart for that and would have to find out the truth sooner or later anyway. I might as well rip off the Band-Aid. It was gonna hurt like hell, for both her and me.

I went up to her room and knocked on the door. She opened it. As I looked at her, I knew she'd been crying. Her big blue eyes were red rimmed, and her face was stained with tears. Her nose was also running. "So, what did you find out? What did Sarah tell you?"

"Amelia, honey, Sarah told me that your biological father is named Baron Wicker. He's a rich guy. Lives in Dallas, Texas. He's an heir to an oil fortune. Now just because Sarah says Baron Wicker is your father doesn't mean it's necessarily so. Sarah could be lying. But I thought it was important for you to know there's a possibility it's true."

Amelia crossed her arms in front of her. "Are you telling me my dad is involved in destroying the environment?" She shook her head. "That makes me mad. I don't want a guy like that to be my dad. I want you to be my dad."

Her lips were quivering. I stooped down to her level, and tousled her hair. "Kiddo, I know you don't want to hear this, but I *am* your father. No matter what, I am your father."

"I know you are. You'll always be my dad. Why do I think—"

She couldn't say more. She wrapped her little arms around me tightly and I squeezed her hard. I held her as she cried. "You'll always be my jellybean." *Jellybean* was my nickname for her, both because I thought she was multi-flavored like a handful of jellybeans, and also because when I saw her for the first time on the sonogram, she looked just like a little bean.

Nate came out of his room. "Hey, Dad." He looked over at Amelia. "What's wrong with her?"

I didn't know what to tell him. He was already having so many problems with my divorcing Sarah and now this. There was a possibility he would lose his sister and there was just no way to tell him the truth.

Amelia looked at me, wondering if I would tell him. I just shook my head at her. I wasn't ready to deal with him.

I wasn't ready to deal with any of this, but here it was, coming at me like a freight train.

Chapter Eight

I HAD to get back to Heather because Beck's next hearing was coming up shortly. When he first came in front of the judge, for his initial appearance, he told the judge he would try to find a private attorney. The judge gave him a two-week continuance to find an attorney, so it was almost time for Beck to be in court again. That meant I had to make a decision soon on whether or not to take him on as a client.

I specifically had to find out what Beck meant when he told me Heather had killed a man. If that were the case, then Beck certainly could do damage to her if he wanted. That was the last thing I wanted. I supposed that if Beck had something on Heather to where he could destroy her life if he wanted, I'd probably take him on as a client. I had grown rather fond of Heather and didn't want to see anything happen to her. If I had to take Beck's case to protect her, I would do it.

I would be kicking and screaming the whole time, but I would do it.

Heather came to my office. She laid her purse down in

front of her. "Okay, you wanted to see me? Did you see Beck? Did you find out anything? Are you going to take his case?" Her questions were coming fast and furious.

"Slow down. One question at a time. Actually, strike that. I need to ask you a question."

Her eyes didn't meet mine. I had a feeling, as I looked at her expression, that Beck probably was telling the truth. Heather probably did kill a man.

"What do you need to ask me? Go ahead, I've got nothing to hide."

"Beck told me you killed a man. Is that true?"

Heather's eyes got big. "I can't say anything to you about that." She shook her head. "I can't say anything to you about that."

I took a deep breath. I could try to sign her up as a client, although that would end up being a conflict of interest in the event Beck knew something about her and what she did criminally. I couldn't represent Beck and her at same time. Yet, I also knew that if I were her attorney, and Heather told me something incriminating about herself, I couldn't reveal it.

I steepled my hands, wondering how to approach this. Heather had come to me for help. I had to know what was going on. That was the only way I could know what to do with Beck. If he knew something serious about her, even more serious than what she told me about burglarizing the jewelry store, I'd have to do all I could to make sure Beck kept his mouth shut.

"Heather, I can't become your lawyer. I believe that if I did, it would be a conflict of interest. But I will tell you one thing – you have to tell me what you did. I have to know what Beck has on you. As it stands, I don't want to take him on as a client. I don't want to have anything to do with that man. But if your life depends upon my representing him and getting him off, then I'll do it. You have to tell me if that's the truth."

"It's my mom," Heather blurted out. "My mom, she worked for this creep. His name was Reverend John Scott. He was a horrible man. A truly horrible man."

"I know about him. That was how you came to know Harper, right? Your adoptive mother was also involved in that church – right? And the Reverend Scott was brainwashing all of his congregants into killing gays, lesbians and trans - isn't that right?"

Heather nodded. "Yeah, that's what happened. My adoptive mom went bat-shit crazy because she was going to that church all the time and learning from Reverend Crazy that we LGBT folk are corrupt and need to be killed. So my adoptive mom decided to kill me one day and came after me with a butcher knife. I killed her in self-defense."

"Okay, so what happened?"

"Well, the crazy Reverend went to prison for a while. He was convicted of all those murders that happened in his church because he brainwashed everybody into killing their kids. He got some attorney who was apparently even crazier than him and that attorney overturned his convictions. He got out of prison and waiting for a new trial."

I seemed to remember reading something about that. There was something in the paper about how the Reverend Scott got his convictions overturned because there was a lack of evidence that he was behind those murders. I wasn't surprised, necessarily. It was kind of a novel theory to begin with – the man did not actually commit any murders but he brainwashed people into doing so. It worked, of course, with the Manson trial, but that didn't mean it was a widespread theory accepted by everybody.

The Hate Crime

"Okay, so the Reverend was out of jail on bail, awaiting a new trial. So what happened?"

"Well, my mom, her name is Louisa Garrison, she used to work for the Reverend Scott. In fact, for the longest time, she admitted she, too, was brainwashed by the crazy rev. She thought people like me were the work of the Devil. Satan. And, naturally, because people like me were the work of the Devil, we were to be wiped off the face of the earth. At least, that's what that church believed. But then she got away from that church and got into another faith – first Lutheran and then Unity. She learned in those churches that Christ and Jesus were about love, not judgment. And she learned we're all God's children, even people like me."

I was a bit astounded people could be so easily influenced to believe certain things. It was always something that fascinated me. I knew it was human nature to believe people you looked up to, whether it was a priest or other religious figure, a leader, a teacher, or a parent. I didn't necessarily believe people were weak-minded, *per se*. At least not in the sense that it was some kind of an insult, because I believed everybody was susceptible to persuasion. I knew the reason why the Reverend Scott was so successful in poisoning the minds of his cult members was that they wanted to believe in him. And if he was telling them trans and gay people were the work of the Devil, that would be accepted as gospel. No pun intended.

Yet, when you get out of that environment and go to an environment of acceptance, it's a different story. You suddenly realize people who are different than you are to be loved for who they are. No matter the color of their skin or sexual orientation. That was something I've always believed but I came to that on my own. I was never a religious man, and had never been exposed to some kind of environment that said people who were different were somehow lesser. I was never a person who would fall victim to tribalism, but I knew plenty of people were, even highly-educated people.

"Okay so she got into another faith, and you and she have become close. Right?"

"Well, yeah. I mean, I never even knew the mother who raised me was my adoptive mother. I didn't know that until I killed her in self-defense. What I knew was that she and I never got along. She never accepted me. She always tried to change me. It wasn't just that she tried to kill me with a butcher knife, but she also tried to kill me with a pillow, earlier. Well, not really tried to kill me, but I woke up one day and she was standing over me with a pillow, like she was going to smother me. It was like that scene in that *Star Wars* movie where Luke was thinking about killing Kylo Ren while Kylo slept. Luke thought he had to kill Kylo because he thought Kylo was evil, which he actually was. My mother apparently thought the same way about me – I was evil, therefore she had to kill me. And that was all the work of Reverend Scott."

"Okay, so that was what happened with your mother. Now tell me about Louisa."

"Louisa's pretty cool. I haven't had the easiest time. I got mixed up with the wrong dude and he had me run drugs for him. Charlie. And Charlie kicked me out and I didn't have a place to go. Louisa took me in. She don't have a lot of money because she don't have a lot of skills. I mean, she worked for that church, worked for the crazy Reverend, doing bookkeeping and things like that, so that's what she's doing now. She's a bookkeeper. For a small construction company out in KCK. So you know, she's making about $15 an hour, which doesn't go very far, but that don't matter. She still took me and made sure I had what I needed. Then I started working here and making some money. I'm going to paralegal school. So it's going pretty good. But I won't forget that Louisa, my mom, took me in when I really needed to be taken in. So yeah, I'm a bit protective of her."

"How protective of her?"

Heather crossed her arms in front of her. "Let's just say that if somebody is coming into our house and threatening her life, I'm won't take that sitting down. If someone's going to threaten my mom's life, I'm going to kill that mother fucker." She looked away.

"Is that what happened? Did the Reverend Scott come into your house one day, and threaten your mother?"

"Yeah, that's what happened. Me and my mom were out one day at the grocery store. We come home and there's the Reverend Scott sitting right there in our living room. Just sitting there, waiting for us to come home." She shook her head. "It was fucking scary. I mean, at my murder trial, my mom testified on the stand that the Reverend Scott was poisoning people's minds, getting them to kill their children if they were gay or trans. She was incredibly brave, and she was the reason I was acquitted. If it weren't for her, I'd be in prison right now. I know that. So I owe her that too. Well, mother-fucking Reverend Scott was waiting for us to come home and had a gun with him."

"Heather, you know you have the right to shoot somebody who comes into your house, especially if they have a gun? The Castle Doctrine. All you have to show is that you're the lawful resident of the house, somebody is there unlawfully, and you presumed harm would occur. In this case, the fact he was sitting there with a gun meant you could've shot him for sure. So, please tell me you didn't do anything stupid with the Reverend Scott."

Heather shook her head. "I *did* do something stupid with him. I didn't know about the Castle Doctrine. I admit, I probably should have, since I've been doing legal research for Harper and some for you as well. But I didn't know about it. And you have to understand, I've already been tried for murder that was self-defense. I thought that was gonna work against me. I thought the prosecutor could bring in my prior arrest for killing my adoptive mother and here I go again, killing somebody in self-defense. I thought the jury would have a hard time thinking I was a two-time loser. So yeah, I killed him. I rushed him when I got in the door and saw that gun, we struggled, and I shot him. I shot him and I panicked."

By now, Heather's head was bobbing back and forth. Her hands flew up to her hair and pulled on it and then she brought them down and tugged on her spiked necklace around her neck. She looked a little green, like she was about to get sick.

"Heather, the prosecutor couldn't have brought in your prior arrest in a different trial. I think you know this as well." I had the feeling Heather wasn't telling me the whole story.

"Whatever. It's not like I'm doing legal analysis when I'm facing a motherfucker with a gun in our house."

I sighed. "Why do I have the feeling that somehow, someway, Beck helped you out with all this?"

She nodded her head rapidly. "You're goddamn right, he helped me with it. I shot that bastard and didn't know what to do. All I knew was I was a two-time loser, and the jury wouldn't buy that I ended up in the same goddamn position twice in a row. Killing somebody in self-defense, twice in a row. So I panicked and called Charlie. You have to understand that Charlie's kind of a little fella. And he wouldn't help me out no-how anyway. Plus, when I called him, he was high. So he refused to come out and help me but he sent Beck over to help me instead." She sighed. "Beck came over, and, like with Charlie, he told me if he was gonna help me, I was gonna have to help him. I said sure, anything you want. So that's the real reason why I burglarized the jewelry store. That part was true. I burglarized it and I did it for him. If I didn't do it for him, he was gonna kill me. At least, that's what he said."

"Heather, you didn't burglarize a jewelry store. Please tell me the truth about what you did for Beck."

She rolled her eyes. "Fine. I drug-muled for him. Three times. I put cocaine up my ass and brought it over the border." She sighed. "I don't know why I told you I burglarized a jewelry store. I guess I thought it sounded much more decent than what I really did. More glamorous somehow." She smiled. "You can imagine Catherine Zeta-Jones burglarizing a jewelry store, but you can't imagine her putting dirty cocaine balloons up her hoo-ha."

Great. Just great. Beck was a bad dude. Yet, it seemed he hadn't ratted on Heather yet, so I would have to help him out. I would have to give him my best to get him off that charge.

"So, what did you guys do? Did he help you dispose of the body?"

Heather nodded. "Yeah. That's what happened. He came over and between me, my mom, and him, we wrapped the body in a rug, put it in the back of Beck's pickup, and drove two days into the Arizona desert. We dug a hole 10 feet deep and threw him in. And that's what happened to him. I'm sure you read in the paper about him being missing, right?"

I hadn't been reading the paper all that carefully lately,

so I didn't see that story about him. I thought he got what he deserved, considering all he did to hurt people, but that didn't help Heather's case at all. Heather would be in deep shit if any of this went south. Not just because she helped get rid of the body, but also because she killed a man. If she just did the right thing and called the police after she killed the reverend, she probably could've gotten off scot-free. Her mother was a witness and everyone knew this was a bad guy. The cops knew it. After it became publicly known his church, the Church of the Living Breath, was involved in killing gay and trans youth, the church not only shut its doors, but the cops investigated it and the shady reverend. That was why he went to prison in the first place. I was sure the cops had his number and if Heather would've just called them, she probably would've been okay.

But she didn't call them. She acted guilty by getting rid of the body, and anybody would know Heather had reason to kill him. Whether or not he was in her house, she had reason to kill him. After all, her adoptive mother almost killed her because of him. Louisa also had a reason to kill him, but Heather actually did the deed.

Did she? I wondered if Heather was not the actual person who killed the reverend, but maybe it was Louisa. Heather might've just been covering for her. I took a deep breath. "Heather, did it really happen like you just told me?"

"What do you mean?"

"I mean, did you tell the truth about how you killed the reverend? That he came to your house and was waiting for you with a gun? Or is there another story I need to know about? Maybe you're actually covering for your mother? Come on Heather, you have to tell me the truth here. I have to know how much liability you'll be facing if all of this goes down."

"Why do you think I'm lying to you?" She was getting defensive again.

"I think you're lying to me because it doesn't make any sense. You've been working for me and Harper doing legal research. You should know about the Castle Doctrine. You should also know Missouri recently passed Stand Your Ground. That would mean you had even more reason to have shot that man if he happened to be in your house. You should know all that. Yet you acted guilty by covering up what happened, by taking this man's body out to the desert and burying it. Why would you do that?"

"Listen, I don't need to take this from you." She crossed her arms in front of her and glared at me. Her lips, with the black lipstick on them, were pursed. She narrowed her eyes. "I'm not lying to you."

"I think you are. I think you're lying to me, because I think you're covering for your mother. Why do I have a feeling your mother went after him with a gun and killed him in cold blood? And then you told Beck it was you who did it and he had to help you get rid of the body, because you didn't want your mother getting into trouble. That makes sense to me. I would do something like that myself if someone I cared about got into some kind of trouble like that. So you can tell me the truth."

"No I can't. You're not my lawyer. I can't tell you the truth because if I did, you can go to the authorities. I can't have that happen."

My hunch was right. "Heather, I won't go to the authorities." She was right, though. I would have a certain obligation if she told me something about her mother killing the Reverend Scott in cold blood. I wasn't her lawyer, so I could be forced to testify against her, or her mother, and I also had a duty to report these things to the police. I took an oath to uphold the law so that would leave both of us vulnerable if she told me the truth.

It was bad enough she was telling me she killed the man in self-defense, but if she or her mother killed him in cold blood, there would be little I could do for her. According to her story, she didn't break any laws, as far as killing the reverend. She broke the law, however, when she went out to the desert to bury him. But that was minor, in the scheme of things.

But if there was cold-blooded murder involved – that would be a whole different story.

"I think you'll go to the authorities," Heather said. "So I won't tell you a goddamned thing." She bit her lower lip.

"All right then. I've a feeling this is all more serious than what you're telling me. I'll get the story from Beck. Even so, he'll tell me what he knows, but I think even he probably doesn't know the truth. He only knows what you told him. And I have a feeling you lied to him too."

She rolled her eyes. "Whatever. Are you going to take his case or not?"

I sighed and looked out the window. Goddammit, I did not want to take this man's case. That was the last thing I wanted to do. Yet, I knew I would have to. I would have to take his case and try to win it for her – Heather. I had to keep Beck happy, because if I didn't, he had information that could really sink Heather and/or her mother. I cared about Heather. She was my friend. And I would always do anything for a person I cared about.

"Okay. I'll take Beck's case and I'll try to win it. However, I have to tell you it doesn't look good for him. He was the last one to see the victim, and I'm sure there are

The Hate Crime

plenty of witnesses from the Zoo bar who will testify that he and Adele Whittier left the place together. Adele was found by the dumpster by his apartment. I'm telling you, this is not looking good."

Heather seemed to visibly relax. "Well, you pulled a rabbit out of the hat before. You can do it again, can't you?"

"Heather, I don't know about that." I took a deep breath. "I'll do what I can, though. I just wish you would tell me the truth. I know why you won't and I don't blame you. If you told me, I would have an obligation to perhaps tell the police about what happened or testify against you, because I'm not your attorney. You're right about that."

"Thank you. I know what you're saying and I wish I could tell you the truth. But the less you know about it, the better off both of us will be."

"I guess you're probably right. At any rate, I guess I'll visit Beck today in jail and tell him I'll take his case."

Heather looked like she was about to cry. "I'll pay you back. I swear to God I will. It's going to take me years, but I will."

"Don't worry about it. Listen, if I have to take Beck on a *pro bono* basis, I will. I have to do so many *pro bono* hours anyway, so I might as well just do it like this. Don't worry about it, don't sweat it, I've got this. Now, if I can just figure out how to defend this guy, we'll be in business."

At that, Heather actually did start to cry. Her tears ran down her face, smearing her mascara, and I gave her a Kleenex. "Heather, it'll be okay. I promise you that. I mean, I can't make promises, I shouldn't have said that. But I'll at least take his case and we'll have a chance. We'll have a good chance."

I was sorry I was saying these things to her. I knew in

my heart we didn't have a good chance. It wasn't like we had no chance, but it definitely wasn't looking good. I had to admit that.

"Thank you again. It seems like I'm always pulling my ass out of the fire with the help of people. I feel like I owe everybody in the world."

"You owe your mother. At least you feel that way. She testified for you in your trial and she was why you were acquitted. And she took you in when you needed her. You repaid her by killing the reverend, right? I mean, either you killed the reverend in cold blood or Louisa did. Either way, I have no doubt you were actually protecting her. I just wish I knew the truth about what happened that night."

"I wish you could know the truth too," Heather said. "But I'm sorry, I can never tell you the truth. So please don't ask me."

"I won't."

I knew it would be helpful to me if I knew the truth, but, at the same time, it would be dangerous if I did.

I might never know the truth, and I was okay with that.

Chapter Nine

I WENT to see Beck after I spoke with Heather about what he had over her. He was in jail, still. He had not yet had his next court appearance.

He came out to see me, swaggering as usual. He saw me sitting there and he smiled. "Yo, dog, what's up?"

I motioned to the seat, and he sat down. "I talked to Heather. I now know what you have over her. At least, I think I know what you have over her."

He nodded his head. "Yeah, it's something good, ain't it? I told you. I told you I got something over that bitch."

"Yeah, I guess you do. So that's what I need to speak with you about. Now she told me you helped her bury a body out in the desert. Reverend Scott. I did my research on the man and found he's been reported missing for several weeks. He was awaiting his new tria and it was a famous case, really. So the fact that he's disappeared is a big story. I don't know why I missed it, but I did."

"Yeah, so what? So what, some kook-ass dude goes missing? That guy was fucking insane and got what was coming to him."

"I agree. That guy was insane and got what was coming to him. But that's a bit besides the point, isn't it? Just because he was insane and hurt a lot of people doesn't give anybody a reason to kill him in cold blood."

Beck leaned back in his seat and nodded. "Goddammit, I could really go for a smoke right now. You got any on you?"

"Now, come on. You know better than that. We can't smoke here. Now let's get back to the topic of the Reverend Scott. What can you tell me about how he died?"

"Oh, that's a mystery, now isn't it? Wouldn't you like to know?" He started to laugh. "Now you got two mysteries on your hands, don't you? Who killed Reverend Scott and who killed Adele Whittier. I can tell you one thing. I killed neither of them. But that's all I can really tell you. I don't really know who killed Reverend Scott and I sure as hell don't know who killed Adele."

I thought he was lying. "You have a good idea about who killed the Reverend Scott, though, don't you? I just have a feeling it wasn't Heather. However, I understand it looks bad for her. I know you probably think you have enough evidence to go to the cops about Heather if it came to that. That's the reason I'm taking your case. That's the *only* reason I'm taking your case."

"Yeah, you better do a goddamn good job of it. You better not be fucking hanging me out to dry. You don't phone that shit in, do you hear me? I'm serious man, you better take this case to win. Don't be judging me by my tattoos, by my past. You get in this case, you better go balls to the wall. Balls to the fucking wall."

"Don't worry. I don't usually take cases in an effort to

The Hate Crime

lose them. Now, here's what I have to tell you. You have another hearing in a couple of days. It's just an initial appearance. What that means is the judge will read you your charges again and ask you to enter a plea of guilty or not guilty, and at that point I can probably try to ask for bail. Is there anything you can even afford if you had a bail bondsman who can get you out? Is that something you could do?"

He shrugged. "It depends."

"What does it depend on?"

"It depends on how much it is. I mean, if you get it down to a million dollars, I could probably come up with the 10%. I got some homeys, they got money, don't ask where they get the money, just that they got it. They might be willing to put the money up for me. But if it's more than that, no dice."

"Okay. I'll see what I can do about asking for $1 million bond, 10%, or the possibility of using a bondsman. However, I don't think the judge will go for that. This is a very serious charge. Strike that. It's the most serious charge. It's not like you're being charged with jaywalking or something dumb like that."

"Yeah, that's bullshit."

"Why is it bullshit?"

"It's bullshit because they're going by my past and assuming this is a hate crime. Listen, my Aryan Brothers in prison, most of them don't care about chicks with dicks or gay dudes. They couldn't give shit less about that. Yeah, they be talking about faggots and things like that, but they don't want to kill them. They're no threat to us."

"Okay." I nodded. I knew plenty of AB in my stint in prison, and, while they didn't exactly like LGBT, they didn't actively hate them. Beck made a point. "I'll try to get the prosecutors off the hate angle and I'll try to make sure your background isn't used against you in trial. After all, if the Aryan creed says nothing about hating on LGBT, I can make the argument that your background as an AB in prison has nothing to do with the death of Adele. It's not relevant."

He shook his head. "Goddammit, you don't listen to me at all, do you? Of course my background as an Aryan Brother has nothing to do with the death of Adele, because I didn't kill her."

"Regardless-"

Beck sighed and hung his head. "Dude, you don't know what you're talking about. But whatever. Seriously, you don't know what you're talking about."

"I guess you're probably right. Anyhow, at this point, that's neither here nor there. What's important, at the moment, is getting you a bond, entering a plea of not guilty, and getting the show on the road. I have an investigator, his name is Tom Garrett, who can try to track down anybody who might've had it in for Adele. What can you tell me about Adele? Anything at all?"

"No, dude. I just met her that night. In a way, it's kind of embarrassing I didn't figure out she was a dude. I mean, her voice was pretty good. She sounded like a woman. She had a scarf covering her neck, so I didn't get a chance to see if she had an Adam's apple. You know, her boobs looked pretty real. There wasn't nothing that really told me she wasn't a woman." He shrugged. "And, you know, she was a pretty hot bitch. I wanted to tap that. I was horny. There wasn't nothing more to it."

"Okay, then. I guess I have my work cut out for me. You don't know a thing about her so you probably don't know of anybody who might have had it in for her.

Right?" I thought he might be lying to me, but I wasn't sure.

"No, I don't."

"And you have no idea how she would've ended up by the dumpster next to your apartment complex? That's the part of the story that's not sitting right with me, I'll be honest with you. You told me earlier the two of you went out to your car, and you wanted to mess around with her, right?"

"Yeah, that's what I said."

"And you grabbed her crotch, which was when you found out she was a man. Right?"

"Yeah, that's right. You got it. You must be taking good notes."

I was. "Now, the Zoo Bar is a good 5 miles away from your apartment."

"Yeah, so what?"

"So what? Listen, your story is that you went to the bar, you met Adele there, the two of you went to your car right outside the bar, and then you messed around. You found out she was a biological male and you kicked her out of the car. And then you drove off."

"Yeah. That's my story. So what?"

"How did she end up 5 miles away from the bar, right by your apartment? It's not like your story is that the two of you went back to your apartment, you messed around and then you kicked her out. That would be one thing. That would explain how she would've been in your neighborhood. But, what you're telling me makes no sense to me at all. Your apartment is about 5 miles away from that bar and she lived 3 miles in the other direction. That means she wasn't in her neighborhood when she was found and she wasn't near the bar, either. That means that either it was a terrible coincidence she ended up in the neighborhood of the person who was last seen with her, or…"

"Or what? You still think I did it, don't you?"

"I don't know. Listen, it's not anything against you. I always have to look at these cases with a cynical eye. If I don't look at them with a cynical eye, I get into trouble. So yes, I do question it. I'm not going to say I think you're innocent, not at all. Truth be told, I never know if the people I defend are innocent or guilty. You're no different. And it doesn't help that you gave a confession to the cops. That doesn't help at all."

"Yeah, dog. I got ya. I was in the joint. All the dudes in there be innocent." Then he laughed. "Or so they say. I know almost all of them were good for what they were charged with. Including me. Yeah, I held up that liquor store. I'll admit it. I did it. I ain't never told nobody differently. I don't be telling even the dudes in prison different. So I sure as hell ain't going to tell you differently. I own up to the shit I do. I always be owning up to the things I do."

"Well, I hope you're right. It just doesn't look so good."

"You're acting like this is some kind of a hopeless case. You best not be approaching it that way, though. You best be looking at this case and saying goddammit, I can win this. No way am I going to the joint for something I didn't do. No fucking way. And if I go to the joint for something I didn't do, you best know I'll be rolling on Heather for the murder of the good Reverend Scott." He nodded his head. "That's what I'll do. I got something up my sleeve, something that'll hopefully get my sentence shortened, and that's rolling on her for that. I know cops always be looking for a good witness to a murder. So, that's a fair warning to you. If I go down for this case, I'm bringing Heather down with me."

"I figured as much. And you're right, that probably would be a piece of valuable information to the cops. The reverend has gone missing and it's been kind of a big deal. Not that anybody will miss him, aside from the people who still were brainwashed by him and thought he walked on water. And there are quite a few people still like that. People who still believed in him, and thought that what he said was true. But since you know where the body is buried, and you probably could lead the cops to the area, you're right about one thing – that would be valuable information, and, if you get convicted for this case, you probably could use that to get your sentence shortened." That was the reality, which made this entire situation extremely precarious for Heather and her mother.

"Yeah, I know the score. So if you want me to keep my mouth shut about Heather, then I suggest you don't lose this case. So you better be getting to work."

"I know. Believe me, I know."

Chapter Ten

WHEN I GOT BACK to the office, I wanted to talk to Harper. I hadn't yet confided in her about what was going on because I was so on the fence about taking the case. Once I found out how serious things were for Heather, I knew I had to take Beck's case and would have to talk to Harper about it.

I got into our office suite, headed over to her office and lightly knocked on the door. She was on the phone. She was talking quietly, and I heard her daughter's name, Abby, a lot.

I didn't want to barge in on her. I knew she was still having problems with Abby, as far as her having a drug problem. Not that Abby had backslid, but Harper was paranoid she would, so she was on top of her all the time. They were going through family counseling and Harper was finding out that not only was Abby having problems in school, she was also having nightmares about her mother being murdered. From what Harper told me, she had suppressed this all this time. That was why she was so shy and withdrawn before. Rina apparently had a different way of dealing with her mother's murder. She dealt with her mother's death by being boisterous and loud and acting like she didn't give a damn about it. But I knew she, too, was affected, as much as Abby was.

Since Abby tended to keep her feelings bottled in, she was at a much higher risk of becoming addicted to drugs than her sister was. She was also much more prone to being depressed than her sister. Harper had confided all this to me and I had a great deal of sympathy for her.

I knew what it was like dealing with a sick child, and, at the moment, I also knew what it was like dealing with an emotionally unbalanced child. Ever since Amelia found she possibly was not my daughter, she had been acting out. Acting out in school and acting out at home. She was becoming a disciplinary problem in both places, and I was at my wit's end. She was in a private school and she would possibly be expelled from that school. She was starting fights on the playground, cussing at her teachers, and even cussed out the principal. We were doing family counseling of our own, and I got a recommendation from Harper who told me her therapist, Dr. Morrow, was one of the best in the business. I had an appointment with Dr. Morrow for the following week.

Harper looked up at me and put her finger up. I nodded. She hung up the phone and smiled. "Sit down, sit down," she said. "What's going on?"

"How are things? How's Abby?"

"Abby is Abby. I just can't believe I didn't see it. I just can't believe I didn't figure out the real reason she was doing drugs was because of what happened to her mother. How awful is it to lose your mother at such a young age and so violently? Of course she was affected by what happened.

Of course she was. Anybody would be. Anyhow, the counseling is coming along okay. I'm finding out a lot about the girls and their feelings about what happened to their mom. Abby started to open up and her sister has been telling me she and Abby have grown very close within the last few months. So I guess there was a blessing in what was going on with the girls."

"There's always a blessing. In just about anything that happens, there's a blessing." I didn't tell Harper about what was happening with Amelia and me yet. I didn't know how to put that into words. I didn't want to acknowledge, even to myself, I would probably lose her. I couldn't face that, so I didn't tell anybody about it.

"So, what brings you here?" Harper asked. "You look kind of worried."

I took a deep breath. "I don't know how to tell you this, except to come out and tell you. But Heather is possibly in trouble."

Harper blinked rapidly. "Oh God, why? What's going on with her? Is she drug running again? Goddammit, I told her not to do that anymore. I told her she would get caught for that. Don't tell me, she came to you to represent her because she got busted for drug running. Is that it?"

"No, that's not it."

"Then what is it? What happened?"

Another deep breath. "She's in trouble, because…"

Harper's face changed. "This is about the Reverend Scott, isn't it? I've been reading in the news that he's been missing for the past few weeks. He didn't show up for his new trial and people who knew him were telling the police he's been gone a while. This has something to do with him, doesn't it?"

"Yes. It does." I didn't know how Harper changed gears

so quickly, but she certainly did hit the bulls-eye rather quickly. I was impressed.

"Oh, God. Please tell me she didn't kill him. Please." Harper hung her head. "Heather has been like a third daughter to me. I've always felt very maternal towards her. She's so lost and has such a hard shell. But underneath it all, there's a good woman in there. She's gone through so much in her life. Please tell me she's won't go to prison for something like killing Reverend Scott. Not that he didn't have it coming, because if anybody in the world needed to be killed, it was him."

"Heather won't go to prison if I can help it."

"So she hired you to be her attorney?" Harper looked hurt. "I don't know why she came to you to hire. Why didn't she just come to me? In fact, why didn't she tell me anything about any of this? All this time and she never mentioned a word about it."

"Well, I think she didn't want to disappoint you. But no, I'm not representing her."

"Who is representing her, then? Who did you find for her?"

"Nobody. As of now, nobody knows what she did. In fact, I don't even know exactly what she did. She told me a story but I think it was a lie. I think she was covering up for somebody. What I think happened was that her mother, Louisa Garrison, killed the reverend and Heather took the fall. What happened was that my current client, Beck Harrison, helped Heather get rid of the body. Heather told Beck she killed the guy. The story she gave me, and I believe the story she gave Beck, was that the Reverend Scott came into her house with a gun. She struggled with the reverend to get the gun out of his hand, the gun went off, and he was killed. At least that's the story she told me. The real story, I think, is something else. I don't quite know what, but the story she told me doesn't make any sense."

Harper shook her head. "No, it's not making sense. She knows better than that. She knows she has a right to kill Reverend Scott if he's threatening her or somebody else or if he was just in their house. Even if he was in their house without a gun, she had the right to kill him. All she had to do was call the cops."

"I know that. What she told me was she was afraid she was a two-time loser and that the police would never believe her. Or the jury would never believe her. So she panicked and enlisted Beck to help her bury the body in the Arizona desert. I think the story is something else. I think it's much more serious. At any rate, Beck has the goods on her and told me he's more than willing to serve her up on a platter if his case goes south."

"And what is his case?"

"He's accused of killing a transgendered woman, Adele Whittier. His case is a dead dog loser. At least, at the moment it is."

"Why is it a dead dog loser?"

"It's a dead dog loser because, number one, he confessed to the crime. He claimed he confessed after he asked for an attorney and was refused. They kept questioning him. He told me he knew his rights and figured that if he gave them a confession after he asked for an attorney and his request was refused, the confession would be thrown out. Which is true. If we can prove he asked for an attorney and the request was refused, that confession will be gone. That's the rub – we have to prove that happened."

"Why did he confess?"

"He told me he confessed because the cops were telling him they got the goods on his younger brother, Matt, who is

15 years old. Beck knows his brother's been dealing drugs and the cops know that too. They told Beck that if he confessed to the murder of Adele, they wouldn't press charges against his younger brother. He figured that since he asked for an attorney and was refused, his confession wouldn't be valid, so he might as well sign the confession to get his brother out of trouble."

"I suppose that's reasonable. Any other reason why he would confess? Was he coerced?"

"No. Unless you consider they were offering his brother's freedom in exchange for his confession to be coercion, but that's not really the case. It's on the line but not over it. And, as it turned out, it was a lie. The brother wasn't really in trouble. So, the cops lied to him. What's new?"

"So that's how you'll get the confession thrown out? We have to show the cops violated his Miranda Rights? Is that it? Is there anything else about this case that'll be challenging?"

"That's one reason why I think the case is a loser, but that's not the only reason."

"What other reasons do you think that?"

"Well, Adele's body was found by his apartment complex and the story was that he and Adele were at the Zoo Bar and went out to his car to mess around. He said he felt a lump in her crotch and he kicked her out of the car. In other words, he said he didn't take her home, so how did her body end up next to his apartment complex? And no, she doesn't live around him, either."

Harper nodded her head. "Well, I suppose it's pretty obvious. Somebody had it in for Beck and also wanted to kill Adele. For whatever reason. That's usually how these cases go – somebody kills somebody else and frames another person who they're mad at. So, as usual, you have to look for the intersection between who might have had it in for Beck, and, at the same time, had it in for Adele. Now you say Adele was a transgendered woman? Is that right?"

"Yeah. She was."

"Well, I suppose you can look for somebody who has it in for Beck who might or might not have known Adele. As long as the person has a hatred for transgendered people, that would be two birds, one stone right there. Tell me a little bit about this Beck person. What's his background?"

"He was imprisoned for 5 years. Rob One. While he was in there, he joined the Aryan Brotherhood. He told me the reason he joined was for protection. He said he was getting jumped by black guys inside and needed protection. So he became a part of that gang."

"Okay. Well that's not tragic. From what I understand, the official creed of the Aryan Brotherhood has nothing against LGBTQ. They're mainly focused on racial differences, and, at the moment, they're also a part of organized crime. You probably know this. You were in prison."

"Yeah, I know that. I knew quite a few people in the Aryan Brotherhood when I was in the joint myself, and you're right, for the most part, they could care less about gay or transgendered people. Regardless, because he's been involved in a hate group, prosecutors charged Adele's murder as a hate crime. So that's another wrinkle in the case."

"What else do you know about this Beck person? What does he do for a living?"

"He works for a sanitation plant. So you might say he has a shitty job." I laughed. "Sorry, bad pun."

Harper laughed as well. "But it was funny. Anything else you can tell me? I mean after all, if he was part of the Aryan Brotherhood, he's probably involved in some kind of activities on the outside. You should look into that. See if he's got any connections with drug runners or things like that."

"Well, I know he has at least one connection and that's Charlie, Heather's ex-boyfriend. Charlie sent Beck over to Heather's house when Heather called Charlie to help her get rid of Reverend Scott's body. So, Beck and Charlie are friends. I don't know what that means, necessarily, but I suppose it's a good bet Beck is probably into drug running on the side."

"Find out what you can about him," Harper said. "Of course, the problem is that since Adele was transgendered, it could very well have been a random person who killed her. There are a lot of people out there who have it in for transgendered people. And obviously you can possibly narrow it down by finding out who in Beck's circle would have done something like that, because she ended up outside his apartment complex."

"I agree. Do you want to second-chair this?"

"That goes without saying. Of course I do. I don't know how Heather will feel about that, however. After all, she didn't tell me about what was going on. She's probably too embarrassed to tell me about what kind of trouble she's in. But that's okay. I'll let her know I love her unconditionally. Maybe she'll tell me the truth about what happened to the Reverend Scott if she knows I won't judge her."

"I don't think she'll tell you the truth about that," I said. "You're not her attorney. I'm not her attorney, either. I can't be her attorney, because of the conflict of interest issue. And, since you're in the same office as me, you can't be her attorney either. So, if she told either one of us the truth, we'll have to testify against her if it came to that. We can be compelled. The story she gave me indicated she committed a crime, but not a serious one. What she told me was she helped dispose of the body. On the facts of what she told me, however, it wasn't murder, which is why she felt comfortable enough to tell me about it. However, I think the truth is much more serious than that. I have a feeling there's a first degree murder involved in this whole scenario, and there's no way she'll tell either of us about that."

Harper looked pensive when I said these things to her. She looked down. "You're right. Of course. She would be open to liability if she tells either of us the truth. We shouldn't try to find the truth. It's not our business. And, I think you can agree, that guy got what was coming to him." She chuckled. "That's been the story lately, hasn't it? Victims who are better off dead. Sometimes you just want to hand out a medal for killing somebody like your father or the Reverend Scott. He was definitely somebody who needed to be dead." She nodded. "Some people just need to be dead. That's a fact of life. Reverend Scott was one of those people, as was your father."

"Well, I thought I'd tell you about what's going on with my case."

Harper sighed. "We have to win this, or else Heather will be in big trouble. So we'll have to really throw ourselves into this. Leave no stone unturned. If Beck doesn't get convicted for murdering Adele, he won't have any reason to roll on Heather for anything."

"True. So yes, I'm going to have to throw everything I can into this case. And you will too. You'll help me, right?"

"Goes without saying." She shook her head. "If Heather gets in trouble, I don't know what I'll do. I'll feel like I lost one of my daughters."

When she said that, it was like she stabbed me in the heart. After all, I possibly *would* lose my daughter. Not to cancer – thank God, she was still in remission– but to Baron Wicker.

I turned around and saw somebody standing in the suite. He was standing in front of Pearl, who was answering the phones. He glanced at me, and, before I could duck behind Harper's desk, he rushed over to me.

Goddammit. I instinctively knew who he was before he even said one word to me. Not that I'd recognized him. I didn't. Yet I somehow knew who he was.

"Damien Harrington?" the man asked when he saw me.

I was tempted to tell him my name was not Damien Harrington, but I knew that would be pointless. I was sure he had a picture of me.

"Yeah. I'm Damien Harrington."

At that, he handed me a copy of a petition.

"You've been served."

Chapter Eleven

I LOOKED OVER AT HARPER, who was staring at me with her mouth agape. "What's going on?"

I took a deep breath. "I think I told you Sarah has been harassing Amelia, telling her I'm not her father. I told you that, didn't I?"

Harper looked shocked. Her eyes were wide and her mouth was open. She shook her head slowly but then nodded. "Yes, I remember you talking about that. So what's going on?"

I took a deep breath. "It's Sarah. She apparently had an affair with a man by the name of Baron Wicker. She's been telling me this Baron guy is Amelia's father. She claims she already had him take a paternity test which showed he's Amelia's father. So now, apparently, Sarah wants Amelia to get to know this guy. " I looked at the petition. "And, it looks like not only is she trying to establish paternity for this Baron Wicker person, but she also apparently…"

"Apparently what?" Harper looked genuinely concerned.

The Hate Crime

I took a deep breath as I read through the rest of the paternity petition. Not only did the petition seek to establish Baron Wicker was Amelia's father, but there was an attached parenting plan on the back of the petition. I read the parenting plan and then re-read the petition carefully. I was shocked to see that, at the end of petition, where her attorney asked for a remedy, she asked for my parental rights to be severed.

"Oh my God. Oh my God. This can't be happening to me." I closed my eyes. "This can't be happening to me."

"What's happening to you? What's going on?"

"Sarah wants my parental rights to Amelia to be severed. She can't do this to me. She told me on the phone she just wanted Baron to get to know Amelia. That's what she said. She just wanted him to meet her. And now, here she is, asking on this petition to have my parental rights severed from my own daughter. How could she do this to me?"

Harper stood up and put her arm around me. "Now, calm down. Just calm down. You know as well as I do that no judge will sever your parental rights, not when you're the only father that girl has ever known. Even if it's proven that you're not the biological father of Amelia, you're still the presumed father. And it's definitely not in the best interest of Amelia that she be taken from you and given to somebody else. So don't worry." She lightly massaged my shoulders. "She's not a coffee cup you give to somebody else."

"You don't understand. Baron Wicker is one of the richest men in America. He's a Texas oil billionaire. He's got more money than God, which means he can hire the best attorneys to come after me. And he also has the money to bribe the right judge. Or blackmail him or her. You know how those rich guys roll. When they want something, they'll get it. And this man apparently wants my daughter." I put my head in my hands. I was shaking all over.

"He won't get your daughter. Have you taken a paternity test? Have you given your DNA to find out if you're the father of Amelia after all?"

"No, I haven't taken a DNA test yet. To be honest with you, I'm terrified to do that. I'm terrified of finding out I'm not really her father. And, I know what you're saying, any non-corrupt judge won't sever my rights to her. Not after what I've gone through with her. The judge will know Amelia and I are very close. I'm her only parent. I've been her only parent for quite a long time. When Sarah left the family, when Amelia was sick, I was there in the hospital room every night when she was sick. I took her to the doctors. I held her while she cried. I did all that. I was there for all that, not Sarah. Goddammit, it's so unfair. How could she do this to me?"

I felt so agitated. I was jumping out of my skin. I felt like I did when I was 15 years old and had just killed my stepfather. I was so angry when I killed him. He was beating on me all the time. He came home and beat up my mom and I lost it. I just lost it. My mom couldn't necessarily fight back. She was a small lady, very thin and little, and I thought he would kill her that night. He was a strong man, and when he drank, he had the strength of 20 men. So I shot him while he slept. Killed him in cold blood. The prosecutors knew I did the world a favor, so they went easy on me.

And, at the moment, I was feeling about Sarah the same way I felt about Stephen all those years ago. I hated her with the passion of a thousand suns, and if I could get away with it, I would kill her. I closed my eyes, knowing I could not get away with killing her, no matter how much I wanted to.

And I wanted to. I really did. That was why I always had a ton of sympathy for my clients who killed somebody when they were angry. Sometimes I actually admired them for having the courage to do something about the people who tormented them. I didn't have the same courage. If I did, I would've killed Sarah.

"Damien, are you okay?" Harper was very concerned. "Listen, I'll find you a good family law attorney. I'll help you find the best one. You're going to fight this. You're going to win. I think you should ask that even if Baron Wicker is proved to be the biological father of Amelia that he not have contact with her. Don't even open the door to him seeing her. Don't let the camel get his nose under the tent."

"It goes without saying that I'll try to do just that. I don't know how successful that'll be, though. Sarah tells me that because this Baron Wicker guy is a rich guy, he can give her things I can't."

"Since when does a judge factor that kind of thing in the 'best interest of the child' analysis? You make a good living. You can give her everything she needs. You're sending her to a private school, and I know you have a good college fund going for her. You have excellent insurance for her and you've been there for her through all her sicknesses. That's what matters to a judge, not the fact that there's some richie-rich guy trying to get his hands on her. Why would he be better than you? He could take her on a private plane? He could sail around the world with her? What exactly can he give her that you can't? At least, in the big scheme of things?"

"Nothing. Of course. But that's not what I'm worried about. I'm simply worried about the fact that... Well, I'm worried the relationship with my daughter will change. She's so incredibly bright. She knows what's going on and doesn't like it. I don't know. It's weird that, even if I beat this custody case down, I'm not her father. At least, I'm not her biological father. And I just think it'll change things between us and I don't want it to."

"Of course you don't want things to change. And it won't. Yes, it might be weird at first, but you guys will get through it. You have to understand one thing – family bonds don't come from blood. Look at me – my daughters are adopted. I have just as much love for them as I would for any other child. Biological or no. Granted, Abby is having problems right now, but that's mainly because she lost her mother in such a way. Rina is having the same kind of problems but it's not as obvious with her. But we're getting through it and they love me just the same as they did their mother. At least that's what Rina and Abby both told me. So, don't worry about it. You're still Amelia's father, and you always will be. You always will be."

I smiled. "Thanks. I know you're right. Now, I just have to get an attorney and answer this petition. I have to face it. And I'll do a DNA test to see if I'm her father. I have a feeling I'm not. You know, I get so angry about Sarah having an affair with somebody while we were married. But then I think to myself, if she had an affair and that person actually fathered Amelia, I should be grateful she cheated on me. I know it seems kind of weird, but, if you think about it, if Sarah never had that affair, I wouldn't have Amelia right now. She's the light of my life. She really is. I can't imagine what my life would be like without her. So, yeah, I hate Sarah for many different reasons, but I can't hate her for cheating on me and having Amelia through this affair. I just can't."

"You're looking at this in a way most people wouldn't." Harper nodded. "Keep looking at the bright side. Because, as you say, there's always a bright side. There's always a blessing. And your blessing was Amelia. So, no matter what happens, you just fight this with all you have. Amelia doesn't belong to him. And, the way Sarah has been acting, Amelia doesn't belong to her either. Amelia belongs to you. And that's all you need to know."

I took a deep breath and stood up. "Well, I think this is enough bad news for one day. It's time to make an appointment with an attorney and get going on this. I have to think about the whole Beck thing. His first court appointment is in a couple of days. I'll try to get a bond reduction for him and I'll also talk to the prosecutor to see if they can drop the hate crime designation. The only reason why they're looking at this as a hate crime is because of Beck's background in prison with the Aryan Brotherhood. You're absolutely right, the official creed of the Aryan Brotherhood has no problem with LGBT. So, technically, there's no reason to use his background as an enhancement in this case. I'll start there. If I could just get the prosecutors off the hate crime thing, that's one victory I can claim. Of course, I can't be satisfied with that. I have to move ahead and hope I can find out who really killed Adele, assuming Beck didn't do it."

"Of course, you'll have to show Beck didn't do it. Because if you don't, Heather will go down for that murder. And we can't have that happen." Harper nodded her head. "I'll do all I can to help you too. I'll approach this as if Rina or Abby are the ones in trouble. That's how I feel. I feel like one of my daughters is in trouble."

It was then I noticed Harper had tears in her eyes. It was my turn to comfort her. "Harper, don't worry. We'll fight this and win. Don't you worry." I took a deep breath. "I'll find out who really killed Adele. It'll be fine. You'll see."

"I hope you're right. I really hope you're right."

Chapter Twelve

I MADE AN APPOINTMENT WITH TOM, because I needed to see if he could tell me anything about the victim, Adele Whittier, or Beck. I hoped Tom had some good information to go on.

I went over to his house for dinner. Or, rather, his apartment. Tom lived in Kansas City, Kansas in a tiny one-bedroom apartment with hardwood floors. He had a little tiny dog, a Maltese mix named Trudy. He recently bought her a companion named Max, who was also a little tiny dog. Tom explained he loved dogs but his building had a weight limit on the dogs that could stay there. That was the reason why he had to get these tiny things. Still, I thought it was funny that a big beefy guy with lots of tattoos, like Tom, would have such little froufrou dogs. It didn't seem to match his personality, or the way he looked, but that was okay.

They were sweet pups, and when I went over there, they both leaped on my lap and licked me on my face.

"Trudy, Max," Tom said. "You get off him. I'm so sorry.

I try to teach them not to do that, but they just can't help it. They're full of love."

I had to laugh. "I know, they *are* full of love. I want to get Amelia and Nate a dog. I haven't wanted to get them a dog before this, because Amelia was so sick and her immunity was so low. I was worried a dog might make her sicker. But they've been asking me for one, and I'll get them one. Amelia wants a French bulldog and Nate wants a pit bull. I think I could make them both happy by getting one of each."

"If you want a pit bull, start at the animal shelters. They're full of pitties who will love you until you die. Frenchies are different - you won't find them in any shelter. They're so valuable, people have been held up at gunpoint to steal the dogs while the owner takes them out for a walk. If they're that valuable, you won't find them in a shelter. But pitties, yeah, they're in shelters all the time and desperately need a good home," Tom said.

"I agree. I'll adopt a pittie from a shelter and buy a Frenchie from a breeder."

I immediately thought about Amelia and how I was in danger of losing her again. Somehow, I thought that if I bought a dog, she would stay with me no matter what. No matter what the judge said, she would stay with me, if I just bought her a dog. I know it wasn't rational to think that way, but that was going through my mind.

Tom didn't know about any of this. I was going to tell him, because maybe he could help out. If Tom could dig up some dirt on this Baron Wicker person, that would be my best bet to make sure my parental rights weren't severed from my own daughter. After all, Baron Wicker was a very wealthy man, which meant he probably was involved in something shady along the way. I doubted he was squeaky clean.

So that was the first thing I asked Tom to do. I asked him to look into Baron Wicker's background.

"I'll find something on him, don't you worry," Tom said. "I'm sure he's been involved in all kinds of shit. I've seen his name in the paper a few times. He's always seemed like a bastard to me."

"I'm sure he is. Hopefully the things he's done in his life have been worse than the things I've done in my life. But I wouldn't count on it." I grimaced. I hated that my juvenile record had been unsealed. It wasn't fair that it could be used against me. But I knew why it was – I knew the governor had to have some kind of revenge for my blackmailing him. And he got his revenge by unsealing my record. That meant that shit would follow me around no matter what I did.

"Anyhow, what did you find out about Beck Harrison?" I asked Tom. "Anything good about him?"

"Yeah, I found out he's a piece of work. I mean, I'm sure you know about all that. The Aryan Brotherhood membership, the robbery, all that. So I'm not telling you anything new here."

"No. You're not. But go ahead. What else have you found out about him?"

"Well, I'm sure this will come as no surprise to you, but he killed a man in prison. It was an initiation into the Aryan Brotherhood. They required him to do it and he did." Garrett shook his head. "The guy he killed was a guy named Jackson Benner. He was a black guy who was rather powerful. He was also a member of a rival gang by the name of the Black Guerrilla Family. The BGF is one of the most prevalent and powerful black prison gangs in America. From my research, I found that the BGF has somewhat lofty goals. Their stated mission is to get rid of racism and topple the American government. They recruit black gang members in prison on the outside to become a part of their gang on the inside. This Jackson Benner was one of the most prominent members of the BGF, so the Aryan Brotherhood wanted him gone. And, since Beck was one of the newer members of their gang, they assigned him to do the dirty work."

"How? So what happened? Did anybody find out about it? By anybody, I mean any of the prison guards or anybody else in authority in Cameron?"

"No, of course not. Prison code, you know. Nobody would talk. So, nobody knew Beck killed him. The only reason why I know he killed Jackson is because I've been on the street talking to other former members of the Aryan Brotherhood and the BGF, and that's the story I've been given."

"Well, that's interesting. I guess I should look at former BGF members. They might've wanted Beck to get into trouble, so they killed Adele and pinned it on him. Although I have to admit that's a far-fetched theory. I mean, if they wanted to get Beck, they just would have. They would've killed him." I shook my head. "I'll put it in my back pocket, but I don't think it'll necessarily bear fruit. What else did you find out about Beck?"

"I found out about his family life. His father is serving time in prison for Murder One. If Beck has any kind of white supremacist leanings, chances are he got them from his dad. His father is not a member of any white brotherhood gang, or anything like that - not in prison and not on the outside, either. However, from what I understand, he's a hateful person. Seems his mother, Beck's grandmother, was murdered by an African-American man. Because of that,

Beck's father, whose name is David, apparently hates black people. He went to prison for murdering an African-American man who he worked with at a local restaurant. The guy's name was Tyrell Washington, and, according to my understanding, David Harrison killed Tyrell for no good reason. I got ahold of his file and he kept a diary where he talked about all kinds of vile and hateful things about other races."

I worked that out in my head. "Sounds about right. It sounds like the apple didn't fall too far from the tree. So his father was a white supremacist and hated black people. And now he's serving time in prison for murder one. Is he LWOP?"

"Yeah. He is. So there you have the father."

"What about his mother? What's her story?"

"Her story is she's on SSD at the moment. She lives in a trailer out in the country, in Harrisonville. Apparently she's suffered from debilitating depression her entire life. She recently has also been diagnosed with schizophrenia. She'd been in the state-run mental hospital a few times, but they always let her go because she wasn't necessarily bad enough to stay in one of those places. And you know how it is – if you don't have insurance, which she doesn't, then you don't get to stay anywhere. Not in state-run hospitals and certainly not in private hospitals. So, the upshot is she's schizophrenic, but, because she doesn't have the money to actually get treatment, she's just living in a trailer and apparently she's not well. To say the very least."

"Okay. I can already see how this is shaping up. His mother is schizophrenic, his father is imprisoned. What about his little brother, Matt? What's going on with him? According to Beck, Matt's been dealing drugs and that was why he confessed to the cops he killed Adele. He said the cops told him that if he confessed, they would not press charges against Matt. It turns out Matt wasn't arrested for anything. Did you find anything out about him?"

"Yeah. I did. Matt's been going down the same road as his brother. He's been dealing drugs, assaulting people, and he's also been involved in some hate incidents. He was caught tagging a highway underpass with Swastikas. He also went to a dorm room of an African-American kid and put a noose on the door. So he's going down the wrong path, to say the very least. But he's not gotten arrested for anything major. Again, I only know these things because I know people on the street who know him. They even tell me all the things he's been doing."

"Good Lord, does Beck have any normal family members? Anybody who's not in trouble?"

"No. He doesn't. At least, his blood family isn't normal. He does have a half-sister, Charity, who seems okay. She's on the dole with two kids, but compared to the rest of that clan, she's a fucking CEO." He laughed.

I made a mental note to investigate Charity and see what she could tell me. "Now Beck told me he's a changed man. He told me he was in the Aryan Brotherhood while imprisoned but that he doesn't believe in that kind of philosophy anymore. Plus, he said he only joined the AB in prison because he needed protection from some black guys who were jumping him all the time. Do you know anything about that? From what you've found out, is that true? Is it true he's renounced the ideology of the Aryan Brotherhood? Or, he never even really adopted it?"

Garrett drummed his fingers on the table, while he seemed to contemplate what I was asking him. "I don't really know about that. It seems that maybe he has, at least that's what his peeps tell me. He doesn't say hateful things and hasn't hung out with his AB brothers on the outside. A lot of the hate crimes you've been seeing around the country, more and more these days, is the work of not only the Aryan Brotherhood but other members of the far right. The people who believe America should be white, and anybody not white doesn't belong in this country. He hasn't been hanging with people like that."

"Have they been trying to recruit him on the outside? I personally couldn't see how Beck could get away with renouncing the AB. After all, the AB spent 5 years protecting his butt in prison. They're going to want loyalty on the outside as well. You don't just leave an organization like that. Especially not when you go as whole hog as Beck did. I would imagine they're harassing him at the very least. But, more likely, they're probably threatening him. Threatening his life, threatening his family, threatening everything about him."

"That's what I'm trying to figure out. Nobody's talking about that."

"Then it makes sense this happened to him."

"What do you mean?"

"Think about it. What's the best way to get back at somebody refusing to join your gang outside the prison? Besides, of course, killing that person?" I nodded. "I'll tell you the best way to do that. Killing somebody and pinning it on him. Especially if that somebody is a part of a marginalized group as Adele was. That would be my first instinct - look at somebody in the AB who had it in for Beck. Maybe the whole murder of Adele was some kind of ritualized initiation act. Kill the transgendered women and pin it on somebody renouncing our ideology. Two birds one stone." I clapped my hands together as if I was getting dust off them.

Tom nodded. "That makes a lot of sense. I'll keep my

ear to the ground and find out who knows AB peeps who might know something about what happened to Adele. Although, I have to say, it'll be difficult trying to get people to talk about that. They're pretty tight-lipped about the things they do and are very protective of one another. I don't think I'll find a snitch who'll tell me something like that. But I'll certainly try."

"What else did you find out? About Beck or his family?" I asked.

"Well, apparently, as I mentioned, Beck also has a half-sister. Her name is Charity Harrison. She was born while Beck's father was serving one of his prison sentences. She lives in Raytown."

"And what does she do?"

"She has two kids so she's a stay-at-home mom. But she's living on the dole. You might want to give a shout-out to her because she can probably tell you a lot about the family. Of all the Harrisons, I think she's the most normal. By normal, I mean she's not in trouble with the law. At least not yet."

I made notes. I thought the most logical place to start looking for an alternative suspect would be in the AB. But at the same time, I hoped that was not the path I would have to go down. I certainly didn't want them coming after me or my family. And I knew they would do just that.

"Okay, then. I'll pay a visit to Charity in Raytown."

"Okay," said Tom. "I'll do some background research on Adele. There might be something shady in her background that would help you out as well. I don't know enough about her, but I'll find out very soon."

Tom and I talked a bit more about this and that. I knew he would at least try to find something out about Baron to help in my custody case. That would be the most helpful thing for me. At the moment, I was heavily involved with Beck's case, mainly because I wanted to protect Heather. However, my custody case was most important. I had to protect my family at all costs. Nobody would take my daughter from me.

Nobody.

Chapter Thirteen

I WENT to see Charity after I spoke with Tom. I made an appointment with her and she told me I could come by anytime. She explained she was usually home. She sounded a bit apologetic, saying she was looking for a job, but it was difficult to do with two kids at home.

"The father's not around," she explained over the phone. "And it was the same father for both kids. Just in case you're wondering."

"I wasn't wondering, actually. That's really none of my business." I didn't want to judge Charity before I saw her. She might end up becoming a good witness for me and she hopefully had a lot of information about Beck I needed to know.

I got to Charity's apartment, which was a run-down place probably built in the 1960s. Outside the complex were older cars, many from the 80s and 90s. There were very few cars I recognized that would have been manufactured post-2010. I went to her apartment unit, and knocked on the door.

Charity answered the door with a small child on her hip. The child was a blonde and blue-eyed little girl who was button cute. The kid was probably less than two years old. Behind her, on the floor, was a small boy about the age of three. He was playing with a train set on the floor, making choo choo sounds as he made the train go around and around the track.

Charity herself was a very attractive young woman, probably around 20 years old. She was petite and thin, and had washed-out blonde hair she wore in a ponytail. Her teeth were slightly oversized, as were her eyes and lips. She almost looked cartoonish, but she was pretty in her way.

She smiled big and motioned to a threadbare couch in the living room. "Have a seat," she said in a slightly southern drawl. "I gotta put Heaven down," she said motioning to the little girl. "It's time for her nap." The little girl clawed at Charity's hair and started to cry a little bit. "She's getting a little cranky." At that, Charity disappeared into the bedroom and came back out five minutes later.

"Now, you wanted to talk to me about my brother Beck, right?"

I nodded my head. "Yes. As you know, he's been accused of murdering a transgendered woman. I wanted to talk to you and see what kind of background you can give me on your brother."

"Well, good luck with that, I mean defending him." Charity shook her head. "My brother has been in trouble for most of his life. As I'm sure you know. He went to prison when he was only 21. Rob One. He was in there for 5 years. Personally, from what my mother tells me, Beck probably shouldn't have gone to prison for so long for that. However, he had a shitty attorney. The prosecutors were trying to get him to roll over on the person who put him up to it, a known drug dealer in the area. However, Beck wouldn't do it and I think the prosecutors wanted to punish him. That was why he went down for so long."

"Who were the prosecutors trying to get him to roll on?"

"His name is Larry Rodriguez. He's still pretty well-known in the area, but, from what I understand, he's dealing less now and is more into the sex trade. Although he does still do a lot of dealing."

Larry Rodriguez. I wondered if he was the same guy as Tina's pimp and dealer. "Where is Larry now? What do you know about him?"

Charity shrugged. "Not much. From what I know, he's being held in the jail. He got caught dealing, and with a gun. He was holding up another drug dealer and that other drug dealer ratted on him. He's a felon, he's got a gun, and he's dealing, so the feds will take a bite out of his ass. That is, of course, unless he decides to roll on somebody over him. Higher up on the food chain. And he's the kind of worm who would do it, too." She laughed. "I think Larry knows he's got protection on the streets, so he's not really all that scared about snitching on others."

I wrote down what she was saying. I would have check out this Larry Rodriguez person, his background and everything. I didn't tell Charity about my other case I had with Larry in the middle of it. Tina's case. I'd been working to get her to roll on Larry but she still refused to do it. I would have to find some other way to try to get her charges reduced or even dismissed. Having the charges dismissed, of course, would be the best-case scenario, but one I didn't think would become a reality.

"What do you know about Beck which will be relevant to this case? Specifically, can you tell me how he feels about gay or transgendered?"

Charity looked like she was thinking on the question. She paused for a little bit. "Well, in answer to that question, I don't think he necessarily has a problem with people who are transgendered or gay. I mean, I never heard him say anything about them."

"What about his being a part of the Aryan Brotherhood?"

"What about that?"

"Do you think he's a true believer? Or do you think he just joined that gang in prison for protection?"

She shrugged. "I don't know about that. Our dad, I don't know him all that well, because he's been in and out of prison for most my life, but he's kind of a white supremacist. No, strike that, he's a Neo-Nazi. A true believer. My mom also doesn't know Beck's and my dad all that well. She dated him for just a few months. That's how I came into the world. She wasn't married to him or nothing like that. All she's told me is that he's a Neo-Nazi and she never should've got involved with him. My mom, she's not like that, so she could never stay with David, my dad. So, I guess an answer to your question is I wouldn't be surprised if Beck holds those beliefs. But he's told me he's not a racist. He's told me he just wanted to be a part of the Aryan Brotherhood gang in prison because he needed protection."

"That's exactly what he told me."

"Then maybe you better believe him. Now I can tell you a little something about that Adele person. The one he's accused of killing."

"You know her?"

"I do. I knew her when her name was William Page. In other words, I knew her when she was a he. Now, even when she went by a boy's name and didn't start growing her hair out, wearing makeup, and dressing like a woman, I kind of knew there was something off about her. Him at that time." She chuckled. "I never know what to say about this."

I was a little bit surprised Charity was familiar with Adele. Beck told me he didn't know Adele before he met her at the bar. I guessed it was possible, if a coincidence, that his half-sister would be familiar with her when he didn't know her from before. Then again, maybe he was lying to me about that. Maybe he really knew her from before.

"Did Beck know her, too?"

Charity shrugged. "No clue."

"How did you know her?"

"She worked for a guy I used to know, Jordan Kennedy. Actually, come to think of it, I think Beck and Jordan were friends. So yeah, I guess it's possible Beck knew Adele back in the day before she became Adele. He might have known her when she was going by the name William. That's possible."

"Jordan and Beck were friends?" This was becoming more and more interesting to me.

"Yeah, I guess they were. I don't think they were necessarily tight, but they knew one another."

"What does Jordan do? When you say Adele worked for him, what do you mean?"

"Jordan's a drug dealer. And when I say she worked for him, I mean she was one of his dealers. She became a nurse, so I guess she was trying to go straight." Then she laughed. "But then again, she knew a lot about drugs, so maybe that's why she became a nurse."

"When did she work for Jordan?"

"She worked for him when she was young. Remember, she was a man back then. I think she worked for him when she was around 16, 17. She was what, 26 when she died? So yeah, it's been quite a while since she's worked for him. But I know she used to."

I made notes of this. I wondered if it had anything to do with her being murdered. It might. It might not.

At this point, anything was possible.

Chapter Fourteen

OUR FIRST SHOT in front of a judge was Beck's initial appearance. It was the court appearance that had been continued from before because Beck was looking for private counsel. That private counsel was me, so we needed to go back in front of the judge and try to get a bond reduction and talk to the prosecutor about not charging this murder as a hate crime. If I could get them off the hate crime designation, I'd have an easier time suppressing Beck's white supremacist past at trial because his past would be less relevant.

I got there early to talk to the docket prosecutor, whose name was Molly Brighton. She was new which was why she was doing this particular docket.

I went up and shook her hand and introduced myself.

She nodded. "You're kind of a legend around here."

"I am? Why?" I had the feeling that being a "legend" wasn't necessarily a good thing.

"Because you walked down that murder charge. That

was an exciting case. I mean, who knew the governor's wife would be involved in something like that?"

"I don't know but she is. But you know she'll never serve time for it. Her lackey, Jacqueline Peterson, will take the fall. One thing for sure, this spells the end of Governor Weston's career. I don't think he can still claim to be a family values man when his wife was having an affair and apparently murdered the person with whom she was having an affair. Governor Weston has his own skeletons. They haven't come to light yet, but they will one day. They will. They always do, sooner or later."

"Well," Molly said, "congrats on walking that case down. Now what can I do for you?"

"I'm here on the Beck Harrison case. Now I understand your office has plans to charge this murder as a hate crime, right?"

"That's what I think. I'm not sure about that yet. The higher-ups haven't made a final decision."

"I'd suggest your office leave that alone. I think you know why this case was charged as a hate crime - you guys want to bring my client's membership in the Aryan Brotherhood into the trial. It's hard to prove a crime is motivated by hate and you guys can't prove my client had animus towards Adele just because she's transgendered."

"Your client is a known Neo-Nazi." It was obvious this fact was the be-all and end-all for Molly.

"Actually, he's not. Yes, in prison he was a member of a white supremacist group, but hasn't been active with them since he's been out of prison."

"Once you're in with them, you're always in with them. It's not something you can just turn your back on. You can't just get in with them in prison and then get out and say

The Hate Crime

'sorry I don't want any anything to do with you.' It doesn't work like that."

"Regardless, it's not relevant. The official creed of the Aryan Brotherhood talks about racial purity, says nothing about any kind of hatred of the LGBTQ community."

She laughed. "That's your argument? The Aryan Brotherhood hates people who are nonwhite, but don't care about people who are transgendered or gay? Seriously? Listen, a hate group is a hate group. If you're a member of a hate group and somebody marginalized is murdered, we'll charge it as a hate crime. Not always, but that's definitely something we look at."

"Be that as it may, there's nothing that stands out in this particular murder that would show it's a hate crime. You have any witnesses who'll testify my client was badgering Adele before she died about being transgendered? Any witnesses who can testify that he's been harassing her? Do you guys have anything that will give you evidence to charge this as a hate crime?"

"Not yet."

The judge came on the bench. It was Judge Wilson, who traditionally did the initial appearances for everybody who came through the Jackson County Justice system. I took a seat, the judge started calling the cases and soon got to mine.

"Mr. Harrison, I see you're back. And you have private counsel. Now, I'll read you your charges again, take your plea, and set the case over for a preliminary hearing."

I knew Beck's case wouldn't actually get a preliminary hearing, however, because it was a Grand Jury case. That was how murder cases went in Missouri. They were brought before the Grand Jury, a jury which decided if there was enough evidence to bound the defendant over for trial.

"Beck Harrison, you've been charged by the State of Missouri with one count of murder in the first degree. How do you plead?"

"Not guilty, Your Honor."

"Okay. I see there's a motion for a bond review in front of me as well. Ms. Brighton, do you have any objections to the defendant getting a bond?"

"None, Your Honor, although I would ask for a bond of at least 3 million."

"Three million is pretty steep," the judge said. "I'll set the bond at one million, 10%. The conditions of the bond are that the defendant is not to have contact with known felons, he must wear an electronic monitoring device and he must report to a probation office and submit mandatory regular drug screening."

I looked over at Beck. I had a feeling he could not even do 10% of a million. Most people couldn't. But I was somewhat encouraged that he was even given a bond.

I left the bench and looked over at him. "Any chance you can make bond?"

"Maybe. I just might be able to."

"Really? Who has that kind of money?"

"Don't worry about that." He nodded. "If I find that kind of dough, just don't even ask. It's really not your business."

I sighed. "It *is* my business. If you're getting it from a felon, that's a non-starter. You're not supposed to have contact with anybody who's been convicted of a felony."

Beck laughed. "Yeah? I know. But who else do you think I can get money from? Ain't nobody in my life not a convicted felon. Except for my sister. It's just a matter of time with her. It's pretty much I gotta get the money from somebody who's got a record or I don't get it at all."

The Hate Crime

"Maybe it's best you don't get it at all, then."

"Whatever. Okay," he said as the guard led him away. "I'll let you know if Imma get out of jail or not."

As he was being led away, I had a feeling he would get out of jail.

I also had a feeling that his getting out of jail, somehow, someway, would lead me to the key to this case.

Chapter Fifteen

I KNEW I had to find an attorney for my paternity case and knew I had to do it quickly.

I got the devastating results of my paternity test on the Friday after I took it. I got the results expedited and found out, indeed, that Amelia wasn't my daughter.

The envelope came in the mail and I didn't want to look at it. Yes, I knew that no matter what, Amelia was my daughter. Even if I did not actually supply her DNA, she was always my daughter. But that didn't matter. What mattered was that she was my *biological* daughter.

So, when I got the results in the mail, which showed I was not her father, I had a minor breakdown.

No, scratch that, I had a major breakdown.

I called up Sarah. Somehow, even though I'd known this was a possibility all along, I kept it together. I hoped none of this was true, so I was calm. However, once I found it *was* true, I decided it was time to tell Sarah exactly what I thought about her and her little plan to take Amelia away from me.

"Hi Damien," Sarah said as she picked up the phone.

I took a deep breath. *Calm down Damien, calm down.* However, I couldn't calm myself down. I just wanted to tear this bitch limb from limb. How could she do this to me? Even if she knew all along I wasn't Amelia's father, how could she break us up like that? That was the secret she should've kept until she was dead.

Which, if I had my way, would happen sooner rather than later.

"Don't fucking 'hi Damien' me," I said to her. I took a deep breath. "I got the results of the paternity test." I chuckled ruefully. "And yes, you're right. I'm not Amelia's dad. But that doesn't matter. I'm going to stay her dad if it's the last fucking thing I do. If I have to fucking come over and flay you alive, bit by bit, I'm gonna do that, if it means that's what I have to do to keep Amelia with me."

Sarah, on the other end of the line, remained calm. Maddeningly so. "Damien-"

"What? What can you possibly say to me at this point? I could kill you at this point, and I don't think there's a jury in this world that would convict me for it."

"Listen, Damien-"

"No. You won't do this. You won't succeed. I'm gonna find out things about Baron Wicker and there's no judge in the world who will allow that rich asshole to take Amelia away from me. This is where she belongs, and this is where she'll stay."

"Baron's her father."

"No, he fucking is not. He wasn't the one who was there when Amelia was sick, and possibly dying. For that matter, you weren't there either. I was there. I was the only one there. And why do I think Baron has known all along that

Amelia was his? Why do I think you told Baron a long time ago and he didn't give a shit?"

Sarah was quiet for a spell. "Damien, you're right about that. I told Baron, when Amelia was born, that I thought she was his. And I kept him in the loop about her all these years."

"You kept him in the loop, seriously? So you told him when she got sick, and would possibly die that she was in that state? You told him about all that? And what did he say? He didn't give a crap, did he?" By that time I was shaking with rage. I wanted to throttle her and Baron.

"He knew about it, but, Damien, I wouldn't put him in the middle of all that. You and Amelia, the last thing the two of you needed was baby daddy drama. I did this for you."

"Bullshit! You've never done anything for me, and you sure as hell have never done anything for Amelia. What's the real reason Baron never got involved in Amelia's life, prior to this? Because I'm not buying that you were looking out for mine and Amelia's feelings. I don't believe that for a second. I'll find out the truth. The truth will always win out, and it won't look good for you or Baron."

"Here's the truth, Damien. What would've happened, if I would've announced to you, years ago, that Baron was Amelia's father? I couldn't say anything about that because you and I were trying to work things out. And now we're not trying to work things out, and you've made it clear you want nothing to do with me, so I just figure that it's time for Amelia to know who her real father is. Plus Baron wants to raise her. He'll be a good dad. He doesn't have any other children and he's very well off. He can spoil her, the way she wants to be spoiled. The way she needs to be spoiled."

I shook my head. "No thank you. I won't allow her to be

spoiled like that. She'll have a normal life right here with me. And there's nothing that will change that."

Little did I know I was actually right about that. There was a piece of information, about to come to light, that would throw a monkey wrench into all of this.

And it was something I never, in a million years, expected.

Although I probably should have, knowing sneaky Sarah the way I did.

Chapter Sixteen

SOMETHING WAS NAGGING me about Larry Rodriguez. He had popped up in this case quite unexpectedly. He was the one back in the day who got Beck in trouble with the Rob One. And now, apparently, he also got Tina Phillips in trouble. She was his drug mule and he hung her out to dry. At any rate, since he was somehow in the middle of both of my cases, I would have to find out more about him. To do anything less would be malpractice on my part.

I went to see Tina at her halfway house. I was hoping she'd know something more about Larry. Maybe she could somehow be the key to my case with Beck. I didn't know why I thought that but I figured I should cover all my bases.

She was sitting on her porch swing waiting for me. I called her ahead of time to tell her I was coming.

"Hey!" she said as I approached her. "What did you find out about my case?"

"I've been in touch with the prosecutor and been asking them about Drug Court," I said.

She rolled her eyes. "I told you, no Drug Court. I don't want to mess with that shit. I'd rather go to prison."

"I can arrange that." I was annoyed. Yeah, I knew she was a victim too. But if I got something as lenient as Drug Court, she better take it. There was a chance she wouldn't go to prison if she got Drug Court. Granted, it was a small chance, since if she continued to do drugs, she would never graduate from the program. But she would for sure end up in prison if she didn't take Drug Court as her sentence. Yet she was trying to avoid all that. That wasn't making sense to me.

"Does Connor know you talk to me like that?" she asked.

"I'm sure he doesn't. And I don't know how Connor has a thing to do with this."

"He doesn't." Tina looked annoyed. "So tell me, what you got going? What you got cooking?"

"Listen, there's not a whole lot I can do for you unless you're willing to roll on Larry. But you won't, and won't take Drug Court, so I don't think I can do a thing for you."

"So why are you here?" Tina looked suspicious. "I mean, seriously, why do you bother coming down here to talk to me?"

"Because I need to talk to you about Larry. He's popped up in another case of mine and wanted to find out more about the guy."

"What do you need to know?"

"I need to find if he's ever dealt with an Adele Whittier."

"Adele Whittier? You mean the Adele Whittier who was murdered by your client, Beck Harrison? That Adele Whittier?" she asked with a snort and a shake of her head.

"One and the same. Listen, I found out Adele used to go

by the name of William and was a drug dealer herself back in the day."

"Do you think all drug dealers know each other?" Tina shook her head. "That's like saying all black people know all other black people. Or when you tell people you're from a certain city and they're all like 'do you know such and such?' He lives in that city too." She laughed. "You ever get that? People asking you if you know John Brown, because after all, he lives in Kansas City, too?"

I ignored her question. I had to at least try to get to the bottom of this. "What about Jordan Kennedy?"

"What about Jordan Kennedy?"

"Does Larry know anybody by that name?"

Tina shrugged. "I don't know. Why do you ask that question?"

"Because Adele worked for Jordan Kennedy back in the day. When she was a drug dealer, she worked for him."

Tina did not necessarily dismiss that question out of hand the way she did the other one. "Jordan Kennedy," she said nodding. "Actually, I think Larry knows him. Or, you might say Jordan Kennedy is Larry's business partner."

"Business rival, meaning?"

"Meaning Jordan Kennedy was trying to work the same turf as Larry. Larry had to set him straight a time or two. What does that have to do with anything?"

"I didn't know the answer to that question. I just wanted to know if Larry and Jordan were somehow associated."

I tried to work it out in my mind. Larry was the drug dealer in charge of Beck back in the day and was responsible for Beck getting pinched for Rob One. Jordan was a dealer in charge of Adele back when she was known as William.

Larry and Jordan were business rivals.

"Listen, Tina, if you have any information about Larry I need to know then you need to tell me. Don't worry, I'm your attorney, so whatever you say stays with me. Unless you want it to get out to somebody else. But you know you don't have to worry about me telling anybody about what you're telling me."

"Like what? What are you looking for? What kind of information do you need?"

"I don't know." I was having a hard time working it all out in my mind.

Tina scoffed. "Whatever. Listen, if you want some kind of specific information, ask a question and I'll tell you. But you have to ask me something. If you do that, I'll answer you. But as it is, I got nothing for you."

I suddenly realized I was talking to the wrong person.

The person I really needed to be speaking with was Heather.

Chapter Seventeen

I WOULD HAVE to find out a lot more about Adele. There was something sticking at me and I just had to know what it was. It was somewhat unusual that she was a dealer back when her identity was male. And then she became a nurse.

I had a hunch and would have to follow up on it.

The first thing I did was go to her high school, Van Horn High in Independence, Missouri. I needed to find a copy of her yearbook. I needed to find out what she looked like in high school when she had a male identity.

After that, I would get Anna involved in finding out more about her background.

I saw the class picture and I squinted when I looked at William Page. I was struck by how different he looked from Adele. I had seen pictures of Adele, and she had soft features, like that of a woman. She had a small nose, large eyes, soft cheeks, and a rounded chin. On the other hand, this picture of William Page looked very different from Adele's pictures. A large pointy nose, eyes smaller than that of Adele's, cheeks angular and not rounded, as was his chin.

The Hate Crime

I made a note of how different William Page looked than Adele. I thought that was slightly unusual. From what I knew about transgendered people, most of them didn't look all that different when they transitioned from male to female or from female to male. Their same basic face followed them from gender to gender, as it were. Not so with William Page. He apparently did wholesale plastic surgery on his face when he transitioned into a woman.

I wonder why he did that. It was almost as if he made a decision to transition from one gender to another and also wanted to become an entirely different person.

He also wanted to become an entirely different person.

I called Charity. She picked up on the third ring.

"Hello, this is Damien Harrington, I talked to you yesterday."

"Yes, hello. How are you?" Charity's voice was pleasant and I heard the baby screaming in the background. She shushed the baby for a few seconds and then came back on the phone. "What can I do for you?"

"I was wondering what you knew about William Page. Was he your friend?"

She cleared her throat. "I knew him well enough. I went to high school with him."

"Was there anybody he used to date in high school? And, if he dated somebody back then, was it a man or a woman?"

She was silent for a few seconds. "There was, and it was a woman. Her name was Darlene Reich. However, everybody always assumed she was a beard. Even then, I think William was into men. That was before he transitioned into Adele, of course."

"Really? Is there any reason why he felt the need to have a beard? Was your high school the kind of place where that kind of thing wasn't all that accepted?" This was getting interesting to me. I had no idea why, because I was still going down a blind alley, but I was latching onto something. What it was, I didn't know yet. But it was something significant.

"No, nothing like that. I mean, we graduated from high school only seven years ago. So, you know, LGBT wasn't exactly unheard of. We're millennials, after all. There were other transgendered guys and girls. And we had gay guys and lesbians. Nobody really gave a care about what other people were doing. So I don't really know why he wanted a beard. But apparently he felt the need to have one. Anyhow, Darlene Reich probably knew him best in high school." She paused for a few minutes. "So, is there anything else you need to know about William?"

"Yeah. When did he transition into Adele?"

"Let's see…" She took a deep breath. "I don't know the answer to that question. I only know Adele was the same person as William Page because Beck told me this. To tell you the truth, I was as surprised as anybody when he told me about William becoming Adele. It was kind of odd because he acted like it was some kind of big secret. He got drunk one night, came over to my house, and you know, we kinda shot the shit. He's my half-brother, after all. He liked to hang around with me because he felt I didn't judge him. Anyhow, he got really drunk and told me Adele was the same person as William Page. I was really surprised, because I knew Adele, and she looked nothing at all like William Page. I mean, nothing at all like him."

This was getting odder and odder. What I knew, without a shadow of a doubt, was that Beck was lying to me about not knowing Adele before going to the bar with her that night. He clearly knew her, and, what's more, he knew her former identity as William Page. And, apparently the fact she used to be William Page wasn't widely known. Why it wasn't widely known was an open question.

"Did Beck say you weren't supposed to know Adele was the same person as William Page?"

"Actually, now that you mention it, yes. He told me that it was something I wasn't supposed to know. I forget why he told me about William Page being Adele, though. We somehow got on the topic of Adele, I think he was here when he brought her up, and he told me about her being known as William Page back in the day. It's like he wanted to surprise me. You know, 'you remember that guy in high school? Well, look at him now!' That kind of thing."

"Did you later bring up the subject of Adele and ask him about her being known as William Page back in high school?"

"Yeah, I did. I mean, it wasn't a big deal. Not to me anyway. It was kind of funny, if nothing else. I just brought it up to him one day, when we were hanging out again, a few months later. You know, I brought it up casually – 'it's so funny what you told me about Adele.'"

"And what was his reaction when you brought it up to him again?"

"Nothing much. He did what he could to change the subject and chuckled a bit. He acted kind of weird about it, so I didn't bring it up anymore."

"By kinda weird, what do you mean by that?" I was starting to understand what had happened, but I didn't really know *why* it happened. There was some reason why William Page became Adele, and I had a feeling it had nothing to do with him being transgendered. In fact, I had a feeling William Page became Adele through a process known as ghosting - taking a dead person's identity and "becoming" them. I just had to get ahold of Anna and ask her find out if an actual Adele Whittier ever existed. At the moment, however, I was asking Charity these questions because I was interested in seeing how much Beck knew about the transition between William Page and Adele. If I could figure out that, I might, just might, be able to figure out why William Page became somebody new.

Somebody completely new.

"Oh, he said I wasn't supposed to know about that. And then he got real serious. He said I wasn't supposed to know about that. I mean, he repeated himself. And then he apologized. He said he told me something I wasn't supposed to know. And I was to keep my mouth shut about it."

As Charity spoke, I was getting the picture on what went on with William/Adele. If he became a different person, why would he do something like that? That was a big if, however. I didn't want to jump to conclusions until I actually got a hold of Anna and asked her to do a background check on Adele Whittier. I assumed there was an actual Adele Whittier who lived and that this William Page took her identity. It was just a theory I had in my head. But, once I figured that out, I hopefully could get one step closer to finding out who killed her.

"What else can you tell me about William?"

"As I said, I didn't know him all that well. I mean, I went to high school with him and everything, but he wasn't part of a group. He was just somebody I saw around school. I got to know Adele, however. Once he became Adele, I got to know her."

"And Adele, as far as you know, was into drug dealing?"

"Not that I know about. I assumed that when William became Adele he decided not to live the kind of life he led before. But then again, I don't really know if that's true or not. I knew Adele well enough, but she could definitely have led a double life I didn't know about. That's possible."

"Well, thank you. You've really helped me."

"I hope I did. I mean, I know my half-brother Beck has had a lot of problems in his life. But I don't think he would've killed Adele. He had nothing against her. They were friends."

And yet Beck told me he didn't even know her until they were at the bar. That he met her that night. That was a lie Beck told me.

I had no idea why he'd lie, but I was going to find out.

And the first person I'd have to talk to was Anna.

Chapter Eighteen

ANNA WAS HARPER'S HACKER. She didn't hack computers and things like that for bad reasons but hacked to get information about people. She was invaluable when we needed information not open to the public. In this case, I needed more information about Adele Whittier. Not William Page, necessarily, but Adele Whittier.

Anna was a gorgeous woman, in her way. She was heavily tattooed, wore her hair short and was a bit of a tomboy. That was the best way to explain it – she was a tomboy. She wore high top sneakers, tank tops, and blue jeans. But, with her high cheekbones, her big blue eyes and freckles, she was a looker. Not that she really cared she was a looker. She never wore makeup and just wore her hair in the easiest style she could muster because she was a no-fuss girl. She was definitely somebody I found attractive, however.

"Hi Anna," I said to her when I called her. "I have an assignment. I'll pay the usual rates. I just need to track down some information about a woman named Adele

The Hate Crime

Whittier. I don't have any information about her other than her name and approximate age, which was 25 or 26. Also, she was a nurse. I hope you can find something about her. I have to assume she's dead. She most likely died around two years ago."

William Page became Adele around two years ago, so I had to assume that was when the actual Adele Whittier died. I hoped this piece of information would narrow down Anna's search enough. Thank God "Adele Whittier" wasn't an overly common name, like John Smith or something like that. If she had a really common name, I'd would have more work to do, specifically file a motion with the judge to inquire with her employers about her social security number, but hopefully it wouldn't come down to all that.

"Sure, Damien," she said. "What do you need to know about her?"

"Anything you can tell me about her. Anything at all."

"Okay. Give me a couple of hours and I'll let you know what I find out."

I got off the phone with Anna and started to think about this whole crazy scenario. Again, it was only a hunch. It was just unusual that William not only became a woman, but became a woman who looked nothing like what he used to look like. His features were completely different when he became Adele Whittier. That was the first clue I had there was something amiss.

I also wondered about Heather. When she first came to me, she told me Adele was "a transgendered sister." I didn't ask her how well she knew Adele or if she knew her at all. I would have to press Heather on Adele and her relationship with her. There was something Heather wasn't telling me about Adele. Or, maybe it was something Heather wasn't telling me about William. Not to mention what she wasn't telling me about Beck.

That was the weirdest thing about this entire scenario. Beck told me he didn't know Adele, yet he did. I wondered if he knew Adele in her prior life, too. And if he did, why was he keeping these things from me? What was the big mystery? Why was everybody playing games with me? And being so coy?

Chapter Nineteen

ANNA CALLED me back in a few hours. "I found out some information about Adele Whittier," she said. "You're right, she's dead. She apparently committed suicide about two years ago. The poor girl had no living relatives."

"What else can you tell me about her?"

"She was a nurse, as you said. She got her BA in nursing at UMass. Got a master's degree at the same place. She started working at Massachusetts General as an oncology nurse when she got out of graduate school about three years ago and committed suicide about a year after getting that job."

"And how old was she when she died?"

"26."

"Was there anything unusual about her records?"

"Yeah, as a matter of fact there was. I looked at her death certificate online but her last name was misspelled. I actually talked to the clerk who filed the certificate, and found her death certificate was originally filed under the misspelled name, which was Whitter without the extra I.

However, somehow, during a routine audit, that mistake came to light and the death certificate was re-filed under the right name. So, yeah, there was a SNAFU with her records. It got corrected, however."

Hmmmmm… I wondered if the SNAFU with the death certificate being filed in the wrong name was an accident or was by design. I knew the ghosting procedure was difficult because when you apply for a new Social Security card and birth certificate, clerks can crosscheck your application against death certificates. It was convenient, in this case, that the death certificate was not filed in the correct name. Therefore, when William Page decided to become Adele Whittier, he wouldn't have run into a problem with cross-checking the death certificate.

The whole thing just reeked of some kind of set up. It was an extremely lucky coincidence that William Page took the identity of somebody who's death certificate was misfiled.

Unless there was something more to the story.

There had to be something more to the story.

"Anything else you can tell me about Adele?"

"Well, I can certainly try to get into her background more if that's what you're asking me. I'm skimming right now because I could only find out so much in such a limited period of time. I can find out anything you want about her, however. Just ask me some specific questions, and I'll try to figure it out."

"Let me talk to Heather and Beck. And then I'll let you know."

Chapter Twenty

HEATHER SHOWED up in my office later on that day after I called her to come in. There were some questions I wanted to ask her about Adele. Things were rolling around in my mind, but they weren't gelling. They were just hazy.

As things became more concrete, I decided to dig into Jordan's relationship with Adele. I found out that when Adele was William, he apparently ripped him off to the tune of $50,000. I knew what happened when people got sticky fingers with drug dealers, and had to assume William would've been in trouble with Jordan. No question about it.

That explained why William would've become Adele. He obviously decided he was in trouble with Jordan Kennedy, a known drug dealer, so he needed to change his entire look and become somebody else, complete with a brand-new identity. It was like being in the witness protection program, in a way.

However, I did some more research, and Anna looked into it. There was no sign that William Page had entered the witness protection program. Anyhow, I knew something about the witness protection program and they typically didn't ghost their clients. People in that program didn't usually use the identity of a dead person. It would be against the law to do something like that because Adele Whittier would have eventually started collecting Social Security payments from the government. She was also collecting debt in her name, and, if she'd lived, she probably would have eventually bought a house. All in the name of Adele Whittier, who was an actual person at one time. The biggest thing, however, to the government was that she would collect Social Security payments one day. Because of that, I knew it wasn't legal for the federal government, or any kind of government, to take an actual person's identity and give it to somebody else. That just wasn't done.

Which meant that either William Page had decided to do it on his own or got the help of somebody else. If I could figure that out, who did that for him, I'd have another piece of the puzzle. Just a small piece of the puzzle, however, because many things were still not adding up.

The biggest thing that wasn't adding up, of course, was the fact that Beck never told me he was familiar with Adele. And he certainly never told me he knew Adele was once a man by the name of William who had taken Adele's identity. Beck knew all that. So why didn't he say something about that to me?

But the first person I wanted to talk to about this entire situation was Heather.

So, she came to my office and sat down. She picked up a paperweight and her eyes didn't meet mine. "You wanted to see me?"

"Yeah. I did. Thanks for coming in." I nodded as I looked at her. I absolutely needed information but didn't know if she would be straight about any of it. "How well do you know Adele Whittier?"

Heather shrugged her shoulders. "I don't know her," she said. "Why do you ask?"

"You said she was a transgendered sister so I assumed you knew her. But you didn't actually know her?"

I was attuned to people who lied. I'd done enough cases in my life and had known enough people in prison to get a read on people's body language. It was a fine art and a science to judge if somebody is lying or not. It was important to be in the room with them so you could get a read on their eyes, their posture, and whether or not they were fidgeting.

Heather looked at me like she was trying to decide if she should tell me the truth or not. She finally took a deep breath. "Listen, I know you need to have all the information you can when defending Beck."

"Yeah, I do. Now, would it surprise you to know Adele was not actually a transgendered woman? That she was only posing as a woman because she took the identity of somebody else? Now, I don't know enough about William Page, who was Adele's previous identity, but I found out something about him. He stole from a powerful drug dealer named Jordan Kennedy. So what I want to know from you is why you called her your transgendered sister as if you knew her, and, if you knew her, why you told me she was transgendered when she clearly wasn't."

Heather shifted uncomfortably in her chair. "Okay. Okay. Yes, I knew about Adele's background as William Page."

That was all she said. She leaned back in her chair and looked at me with a defiant look as if daring me to ask for something else.

"So you knew her identity. Why do I think you also knew Beck and William knew one another back in the day and Beck knew the real reason why William Page became Adele?"

There was, once again, something Heather was hiding from me and I couldn't quite put my finger on it. She so desperately wanted me to take Beck on as a client, and yet wasn't telling me things she knew about his relationship with the victim, and about the victim herself. Actually, it was time to stop calling Adele "her," because she wasn't really transgendered. She was simply a man posing as a woman because he needed a completely different identity.

"Listen, I know what you're thinking. I know you're thinking William Page became Adele because he needed a different identity, and that's that. But it's not like that." She looked nervous. "Listen, I think I might have even said too much."

I sighed. "What do you mean, it's not like that. It's not like what? What are you trying to say?"

"I knew Adele. And she was a woman. She really was. It wasn't just a convenience thing." She nodded. "And that's all I'm really going to say to you. I can't tell you anything more than that."

"Okay, so you know what the situation was, right? You know William Page became Adele? And I'm assuming you probably also know Adele Whittier was a woman at one time. She was a living, breathing person. She died several years ago of an apparent suicide. I'm assuming you know all that, right?"

"Yeah, I know all that." She seemed very nervous. "I know you know about all that stuff but you really shouldn't. It's very dangerous for you to know it. And all that has nothing to do with the reason she died."

Heather wasn't making any sense. "Heather, I just can't believe you would do this to me. You begged me to take his case. You told me if I didn't take his case, you would be in big trouble. You know what'll happen if Beck gets convicted. You know if he's not acquitted, you'll probably down for something. And I think Beck knows more about what happened that night with Reverend Scott than he's letting on. Yet you keep a key piece of information from me, like the fact that Adele Whittier is the ghost name of William Page and nothing more. Don't you think the person threatening William Page finally caught up to him?"

"No, I don't think that." She crossed her arms in front of her and gave me a scowl. "Listen, you need to get off this line you're on. Trust me on this. I know where you're going with it and you need to get off it."

I took a deep breath and looked at Heather for a little while. "Why do I have a feeling that somehow, someway, the murder of Reverend Scott is tied in with all this?" There was so much she wasn't telling me, it wasn't even funny. "Heather, you need to be completely honest about everything. Absolutely everything. If you don't, I'll have to withdraw from the case. I don't like flying blind, and I don't like you stonewalling me. It's almost like you're protecting Jordan Kennedy. And I don't know why."

She shook her head. "Listen, I'm not trying to protect Jordan Kennedy. I couldn't give a shit about that guy. He's a low-level nobody. The guy served time in prison because William Page rolled on him. He served time in prison. What does that tell you?"

"It tells me there's a bigger fish above him. And that's the person William Page was afraid of, so afraid that he became Adele Whittier." The picture was starting to come into view, but there were still so many more unanswered questions. "And that bigger fish probably killed Adele. That makes a lot of sense. Especially if the bigger fish also had it in for Beck."

"You think you know what happened, but you don't know nothing. You don't know nothing. And you shouldn't be looking in this direction." She looked around the office as if trying to see if somebody had followed her to kill her. "Listen, you're going on a dangerous path that'll go nowhere. I know who that bigger fish is, and, trust me on this, he has no idea William Page became Adele. He didn't know that. As far as he knew, William Page died two years ago. Why don't you do some investigation on that? On what happened to William? The person who helped William become Adele covered his tracks very well. Nobody knew this happened. Nobody except Beck himself."

"And apparently you," I said. "Apparently you knew William Page became Adele. You seem to know everything about William/Adele. Which is odd to me. I don't know why you didn't just come out and tell me about it in the first place. You had to know I'd figure it out sooner or later. That's not something I couldn't uncover during my investigation."

"I was hoping you wouldn't find out about it. I knew if you found out what happened, your mind would go down that road. And that's a dangerous road. Trust me on this, it's a dangerous road. It's a road that'll lead you to a place you don't want to be. And it won't lead you to who really killed her. And yes, I still refer to Adele as 'her.' I know what you're thinking, that Adele wasn't really transgendered. But she was. She really was."

"Again, you're saying that."

"Yes, I'm saying that because it's true. Listen, William had the choice to become somebody else and didn't choose to become another man. He chose to become a woman. That tells you something right there. I knew Adele and she identified as a woman. When William became Adele, it was something he wanted to do in the first place. He always wanted to become a woman. So, Adele was transgendered. I don't want you to be unclear about that."

"Okay. So she was transgendered. Why is it so important that I know that? Of all the things I need to figure out about this case, why is the fact that Adele is transgendered the most important thing on your mind?"

"It just is." She shook her head. "Listen, you have to understand one thing. When somebody goes from a man to a woman, it looks bad on all of us when they do that just for convenience. Like when there's somebody running from the mob or something like that, maybe they enter the witness protection program and decide to become a different sex. They're really underground and want to make sure their tracks are covered. They might even have their fingerprints burned off, they're that scared about being found out. It looks bad for transgendered peeps when someone becomes a different sex just because they're afraid of being found out. That wasn't the case with William. He really identified as female and I just think that's important to know. No other reason than that. I just don't want to ruin Adele's reputation especially because she's dead. That's all."

I thought it was odd Heather was focusing on this minor thing. Then I realized it was probably not minor to her. But, to me, it really seemed beside the point. The point, of course, was the fact that apparently Adele, or William, was afraid of somebody. Another important point was the fact that apparently William wasn't given a new identity by the government. Rather, he took a completely different identity on his own.

Or did he? I did a little research online, and found that it used to be relatively easy for people to change identities. It was easy to get a new Social Security card and new birth certificate. I also found how difficult it was in today's day and age, because of crosschecking death certificates, to get a new birth certificate. Again, I came back to the "coincidence" that the death certificate was misfiled but knew that wasn't a coincidence at all. No, it seemed deliberate. Which meant somebody had to get to the clerks in Massachusetts. I also had a feeling that if I looked into Adele's suicide, I'd find it wasn't a suicide at all. She was probably targeted by somebody who wanted to specifically take her identification.

I would have to find out more from Anna about Adele Whittier to flesh out my theory that she was murdered for her identity. If she was, why was she targeted? Why would William just pick her name out of a hat and set his sights on killing her and taking her identity? It was unfortunate she had no living kin, therefore it would've been much easier for someone to assume her identity than somebody with living family members. That might've been one of the reasons she was targeted, if she was targeted, but there had to be a lot of other people in the same situation.

I had a feeling, therefore, that William Page had help in all of this. Somebody helped him become somebody else. I had no idea why this person would do that. Whoever did that went through a lot of trouble to make sure this happened.

"Heather, who helped William become Adele?"

She crossed her arms. "I don't know. Listen, I can tell you one thing. I didn't know Adele was once William Page until after she was found dead. You have to believe me about that. That's something nobody knew except for Beck himself."

I took a deep breath. "Beck himself. And the person who helped William. Listen, Beck is kind of a low-level guy. He's not somebody who could pull off something like this. I think there was some tampering going on at the clerk's office, because there was a SNAFU with the death certificate and it was just too convenient. I also think William had to have help to target the person whose identity he took. There's somebody who's behind all of this, pulling the strings, and you're afraid of him."

"Yes, I *am* afraid of him." She tapped her foot on the floor. "I'm afraid of him and you should be too. And, as I said, you're looking at the wrong person. The fact that Adele was killed has nothing to do with what happened before, with her stealing money from Jordan. You have to believe me about this. But I can tell you one thing – if you go down this road, you'll be in danger."

"Heather, I have to ask this question. This person you're afraid of, does he or she know what happened with the reverend? It seems you're trying to protect people who could turn you in for what happened to the Reverend Scott. You wanted to protect Beck so you begged me to take his case. And I think you're now trying to protect a person who might also know about it. Am I going on the right track?"

"No, you're not going on the right track. Only Beck knows about what happened that night. Well, Beck and Charlie."

"Why did you trust Charlie in the first place with this? From what you tell me, you and Charlie don't have a very good relationship. Weren't you at all worried that Charlie would turn you in? Why would you get him involved with this entire thing?" That was nagging at me. Charlie, from what Heather told me, was not to be trusted. Not only was he a drug dealer but he really had no love for her. He threatened her life, and she owed him money, which was why she had to do his drug runs. She was much like Tina in that way. Once she paid him back, however, it was my understanding she no longer had a relationship with him. So why was he the first person she called?

There was a buried story in this whole situation and it was making me very suspicious. She knew more than she let on, that much was certain. And what she didn't tell me was extremely important. To say the very least. And now, here she was, telling me not to go down the road I thought would be the most fruitful path of all. If I could get to the nub of who helped Adele become William, I could probably try to figure out the other pieces of the puzzle. However, I also had to find out who the bigger fish was and who William was afraid of in the first place. Heather wouldn't help me with any of that.

Why she wasn't helping me with any of that, I didn't know.

She was still sitting there, watching me. She shook her head. "You need to look in another direction. The person who killed Adele is not the person you think it was. You need to trust me on this when I tell you." She looked around. "I'll give you all the help you need but not if you continue down this path. I just don't want you to get lost in the weeds and try to accuse somebody who had nothing to do with any of it. You're gonna be overlooking the person who really did it. I don't know who that person is, and neither do you, but you need to find out. I'll help as much as I can to find the real killer."

"*Are* you going to help me out?" I suddenly had a feeling she wouldn't help me out at all. That disappointed me, of course, because Heather roped me into this case in the first place. I was doing this case for her and was doing it for free.

Yet, here she was, stonewalling me. I crossed my arms in front of me. "Listen, Heather, I don't have time for your games. I'm helping you out. Or did you forget that? I have to make sure Beck gets a good defense and hopefully gets acquitted. If he's acquitted, then, as far as I know, you'll be in the clear. If he isn't – all bets are off. That alone should encourage you to be straight with me."

Heather nodded. "I wish I could be straight with you about all of this. But I just want you to not go down the road of accusing somebody you shouldn't be. You just don't know how dangerous Jordan's boss is."

"No, you're right about that. I don't know how dangerous Jordan's boss is, because I don't know *who* he is. Care to enlighten me on that?"

"You have to find that out for yourself. I can't tell you. If I do, trust me on this, I'll be in so much trouble."

I sighed. "Okay. I guess if you're going to play games, there's nothing I can really do about it. I can tell you one thing – the more information I have, the better defense Beck will get. I would think that would motivate you to tell me everything you know. I guess not, so..." All at once, I wanted Heather to leave my office. She was pissing me off. I would figure this stuff out with or without her. It just would be easier if she'd cooperate with me.

Her face seemed to soften. "Listen, the main reason why I don't want to tell you who's Jordan's boss is because I don't what you to stop there. I just don't think the person who you think did this is the one who actually did it. Now, I don't know who did it, I just don't –"

"I know, I know." I looked at the clock and saw it was almost time for my next court appearance. I had a burglary client I was going to plead out. "Okay, then. I think we've gone round and round on this enough. If you're not gonna tell me what I need to know, I guess I'll have to find out this information from somebody else and that's just the way it has to be. But, rest assured, I *will* figure that out."

"I know you will. I just want don't want it coming from me. That's all I'm saying."

"Duly noted."

At that, Heather left, and I went to my court appearance. I was still pretty pissed at her, but, in a way, I kind of understood it. Somebody was making her nervous, that was for sure, and that person might or might not have been responsible for Adele's death.

I would figure it out, but it would take me longer.

Chapter Twenty-One

I WENT to see Beck in the jail because I needed to find out exactly what was going on. I needed to ask him what his relationship was with William and why he would lie to me. I had no idea what he would say to me. What excuse he would bring me.

He came swaggering out, as usual. "Yo dog, you know I'm getting out of this joint pretty goddamn soon. I got my homies, they be giving me money to break out of here. So next time you see me, I'm gonna be at Chez Beck. I know, I know, I rock this orange jumpsuit, but just wait 'til you see me in my regular clothes."

I cleared my throat. "I need to ask you some questions. I hope you'll be straight with me because it's clear you haven't been straight with me yet."

"Sure dog," he said. "Ask away. I ain't got nothing to hide."

"You can start by telling me why you claimed to not know Adele, when you clearly did. You knew her when she was William and you knew her when she became Adele. In fact, it's my understanding that you're one of the few people who knew William Page was the same person as Adele Whittier. I have yet to figure out how you know all this, but it seems you do." I leaned back in my chair and stared at him. I didn't know what kind of excuse he would give me or if he would give me any excuse at all.

He grimaced. "How'd you find all that out?"

"I talked to your sister and found out some information about Adele. I found out she changed her identity because she was apparently running from somebody. I'm still trying to figure out why the actual Adele Whittier was targeted by whomever helped William Page change his identity. I'm hoping I can put that puzzle piece together. I think the clue to who killed her is in this whole scenario. But I needed to know why you lied to me."

For once, Beck actually looked kind of scared. Gone was the cocky guy. In his place was a shaking kid who suddenly looked younger than his age. His blue eyes didn't meet mine. He blinked them a couple of times and it looked like he was on the verge of tears.

That was weird. I didn't expect that reaction.

Then he abruptly got up. "Dog, I ain't gonna answer that question."

"You *will* answer the question. Either you answer the question or I find out the answers from somebody else, so it's your choice. You can either tell me in your words why you lied to me and how you knew William Page, or I'll just find out from somebody else what the story is. Plus, I think you knew the actual Adele Whittier, or if you didn't know her, you somehow knew exactly why William Page took her identity. And I think you also know who arranged all of it. I think you know everything. Why you're not telling me everything is beyond me."

He stared at me for a few minutes. I could see, in his expression, that he was trying hard to decide what to do. How much to tell me.

He finally decided, apparently, to come clean. "Adele Whittier, the actual Adele Whittier, she was a chick who pissed off somebody she's not supposed to. You don't get on the wrong side of Larry Rodriguez, I can tell you that. And she did. She pissed him off. You don't piss off someone like him. If you do, you're a dead man, or woman." Beck made a slicing motion with his hand and his neck to prove the point.

I was getting somewhere. "And what did Adele do to Larry to piss him off so much?"

"She was banging some dudes while dating Larry's brother Miguel. Larry's brother lives in Boston which was where Adele lived too. She was living with Larry's brother and getting with every cat in town. A real slut. So, Larry finds out what she's doing behind Miguel's back and has her killed."

"Just like that, huh?"

"Yeah, just like that. So Adele Whittier, the actual Adele Whittier, she's dead. And here comes William, he needs help. He stole from somebody he shouldn't have been stealing from, namely, Jordan Kennedy, who's working for Vincent Sharpelli, one of the biggest mobsters in town. Now, Larry, he's dying to find out more about Vincent Sharpelli and Vince's operation. Turns out William knows a little bit about Vince's operation because he was in it. Larry decides to help him become somebody else. And what do you know, he just killed, or had killed, Adele Whittier out in Massachusetts. Pretty convenient. He just had to figure out how to make William become Adele."

I was getting excited, because Beck was *finally* coming

clean. "So that's what happened? Larry helped William Page become Adele Whittier?"

"Yeah. He did. And he just happened to have a cousin working in the Vital records department of Boston, Massachusetts, so he could doctor up her death certificate. The cousin accidentally misspelled Adele Whittier's last name," Beck said, making air quotes when he said the word *accidentally*. "So it all worked out. William gets a new birth certificate, gets a new Social Security card and becomes Adele Whittier. And that's what happened there."

"I see. Now, can you please tell me why you lied to me about your relationship with her? Don't you think this piece of information was something I needed to know? I mean, come on, there's at least one person in this scenario who had reason to kill her. If not Jordan, then Vincent Sharpelli, would have had reason to kill her."

He sighed. "I just didn't tell you, that's all. Listen, I didn't want you going down that road. I knew that if I told you the truth about William Page, and how he became Adele, you'd jump to conclusions and just assume her past caught up with her. That Jordan or Vincent were behind her murder. But I don't think that."

I hung my head. "Let me tell you how this works. I'm trying to get you off of murder by showing somebody else killed Adele. Which means I need to know anybody and everybody who would've had motive to kill her. And that means anybody and everybody, not just people you want me to look at. So, I need for you to be completely straight with me. I think you're still hiding something. In fact, I know you are. You're hiding the reason why you lied about not knowing Adele in the first place. You told me she was a random person you met at the bar, the two of you went out to mess around in your car, you found out she was a guy, and then sent her on her way. That's what you told me. You certainly didn't tell me you've known her for years."

"Listen, man, I knew William. I hardly knew this Adele person. I mean, I knew her. But not really. She certainly was nothing like William." He nodded. And then he looked away. "She certainly was nothing like William."

For some reason, the way Beck talked about how Adele was nothing like William, I had a hunch. I looked into his eyes and my hunch was confirmed.

"Beck, what relationship did you have with William?" I had to ask the next question but was very hesitant. I knew that asking this question would set him off, either because it wasn't true or because it was. Nevertheless, I felt the need to get to the bottom of it.

"We were homies. We knew each other. We ran around together."

"And when you knew William, did you know he wanted to be a woman?"

Beck shook his head rapidly. "Hell no. I had no clue about that. Trust me, if I would've known about that, it would've pissed me off."

"And why would that have pissed you off?"

"It just would've, man. He was my homie, he was my friend, and I certainly didn't want him becoming a chick."

And here was the question I was going to ask earlier, the question I knew would generate an intense reaction. But it was a question I knew I had to ask.

"Beck, were you in love with William Page?"

Chapter Twenty-Two

"WHAT KIND OF A QUESTION IS THAT?" Beck demanded. "Why would you think I'm some kind of faggot?" He stood up and looked at me menacingly. "Seriously, man, why would you say something like that to me? Do I look like some kind of faggot?" Beck's eyes were wild and he was shaking. "Answer that question. Do I look like some kind of queer? A faggot?"

I tried to be as calm as possible. "I just think your feelings for William were why you never told me you knew him. The real reason why you told me you didn't know Adele. Maybe it's true. Perhaps you believe in your mind that you didn't really know Adele because that was who William became and you didn't like that. Maybe you didn't like that because you liked him as a man."

That made sense to me. If Beck had feelings for William Page, and if Beck were gay, then obviously he wouldn't want William becoming a woman. It would be the same thing as if I was dating a woman who decided to become a man. I obviously couldn't be with her. Perhaps Beck felt the same way about William. William became a woman, Beck decided he didn't want anything to do with him, and that was why he felt he didn't know Adele. Maybe he was telling me the truth when he told me he didn't really know her.

I looked at Beck and realized I struck a nerve. By now, he had tears in his eyes. He finally just lowered his head, and shook it.

"Goddammit," he said softly. "Goddammit, me and William, we had a good thing going. We did. We were talking about living together. Me and him, we were good. Real good. I ain't never experienced something like that, what I had with him."

"How did you and William meet?"

"We knew each other in high school. I always knew he was gay. Everybody knew it. Nobody knew I was gay, though. It's just something you don't really tell people. My dad, if he knew that about me, he would've beat the crap out of me. Shit, he probably would've had somebody come along and knock me off. No way did he want some kind of faggot son."

I wondered about Charity. Did she know about Beck's sexuality? I had a feeling she didn't. If she did, she probably would've told me the truth. She seemed pretty on the level. "Did your sister know about this?"

"No dog, I ain't telling Charity nothing about that. Listen, you don't know my dad. He would've hated me if he would've known I was some kind of a sissy boy. Even though he's in prison, he probably would've sent some of his men after me for shaming him. You know, being gay is some kind of dishonor to guys like my dad. He's old school. Old school. He comes from a time when guys who like guys get the crap beat out of them."

I wanted to ask him a few questions about how influenced he was by his father. After all, his father was an avowed white supremacist. But he was telling me the story about William Page, so I wanted him to keep talking. If anybody would've wanted to kill Adele Whittier, it might've been him, because, after all, he was angry with her for becoming a woman.

Was he angry enough to have actually killed her?

"So you knew William in high school. Did you hang out with him then?"

Beck hung his head. "No. I didn't hang out with him in high school. My homies in high school, they wouldn't want nothing to do with me if I was hanging out with a guy like William. Like I said, everyone knew he was gay in high school, so we dudes were afraid to be hanging out with him. We didn't want people saying that about us."

"So when did you guys start hanging out, then?"

"We started hanging out when we met up at a bar. I saw him over at Side Kicks on Main," he said, referring to a popular gay bar in Midtown. "He comes over to me and says 'I didn't know you were gay,' and then told me he had been crushing on me all through high school. And, you know, I'd never been with a man before. But I was at Side Kicks, so I guess I was curious. And we started hanging out after that."

"Who else knew you were gay?"

"Now let me get one thing straight. No pun intended," he said with a laugh. "I ain't gay. I like women. I fuck women. But me and William, that was a different story. I don't know, I just kinda dug him."

"So were you in love with him?"

Beck stared at me for a second and nodded his head slowly. "Yeah, I think I was."

"So when he decided to become a woman, how did that

make you feel?" I needed to see his reaction. I needed to see if he would give me subtle indications that he was angry enough at William becoming a woman that he killed him.

"I threw a party," he said sarcastically. "How do you think I felt about that? I loved William. At first it was okay, because right after me and William started hanging out, I got nabbed and put into the joint. William visited me all the time while I was behind bars. And so one day he tells me he's on the run from a mobster, and has to get a new identity. I thought, cool. I thought he would get some plastic surgery and just become another dude. But then he tells me he's gonna become a woman who had just died." He shook his head and gritted his teeth. "So he's gonna become a woman. I wasn't down with that. I wasn't down with that at all."

"How mad were you at him becoming Adele?"

"I know where you're going with this. I wasn't pissed off enough to have killed him. If that's what you're thinking."

"I just have to ask the question."

He shrugged his shoulders. "I don't know. It was just weird. All of a sudden, I get this chick visiting me in the joint. I don't know who she is. She says she's William. But she ain't looking like William no more. You know, she's all looking different. And her voice is different too. You know, she got this voice coach that helped her sound like a woman. And she sounded like a woman. She really did. You know how like you see these dudes becoming chicks but their voice still sounds the same? They still sound like a man? Or you see these chicks becoming a dude and they still got a girl voice? Well, that wasn't the case with Adele. Her voice was a woman's voice and she looked like a woman. Completely like a woman."

"The two of you obviously worked it out, right? I mean, you were hanging out at the bar that night. Right?"

He shrugged his shoulders. "Nah, I just ran into her. I see her at the bar, you know, I ain't been out of the joint for that long. When I see Adele come visit me in the joint, I tell her not to come back. I was through with her. But she sees me at the Zoo Bar, we get to talking, it's kind of like old times because I'm drinking. I didn't think of her as being William no more, but, like I said, I like chicks, too. I like banging chicks. So, I'm kinda thinking maybe I can start hanging out with her. I needed to get past the fact she had a dick. That's something I've never done." He laughed. "I've done guys and I've done girls, but I ain't never done someone who's halfway between. But, you know, I loved William when he was William. I thought maybe I could try to adjust to him being Adele. So, she went home with me that night."

I nodded. "So that's why she was found in your neighborhood. Well, that makes some sense. That answers a question that's been nagging me since the beginning. I've often wondered how she would've been dumped by your apartment when you claimed she didn't go home with you that night."

"Yeah. She went home with me. She left my apartment, very much alive, around midnight. I don't know, I tried to mess around with her, but it was just too weird. Like I said, I ain't never done somebody who was not quite a dude and not quite a chick. So, it kinda grossed me out. If you want to know the truth."

This added a new dimension to the case. I wondered if somebody was in Beck's neighborhood who knew Adele and would've had reason to kill her. I would have to figure that one out.

The Hate Crime

I suddenly knew I had another way to look at this case. I was happy Beck finally came clean. However, it still didn't answer the over-riding question I had.

Who killed Adele?

Chapter Twenty-Three

I MET Nick and Tom that night. Tom called and said he had information about somebody else who might have had reason to kill Adele. In my mind, I was looking at Jordan Kennedy. After all, when Adele was William, she stole all that money from him. That was why he became Adele in the first place. What if Jordan found out William was Adele and he killed her? Of course, the only other thing I had to figure out was if there was some reason he also hated Beck. He killed her by Beck's apartment, after all, and from what I understood, Jordan didn't live in the neighborhood. That would had to have meant that, somehow someway, he had some kind of spy who saw the two of them leave together. And that spy followed them home, killed Adele, and dumped her body by his apartment, all in the name of framing Beck for her murder.

But Tom and Nick told me there was another person coming into view. I was anxious to find out exactly who this person was.

We met at a bar. As usual. I got there early and hoped

Tom would not only have information about a new suspect in Beck's case, but might also tell me some dirt on Baron Wicker.

"Hey buddy," I said when the two guys came in. I gave them each a hug, and they sat down. "So what do you have for me?"

"I think I found some pretty decent information about who Adele was working with," Nick said. "I talked to some guys on the street and they tell me Adele was on the up and up, working as a nurse. She wasn't dealing any street drugs. But that's the operative word here – street drugs. Seems like Adele, she didn't want anything to do with dealing cocaine and heroin, but sure wanted to still be in the drug trade."

"Let me guess. She was working in a hospital and was stealing prescription painkillers?"

"Bingo. But she wasn't stealing and selling them. I mean, she was selling them but had a middleman. She had a guy distributing these drugs on the street. He gave her a cut of every sale he made. From what I understand, our victim was making quite a lot of money out of this."

"Who was her middleman?"

"His name is Charlie Williams."

Charlie Williams. I had to wonder if he was the same Charlie Williams who was Heather's boyfriend at one time. The same Charlie Williams who threatened Heather into becoming a drug mule for him. I wondered if that was who Heather was afraid of. When she came into my office, she was obviously afraid of me fingering somebody. Maybe it was Charlie? Maybe Heather knew Charlie was involved? And she wanted me looking in a different direction?

"So what happened? Why do you think Charlie Williams is a suspect at this point?"

"I'll tell you why I think Charlie might've done it," Nick

said. "He had a deal with Adele for her to steal those drugs from the hospital. But Adele apparently told him she wouldn't do it for him any more. She was afraid to get caught, and didn't want to go to prison. You know, she was still technically a guy, so she knew if she went to prison, it would be a men's prison, where she probably wouldn't live very long. At any rate, she was hearing noises the hospital was onto what she was doing. She managed to steal a shit ton of Percocet and Oxycontin, because she worked on the oncology floor, where most of those patients are on some kind of powerful painkiller. She would administer a smaller dose than what they needed and would literally pocket the rest. But the hospital was getting wise and knew it was just a matter of time before she got caught so she told Charlie she wouldn't do it anymore."

"Okay. Now tell me why Charlie would've killed her? Are you saying that just because she told Charlie she didn't want to steal drugs for him anymore, that would've given him reason to kill her?"

"Something like that," Nick said. "Actually, the reason why he might have killed her was because the police were closing in on her. They were getting ready to arrest her at the time she died. Charlie might've gotten word she was about to be arrested and was afraid that if she was arrested, she would've given him up to save her own neck. And Charlie has been on the police radar for quite a long time. He hasn't been busted yet for what he does, but was afraid Adele would change that. He was rightfully worried she would sing like a canary. So that gives him reason to have killed her."

Hmmmm... "I'll definitely have to go down that road. I'll try to find all I can about that situation, but I wonder how Heather, the girl who put me up to this, will think of this. I think she's afraid of Charlie and won't want me to go down that road. That won't stop me. But I should definitely talk to her before I start gathering evidence about this Charlie Williams, and how he might've done this."

"Well, that's what I found out. I also found out some pretty good things about Baron Wicker. There are definitely juicy things I found out about him."

"Oh? What did you find out about him?" My ears were perked up. Ever since I was served with that paternity petition, I had been on pins and needles.

"I found out the real reason why he's suing you for custody of your daughter. And that's not all. I found out something that'll really sink him in court."

I rubbed my hands together in glee.

This was going to be good.

Chapter Twenty-Four

"FIRST OF ALL, I found out that Baron Wicker is definitely not Amelia's father," Nick said.

Huh? "What do you mean?"

"Well, from the people I've talked to, they all say Baron had never been to Kansas City until about a year ago. He never visited the city. Which made me wonder how Sarah would've met him. As far as you know, was Sarah doing any traveling at about the time Amelia was born?"

I shook my head. "No. Sarah never did any traveling around that time. At least she never did any traveling on her own. We went on some trips together. But as far as I know, she didn't travel on her own."

"Right. I figured as much. So, how did Baron meet her? And, I found out there was somebody else your wife was seeing at the time."

"Who? Who was she seeing?"

"She was seeing a guy by the name of Jake Brillis. Jake is your half-brother." Nick shook his head and laughed lightly. "I'm sure it doesn't surprise you that your father had children he didn't know about and kids he knew about but didn't want to acknowledge. Apparently, Jake was in the latter category. Your dad had an affair with a friend of Olivia's back in the day. Her name was Nina Brillis. She worked with Olivia at the nude dancing place. Apparently your father was banging her about the same time he was chasing after Olivia and trying to get Olivia to sleep with him. I guess you might say he had a thing for those girls. Anyhow, Jake was Nina's son. And Sarah got to know him."

"How did she meet him?" This was fascinating to me. I just found out I had a half-brother and he apparently was Amelia's father. That was extremely strange, to say the very least. At the same time I was relieved, if it was true, that Baron wasn't Amelia's father. If what Nick was saying was true, I might have an easier time with this paternity case than I would've before.

"Apparently Sarah met Jake through Olivia. Olivia and Nina are friends. Sarah used to go over to Olivia's sometimes, just to hang out. Nina was there one evening with her son. Later on, Olivia told Sarah that Jake's father was Josh Roland. Sarah knew at that time that Josh was your father as well, so she knew Jake was your half-brother."

I wondered if Sarah slept with him *because* he was my half-brother. She was the kind who would do something like that. "So, how did you find out Jake is Amelia's father?"

"Because I managed to talk to your assistant, Anna. I asked her if she could hack some databases, and she did, and found out Jake took a paternity test back in the day. He took it right after Amelia was born. He's Amelia's father, not this Baron Wicker person."

I didn't quite understand. "So why did the paternity test say Baron was Amelia's father? I don't get that."

"I don't know the answer to that question. What I can

tell you is that Sarah is naming Baron as the father of Amelia because Sarah and Baron are together right now. That's who she's seeing. And Baron needs an heir. You see, his grandma, who comes from old money, is getting ready to die. And she's one of those odd birds who wants to control her family from beyond the grave. She wants to make sure everybody who's in her will has children. I guess it was just important to her that her heirs could pass on the family name. Well, Baron isn't married and doesn't have any kids. I guess her will doesn't specify her heirs have to be married, but it does specify that they must have children before they can collect. Apparently that meant Baron stood to inherit one hundred million dollars, but only if he had a kid at the time of his grandmother's death."

"But what does he care if he gets money or not from her? He's a goddamn billionaire, after all."

"On paper, he's a billionaire. He has assets that make him a billionaire. But he's leveraged to the hilt. He's not that liquid either. So he had a chance to inherit one hundred million dollars in cash, which would make him a lot more liquid. And he went for it. Apparently, he and Sarah cooked up this plan to falsify a paternity test that said Baron is Amelia's father. And they apparently thought they would get away with it."

For some odd reason, I was stifling a laugh. I knew my ex-wife was devious, but I had no idea how devious she really was. But then again, there was $100 million at stake, and probably something in it for her. If she helped him suddenly, magically, obtain a child before his grandmother died, he probably offered her a cut. "And what does Sarah get out of the deal?"

"From what I understand, now this is just hearsay, but

he offered her $10 million to do this. She did it for him but was in it for the money as well."

"I'm sure she was. Now, I guess I have to worry about this Jake Brillis person? He's the real father of Amelia?"

"Yeah. He is." Nick put his hand on my shoulder. "I'm so sorry, buddy. I know it's hard to hear that somebody else is the biological father of your daughter, but at least you don't have to worry about those two clowns taking her away from you. Listen, I actually talked to Jake about it and he told me he has no interest in raising a child. He's married himself now. He told me that if his wife found out he'd fathered a kid out of wedlock she wouldn't be happy about it. She's not the kind who would happily take in other people's children. So I don't think you have to worry about him. I don't think he'll be coming after you for anything."

Nick and I fist bumped. "I guess it's just a matter of proving the paternity results I got in the mail are fraudulent. And then I think both my wife, I mean ex-wife, and her lover, will be in trouble with the law. Falsifying documents like that." I shook my head. "Sarah really must think I'm a fool. She must've really thought she would get away with something like this. After all we've gone through together, and she still doesn't know me that well."

Tom was just sitting there, watching us. He had trained Nick pretty well, because he let him take the lead on this Baron Wicker investigation, and he did a stellar job. He looked over at me and smiled. "Some people, huh? I'm pretty pissed at Sarah, too. I can't believe she would do something like that. Even if she was getting a lot of money out of the deal, I just can't understand why she would do it."

"I figure it's two birds, one stone for her," I said. "She hates me. She has a chance to get back at me by taking away my daughter. She knows that if something like that happened, it would rip out my very heart. And that's what she wants to do. She wants to see me suffer. And if she gets money out of seeing me suffer? All the better for her. That's the kind of person she is. I can't believe I ever loved her."

Nick and Tom and I shot the shit for the rest of the night. I was feeling lighter that night, lighter than I'd felt in a long time. I had the whole paternity issue hanging over my head like a Sword of Damocles all this time. It was threatening to consume me. But I knew now that it was just a matter of showing those two fools for what they were – a couple of charlatans, a couple of greedy whores, who were just after money. As soon as I could show the court they falsified that paternity test, I would get the whole case thrown out.

And Amelia would be with me forever.

Chapter Twenty-Five

ONCE I GOT the information I needed from Beck, Tom and Nick, I knew I would have to talk to Heather. I would have to ask her if she was afraid of Charlie and if that was why she came into my office the other day and told me not to go down the road she thought I was going down. Although I didn't know how she found out I would be looking at Charlie at that time. At that time, I was simply going down the road of looking at Jordan.

I had her come into my office. She came in and sat down and looked at me with a look of attitude on her face. I think she knew she would be cornered and didn't like it. Didn't like it at all.

"Okay, Heather. I need you to come clean with me. I found out Charlie Williams had a relationship with the victim in Beck's case and you didn't tell me about that. Did you know about it?"

When I looked at her face, I knew she was hiding that from me, too. "Listen, I don't want Charlie getting in the middle of this. At least I don't want me to be saying anything to you about him. You forget he knows about what happened with Reverend Scott. He knows about it and could do some serious damage to me."

"Nevertheless, I have to bring him in as a possible suspect. I have to. He had a reason to kill Adele. I mean, Adele was stealing drugs for him. The cops were closing in on her and I did my homework. She was about to be arrested for stealing those drugs from the hospital. And what do you think she would've done if she was arrested? She would've rolled on Charlie. After all, Charlie put her up to it. Charlie was distributing the drugs on the street. Adele was just giving the drugs to him to sell. And I know he's been an active drug dealer for quite a while. I'm sure the cops would love any kind of information to get him. Adele had the information. So tell me why Charlie should not be a suspect in this case?"

"Goddammit, if you bring Charlie into this case, you better not miss. I mean, if you're going to say he's a suspect, you better have your ducks in a row so that he gets arrested for killing Adele and for distributing those drugs. I want him off the street because he's gonna be pissed I didn't prevent him from becoming a suspect in Beck's case. I think he's dangerous and I don't know what he's gonna do to me."

I sighed. "I think you know that's not how it goes. I mean, I have at least one other suspect on my list. The way I approach cases is I try to find plausible individuals who would've done it and bring them all into court and question them. Charlie will be just one of the people I'll bring into court as an alternative suspect in this case. I'm also looking at Jordan. I'm also looking at –"

"I think you should be looking at Larry Rodriguez," Heather blurted out.

"Why Larry Rodriguez?" I was curious about this one.

Beck did tell me how William had become Adele, and I was curious about how it was that William was able to pay for all those surgeries and so forth. And he also told me that Larry was interested in learning information about Vincent Sharpelli's organization, and that he felt that William would be a good source for that. Plus, Larry was the one who, according to Beck, helped William become Adele. He helped her get a new birth certificate, and a new social security card. He also apparently had the real Adele killed, and made sure that her death certificate was misfiled. He did all of that. But I wondered if he did other things as well. And if he did, why would he have had her killed?

Heather's hand flew up to her hair, and she tugged lightly on her braid. "I'll tell you the reason why you should be looking at Larry Rodriguez. He paid a lot of money for William to become Adele. He paid for all the surgeries for her. All those hormone injections. All that shit. That shit's expensive. In fact, he was going to pay for her entire sex reassignment surgery. And why do you think that he did all that? You think he did all of that out of the goodness of his heart? You think he was doing that because she was a charity case? No. He wanted something from her. He wanted her to work for him, and, more than that, much more than that, he wanted her to give him all the secrets of the Sharpelli organization. That's the only reason why he would do something like that. The only reason why."

"And did he get a return on his investment?"

"What do you think?"

"I'm gonna say no. I'm going to say she screwed him over and left him with the bill, and didn't give him what he wanted. Is that what you're trying to say?"

"Let's just say that when William became Adele, he decided, just out of the blue, that he didn't want to do drug dealing anymore. Or, at least, he decided that he didn't want to do street drug dealing anymore. He didn't want to work for Larry anymore. After all Larry did for him, and he turns around and does something like that?" Heather shuddered visibly. "And –"

"Hey, I notice you calling Adele 'him.' You insisted to me that he was really transgendered. Was he?"

Heather shook her head. "I'm sorry about that. I should know better than that. It just gets confusing for me, because this is a confusing situation. I'm trying to say that William was the one that owed Charlie, so that's why I called him by the male pronoun there. Because it was William that owed him. If William did become Adele, if he didn't have a complete change of identity, he probably would've been dead right now. I mean, Jordan would've killed him, and if he didn't, Vinnie would've. Please don't ever look at Vinnie. He had nothing to do with this. Trust me on this, he had nothing to do with this. You can go ahead and try to do what you want with Charlie. I think I can handle him. He doesn't know nothing."

"What do you mean Charlie doesn't know anything? You told me that Charlie was the one that you called when you killed the Reverend Scott. And he was the one who sent Beck over to you. Are you telling me there's a different story?"

She swallowed hard. I could see her Adam's Apple bob up and down as she swallowed. And then she looked at her nails nervously. I think she knew she had told me something she wasn't supposed to. But the cat was out of the bag, and I was going to have to press it. She was lying to me about Charlie. Apparently Charlie had nothing to do with covering up the homicide of Reverend Scott. But I wondered who *did* have something to do with it.

"Heather, you have to tell me about what happened. Listen, I –"

I knew I would have to find someway, somehow, to become her lawyer. Even though I knew there would be a conflict of interest with Beck, it was looking less likely that that would happen. It was a grey area, anyhow. Granted, they were technically co-conspirators, in the death of Reverend Scott, but my case with Beck didn't have a thing to do with that other murder case, so it was a grey area as to whether or not I could represent her.

At any rate, I felt the need to skirt that line so I could get the whole story from her.

"Heather, let's sign an attorney-client agreement."

"But you said we couldn't do that. You said it would become a conflict of interest."

I took a deep breath. "I'm willing to take the chance that if something happens, and Beck turns on you, which means one of my clients turns on another, I can handle the inevitable Bar Complaint. But, since you're technically not involved with Beck's current case, I think it's ambiguous as to whether it really is a conflict of interest at this moment. It might become one in the future, but at the moment, I can plausibly say it's not. So please, please sign this attorney-client agreement and tell me what happened. I have to know this. Because, as it is, I'm going to try to bring in Vincent Sharpelli as one of the suspects in this case. And I have a feeling he's the one you're really afraid of. And I want to know why."

Heather nodded. I gave her an attorney-client agreement, and she signed it.

"Okay. I'll tell you everything."

Chapter Twenty-Six

"OKAY. HERE'S WHAT HAPPENED." Heather looked visibly shaken. She kept nervously fingering her necklace, and her legs were going up and down. Bouncing up and down, up and down, up and down. She looked nervously at the door. "The Reverend Scott was out on bail. I thought when he was put into prison that he would stay there. I thought he wouldn't be a danger to anybody. I thought he would go away for the rest of his life."

"Go on." Somehow, I thought that whatever Heather was about to tell me, it was going to be *extremely* serious.

"Reverend Scott, I guess he went right back to what he was doing, because all of a sudden, he gets out of prison, and all these gay boys and girls ended up dead. Killed by their parents. I knew he was doing what he was doing before. He was brainwashing folks into killing their gay kids. And it made me sick. He was still out there hurting people. Only he was doing it nationwide. He had a videocast attracting people from around the country. He was getting more and more subscribers to his YouTube channel. I took a look at the things he was saying on his YouTube channel, and it was disgusting. Absolutely disgusting. I don't know why YouTube allowed him to continue to be on there. In fact, after a little while, he was gone. His channel was gone. But that didn't matter, he went underground and was still reaching millions of people with his hateful message. So, he had taken his act out on the road and was finding people all over the country willing to listen to what he had to say, and they were murdering their kids."

"Do you have proof he was getting parents to murder their kids?"

"No. I couldn't prove that. But he was doing that before - getting parents to kill their gay and transgendered kids. And trust me, he's the kind of guy who is such a fanatic, and such a believer, that he makes you believe, too. It's sickening, what he does. And he started doing it right when he got out of prison. He was causing people to be hurt, and killed, all over the country. And I couldn't let that stand."

"So what happened? How did you stop him?"

"At first, I was just pissed off. I didn't do anything about it. I was just really, really enraged. But he started to threaten my mom. She showed me emails he was sending to her. And the things he was sending to her were vile and scary. He threatened to rape her. He threatened to kill her. He threatened to burn her house to the ground. He threatened to chain her in the house and burn the house down with her in it, so she would burn to death. He sent her all these emails, disgusting things, and then, one day, he showed up at the house. That part was true. He showed up at our house and had a gun."

"He had a gun? Is this the same story you were telling me before?"

She shook her head. "No. It's not. He had a gun, and he

pointed it at my mom, and he clicked it. She got the gun away from him and found out it was loaded, but it misfired. Which means he was going to kill her. And he would've killed her, if the gun wasn't defective. If the gun was working, she would be dead right now."

"Okay. It sounds like, so far, you have a good case for…"

"For what? I can't just kill the man. Unless he's actually threatening me or somebody around me at the time. You know that. I can't just gun him down, not unless he's actually threatening me or my mom at that moment. Trust me, I wish that weren't the rule, but I know it is, and I respect that. So, my mom, of course, got a restraining order, but that did no good. He still came over. He would be outside the house, looking in at us from across the street. My mom was terrified of him. She knew what he was capable of. And she had all these threats against her. And then, one day, he came over and set fire to her porch. She put the fire out with a fire extinguisher and called the cops. They came over and took a report. They arrested him for violating his restraining order, and for setting fire to the porch, but he got out on bail again. Then he really threatened her. He came over again, and I thought he would kill her."

"What did he do when he came over the second time?"

"He just told her that the next time he came over, he wouldn't be so nice and was going to kill her. He said he felt she was why he was arrested in the first place, because, after all, it was her testimony on the stand that gave the cops enough probable cause to arrest him. He was dangerous. I knew it was a matter of time before he killed my mother and me."

I took a deep breath. "So what did you do?"

She looked around the room, as if she was afraid somebody would come out of the walls and kill her. She blinked rapidly. "My mom, she got an inheritance recently. Her parents were pretty well-off. They died recently in a passenger plane crash. It was a small Cessna that crashed into the Pacific Ocean. So my mom got $100,000 from this inheritance. She told me she would give me that money, every penny of it, to hire somebody to take care of Reverend Scott." Heather shook her head. "I guess mom did her homework and found out that $100,000 was the going rate for a decent, clean hit. She was willing to spend all of her inheritance on this, every penny. It was that important to her that the Reverend Scott be taken care of."

Oh, boy. "Who did you find for that? And how did you find him?"

"I asked around. I didn't find anybody who would know something about that, but I had the money. So I arranged a meeting with Vincent Sharpelli. I heard on the street that he had men who would do something like that." She took a deep breath. "And he did. He sent one of his men out to kill him. And that's what happened. That's where Beck was involved as well. That's how I got to know him."

I drummed my fingers on the desk. "How was Beck involved with this?" I hoped and prayed that Heather wouldn't tell me that Beck killed Reverend Scott. Then again, that made no sense that he would've killed the Reverend Scott, because, if he was, there was no way that he could threaten Heather with it. In that case, he would have much more liability than her. *She* would be dangerous to *him*.

"Beck is the cleanup guy for Vincent Sharpelli. Not all the time. He just does a few jobs for him, here and there. His AB brothers on the outside forced him into helping Vinnie out. But that's all Beck does for Vinnie - cleanups. He did this job. He got rid of the body. I don't know where he got rid of the body. All I know is that he did. And he apparently did a good job of it, because nobody knows where the reverend is. He'll probably never be found. I think Beck does his job well because I think he knows exactly how to get rid of a body."

Well, this was great. Just great. "Heather, you do understand there's a good chance that Vincent Sharpelli was involved in the murder of Adele. You do know that, don't you?"

"No. I don't know that."

"Well, he has to be looked at. I mean, when Adele stole money from Jordan, she was also stealing from Vincent, because Vincent was Jordan's boss. If anybody would have been in a position to kill her, it would've been Sharpelli. He's the most likely suspect in this case."

"Listen, I want you to look anywhere but at him. Anywhere but. I know I can't dictate how you approach this case, but, trust me when I say you don't want to mess with that guy. Seriously. He'll kill you and your whole family without even blinking an eye. You can't just casually bring him in as a suspect and expect things to go well. I don't think he had anything to do with it. He never knew that William became Adele."

"How do you know he never knew that?"

"I just know it. Besides, it doesn't make any sense that he would have done that. Beck did jobs for him. In fact, Beck is probably one of the best cleaners in the business. Even if Vincent Sharpelli was going to kill Adele, he wouldn't do it in that way. I think it's clear, and you know it's clear, that the person who killed Adele either was a rando or somebody who had it in for Beck as well. He or she obviously wanted Beck to take the fall for it. Now, if Vincent killed Adele, he wouldn't have done it that way. He would've killed her and had a cleaner come in and take care of the body, just like he does with every other murder. He wouldn't have been so sloppy about it. Vincent, if nothing else, is a professional. It's not his style just to kill somebody and dump their body, not unless he's trying to frame somebody for the murder."

I thought about it. What Heather was saying was true. She made a good point. Granted, Vincent Sharpelli *was* the kind of guy who would do something like this – kill somebody and dump their body because he wanted somebody else out of the way. Somebody who would take the fall for it. It's like that scene in *The Godfather Part II* where the senator woke up with a dead hooker in his bed. It was clear, in that case, that the senator was the target, not the hooker. So if Vincent Sharpelli did it, he would've done it to target Beck.

I was going to have to look into his relationship with Beck and see if I could find any evidence that Vincent Sharpelli had a problem with him. If that was the case, I would make him an alternative suspect. That was a dangerous thing for me to do. I knew that. But I needed to win the case. And if I could win the case by showing there was a nexus between Vincent Sharpelli, Beck, and Adele, I would do it.

I only hoped that was not the case.

"So you're nervous that if I finger Vincent, he'll come after you?"

Heather nodded. "You're goddamn right. Listen, he can get me in trouble, even while keeping his own hands clean. Trust me on this. He could bring me down. Beck can, too. I got too many fingers in this pie." She shook her head. "I should've just done it myself. I shouldn't have gone to a professional. But I didn't want to do it myself. I've never killed a man before. I mean, I killed my mother, but that was a different thing – it was self-defense. But I've never killed somebody in cold blood. But I knew the Reverend Scott had to be killed. He was hurting too many people, and he was going to kill, or rape, my mother. He threatened her enough times, and I knew that one of those days he would succeed in killing her. I had to take care of him. I just had to."

Chapter Twenty-Seven

THAT NIGHT, I called Sarah to confront her with her shenanigans. Beck's case was bothering me, so I needed to get Amelia's case out of the way so I could concentrate on defending Beck. Heather was certainly getting it from all sides on this case.

That couldn't be helped, though.

I called Sarah. My plan was to be as casual as possible. I was gonna tell her I knew what she did and if she didn't want to go to prison, she better drop the case.

"Hi, Damien."

"Hello, Sarah."

She was silent for a second. "I don't know if your attorney told you this, but we have a court date for the paternity case."

"Actually, no you don't. I mean, I'm sure you have a court date, but you're going to dismiss the case. I'm going to tell you why you're going to dismiss the case."

She was very quiet. "Damien, I don't know what you're

talking about. You got the paternity petition in the mail. You know what we're asking for. A judge will decide this."

"No, actually a judge won't decide this. Oh, wait, maybe a judge will decide this, but, trust me on this, it won't be a paternity judge. It'll be a criminal court judge, because that's who throws the book at people who doctor up official records for fraudulent purposes. And maybe you'll also answer to a civil court judge when I sue you and Baron for emotional distress and seek punitive damages due to your criminality in falsifying a DNA test. Did you really think you would get away with this? Honestly?"

Sarah was silent. Then, with a weak voice, she said "I don't know what you're talking about."

"Oh, don't you? Don't you? Trust me, when I get through with the two of you, Baron's going to be holding a sign begging for money with a barrel covering his ass. That is, if he, and you, aren't in prison for this." I was milking this for all it was worth. Of course those two bozos wouldn't go to prison over something like this. They would both get a slap on the wrist. But Sarah didn't know that. At least, I hoped she didn't.

As for suing her for emotional distress, that wouldn't fly, either. You generally have to have some other kind of negligent tort to anchor a good suit and then add emotional distress into your damage claim. Again, however, Sarah didn't know this. What she didn't know *would* hurt her.

"Damien, I-"

"You, what? What? I mean, really, Sarah, I knew you hated me, but filing a phony paternity action just to get some money? I never thought even you would stoop that low but apparently I was wrong about that."

"Damien, you aren't Amelia's father."

"Oh, I know that. Amelia and I had a talk about that,

but I told her she's staying with me and her biological father won't come for her. Because that's true, isn't it? Jake Brillis, my half-brother at that, won't come for Amelia because Jake has no interest in her. Yeah, I found out the truth. Now, you're going to dismiss that paternity action and we'll all just move on. I won't even come after your sorry and greedy ass, and Baron's neither, if you file a dismissal today. Otherwise, I'm going to the police plus I'll file a multi-million dollar lawsuit against both of you for emotional distress."

Sarah was very quiet. She knew she'd been beat. "I'll dismiss it today," she said in a very small voice.

"I thought so."

"Damien?"

"What?"

"I'm very sorry for all this."

I rolled my eyes. "I'm sure you are."

And I hung up.

LATER ON THAT DAY, I got on the court database and found the paternity petition had been dismissed.

It was over. The damage hit Amelia and me like a freight train, but she would stay with me, and that's all that mattered to either of us.

Amelia and I would be okay.

Chapter Twenty-Eight

THE PERSON who possibly wouldn't be okay was Tina. That was another issue I had to button up so I could give my full concentration to Beck's case. Unfortunately, I couldn't find anything that would make the prosecutors dismiss the case. They offered Drug Court, but Tina said she didn't want that.

Then they offered me a Suspended Execution of Sentence, and I wanted to jump at that offer. What that meant was that Tina would stay out of prison. With a Suspended Execution of Sentence, known as "SES," you're technically sentenced to prison, but that sentence is suspended in favor of probation. As long as you walk down your probation, which meant you didn't catch another case or otherwise run afoul of the rules, you could avoid prison altogether. On the other hand, if you violate probation for one reason or another - maybe you dropped dirty, which meant flunking a random drug test, or you cavorted with other felons, or you caught another case - you had an automatic prison sentence that you would have to end up serving. So, a "3 SES 5" meant three years probation, with a five-year prison sentence hanging out there if you violate.

An SES was contrasted with an SIS, which was a "Suspended Imposition of Sentence." With an SIS, you wouldn't have a prison sentence attached to your probation. If you violated an SIS, you typically would end up with an SES, and then, if you violated your SES, you would end up in prison. It just stepped up from there. A violation of an SES typically meant that you could go for a 120-day callback, which meant you could serve 120 days in prison and then you're called back in front of the court, who would decide if you have to go back to prison or if you could serve the rest of your time on probation. Violate probation on a 120-day callback, and you served the rest of your prison sentence, albeit you typically would serve only 20%, which meant that, with a 5-year sentence, which was being offered to Tina on the back-end of her probation, she would only have to serve an extra 240 or so days before she would be paroled.

The only problem with the SES was that Tina would have a felony on her record. This wasn't the case with an SIS - since the sentence was never imposed, a felony doesn't go on your record.

Still, I felt an SES would be a good deal for Tina, considering the prosecutors were offering her prison time. I went to visit her to bring that offer to her.

She shook her head when I informed her she would be a convicted felon with the SES. "No fucking way," she said. I just wanted to smack her. "I'm not taking no felony. How am I supposed to get a job or an apartment or anything else with a felony on my record? That shit's gonna follow me wherever I go."

I sighed. "Tina, they were offering you five years in

prison. With the SES, you won't have any prison time to serve. I know, it's tough having to take a felony, but come on - you were caught with 5 kilos of coke, with a street value of $70,000. There's not a prosecutor's office in this country who would offer you an SIS for that much coke. They were going out on a limb to offer you Drug Court, but you let it be known that you want nothing to do with all that. If you rolled on Larry Rodriguez, then I might get your case dismissed, best-case, or get you an SIS. But an SES is the best I can do right now, assuming you don't roll on Rodriguez."

I looked into her stubborn eyes, and I felt anger rising up inside of me. Not just at Tina herself, but at Connor. He roped me into representing her, making it my second *pro bono* case in a row. I was doing this for her, free of charge, as a favor to a friend, and doing the best I could to get her the best sentence possible. She wasn't cooperating at all. She apparently thought I was a miracle worker, which was common enough. That was the thing with many criminals - they did the crime but don't want to do the time, and, unless you come at them with an outright dismissal of their case, they'll blame you, the defense attorney, for their plight. It just drove me insane.

Clients like Tina made me question my line of work. The ones that really boiled my blood weren't the hard-core criminals charged with serious felonies, but the whiny low-level drug dealers who felt entitled to have their case dismissed or offered an SIS they'll violate the second they walk out of the courtroom. The ones who caught case after case after case and somehow expected never to end up in prison.

I patted my knees and stood up. "Well, okay, then. Good luck to you. I'm going to withdraw from your case. You'll

The Hate Crime

have to somehow scrape up enough money to pay for private counsel or go with the Public Defender's Office. You qualify for the PD's office with your income, so I suggest you go with them. However, I can guarantee you one thing - if you don't take this offer, you'll end up with something much worse. I happened to catch your prosecutor at a moment of weakness. She's preparing for a big murder trial and doesn't want to deal with your case, which is why she gave me this fire-sale deal. But, as soon as her murder trial is finished, and she has more time for the rest of her cases, she'll ask for prison time on your case again. And, guess what? You'll deserve it."

I walked towards the door, when Tina called my name. "Damien, wait."

Just as I thought. She's going to get religion now. "Yes?"

"I'll take the goddamned SES."

"Thought you would. I'll tee this up for a plea next Tuesday at 9. I'll see you then."

The following Tuesday, she obediently showed up to plead guilty to a felony in exchange for an SES.

I was relieved because that meant I had that much more time to spend on Beck's case.

Chapter Twenty-Nine

December 2 – The First Day of Trial

THE FIRST THING I had to do, on the day of the trial, was to get my motion in *limines* heard by the judge. I knew that when I found out that Beck and Adele were lovers, back when Adele was William, there was no way his past as a white supremacist would be at all relevant. It wasn't relevant anyway, but it *really* wasn't relevant because I could show that Beck and Adele knew one another and had a relationship with one another, therefore it would be very difficult to show this was some kind of random hate crime. That would be a good outcome.

The judge was the same judge I had for my murder trial, Judge Gina Grant, Division 47. I liked her and got along with her very well. I found her to be a tough but fair judge. She was from the defense bar, as she worked for the public defender's office when she was a lawyer, which set her apart from a lot of other judges that came up through the ranks from the prosecutor's office and other places like that. I knew she wouldn't take any kind of bullshit, which was exactly what this hate crime designation was. Bullshit. Always was, and I had the feeling the prosecutors knew that from the beginning. There was no way they couldn't have known that. If they had done their homework for even two seconds, they would've known. Which meant that either they didn't do their homework or were being completely disingenuous when they filed the enhancement on this case.

I got into the courtroom early that morning. I sat at the defense table, waiting for Beck to arrive. I closed my eyes and took a deep breath. I had no idea how this case would go. I had a pretty good idea who really did it, but whether or not I could prove it to the jury was something that remained to be seen.

At first, I was excited to find out that Beck and William had a relationship. But then I realized it wasn't necessarily a good thing for our case. There was the possibility that the two had a lover's quarrel that ended up with Adele dead. It didn't even matter that the two of them broke up once William became Adele. What mattered was that they were, at one time, lovers. However, I didn't think the prosecutors would go down that route because they were so invested in the whole hate crime angle. Why they were invested in that angle, I didn't know. I only knew they were.

Before long, the judge came on the bench, and the prosecutor, Alayna Wilder, and her second chair, Freddy Weinstein, came in the door. "Remain seated," the judge said to us. "Okay, looks like we'll be having a trial today." She looked at me with a skeptical look. "You again, counselor?" She shook her head. "We have to stop meeting this way. I mean, seriously, haven't you heard of pleading out a client or two?" She smiled to make sure I knew she was only joking. Which I did know. Judge Grant liked to joke around a lot behind the scenes. In front of a jury, of course, she was all business.

I chuckled. "I wish. Trust me, I don't like trying these cases any more than you like hearing them. I know that all of us would rather be on the golf course, or, in my case, at the casino, but here we are. I just can't seem to get a guilty client. Sometimes I wish I would get a guilty client a time or two, so I could plead them and give me a break from having to try these cases. Oh, what I wouldn't give for a good plea bargain right now."

Alayna laughed. "Not to mention the fact that the last time you were in front of this judge, you were the Defendant. That's weird, if you think about it."

I turned around and saw Harper rushing through the door. Harper always tended to be a little bit late to court. And when she wasn't late, she was rushing around trying to figure out where her head was. I often wondered how she managed to do as well as she did in the courtroom, considering how frazzled she always was. I would have to talk to her later and see if things were okay with Abby. I knew she was struggling with her still and that Abby was sucking a lot of her mental energy. I knew how she felt. God, I knew how she felt. When I believed I was gonna lose Amelia to that bastard Baron Wicker, I thought I was losing my mind.

As it was, Amelia was not my daughter, at least not biologically. But she also knew she would never leave me and I would never leave her, and that brought us closer. I hated that she knew I didn't supply her genes, but I couldn't help that. Once that cat was out of the bag, it was out of the bag. But the important thing was she knew I loved her, and she loved me, and we would always be together. Crazy Sarah couldn't tear us apart, no matter how hard she tried.

I still couldn't believe how all that shook out. I found out I had a half-brother and that Sarah was banging him when I was married to her.

I still didn't know exactly why Sarah filed that paternity and custody case against me. Yes, Baron Wicker needed an heir, or else he would be cut off from his own inheritance. I just didn't know why the two of them thought they would get away with it. As if I was just gonna lay down and take their doctored documents as gospel. They apparently took me for a fool, but I had the last laugh on them. I had no use for people who were so selfish that they would try to tear a child from her father just because an inheritance was on the line. The dude already had enough money. But apparently it wasn't enough - he wanted more, more, more. He was a rich bastard and money was all he cared about. God forbid Amelia would have gone with him. I had to admit that the outcome that happened was the very best that could have happened. For both Amelia and me, but not so much for Sarah and her boyfriend Baron.

"Hey," Harper said. Her voice was higher pitched than usual and she was shaking. "I'm so sorry, Your Honor, I know I was supposed to be here right at nine, but –"

"I understand counselor," Judge Grant said. "How's your daughter these days?"

"I'm so happy you asked me about her. She's doing just fine. She's not the reason why I was running late this morning." Harper looked down at the floor. "I've just been having some personal problems these days. But they had nothing to do with my daughter."

"Well, counselor, it's okay, you're only five minutes late. Now, I understand the defendant has a motion *in limine* for me to hear. As I understand it, he not only wants the jury to not hear an instruction about this being a hate crime, but he also wants to have his client's white supremacist past excluded from evidence." She looked over at my client, who was dressed in a shirt, that, thankfully, covered almost all of his tattoos. "Counselor, you did a good job of dressing your client today. If he would have had some skin showing, the horse would have left the barn, as far as his white supremacist past." She was referring, of course, to all those Aryan Nation tattoos. I did my best to make sure all of them were covered up.

"You're right about that, Your Honor. If the jury would've been allowed to see his tattoos, it probably wouldn't have been good for him, to say the very least. But, that's not the case, so I can plausibly suppress the fact that my client was once involved in the Aryan Brotherhood. I ask the court to instruct the prosecutor, Alayna Wilder, that she not ask any questions related to white supremacy."

Judge Grant nodded. "I read your motion, counselor, and I've read the prosecutor's rebuttal. I'll tell both of you I'm inclined to agree with the defendant. I fail to see how this could be a hate crime, considering the defendant and the victim had a past together. As I understand it, they were lovers when your client was known as William Page. You'd be hard-pressed, Ms. Wilder, to prove the defendant killed Ms. Whittier out of some kind of animosity against transgendered people. But I'll listen to your arguments anyway."

Alayna looked nervous. Whatever argument she came up with would be ridiculous and she knew it. But she would give it the old college try anyhow. "As I indicated in my response to Mr. Harrington's motion *in limine*, we believe his client's hateful past is extremely relevant. Our theory is that he killed Ms. Whittier in the first place because he was so conflicted about his homosexual tendencies, which obviously clash with the creed he shared with his Aryan brothers behind bars. We believe he was a powder keg just waiting to be set off, and his love for a transgendered female upset his psyche in such a way that he lashed out and killed her."

I rolled my eyes. "That's such a creative argument the prosecutor is coming out with. They could have just dropped the hate crime designation once they found out the true nature of the relationship between my client and Ms. Whittier. But they didn't drop it, so they had to come up with some armchair psychologist cockamamie theory about my client's true nature doing battle with his psyche. However, unless they plan on not only producing an expert witness to back up their cock-eyed theory, but a psychologist who has actually treated my client, then I say, in the most technical terms possible, that this is a load of bull."

Secretly, however, I thought their argument was a good one. If I thought my client actually killed Adele, self-loathing such as what the prosecutor described would be a good reason for him to have committed the crime. I saw firsthand how much my client was conflicted about his feelings for Adele. Beck's homosexual tendencies were eating him alive. However, I was convinced my client didn't actually kill Adele, so I thought the prosecutor's theory, while creative, didn't hold water.

I looked at the judge and saw she wasn't buying it, either. "Ms. Wilder, you're going to have to do better than that. Mr. Harrington is actually correct – if you're planning on bringing in such a theory, you better have your ducks in a row. That means bringing in a psychologist who treated Mr. Harrison along with an expert witness who can testify about the self-loathing you're talking about. I have your witness lists, and you not only didn't designate an expert for anything, but you also didn't bother to have Mr. Harrison evaluated by a psychologist. Therefore, I'm going to have to sustain Mr. Harrington's motion *in limine*. You are not to bring in the defendant's membership in the Aryan Brotherhood, nor may you ask any questions that reference in any way, shape or form, the fact that Mr. Harrison has, what you might call, a troubling past with white supremacy. I agree with Mr. Harrington's motion, and that to do so would be more prejudicial than probative, therefore the motion *in limine* is sustained."

Alayna looked cowed, but she nodded and went into another argument. "Your Honor, in light of your ruling on the defendant's first motion *in limn*, I wanted to clear this with Your Honor before the trial begins. I have witnesses who will testify that Mr. Harrison had a strained relationship with Ms. Whittier because Mr. Harrison struggled with his homosexual feelings for her. That's another way we can establish motive for Mr. Harrison killing Miss Whittier, and I would like to pursue that angle."

"Of course, if you have witnesses who will say something like that, then that's fine," Judge Grant said. "Mr. Harrington will have a chance to cross-examine them, same as any other witness. As long as you don't go into Mr. Harrison's membership in the AB, you may question, with a limited scope, anybody who had personal conversations with Mr. Harrison, where Mr. Harrison indicated that he was having trouble with his sexuality and having trouble with how he felt about the victim. Again, however, the questioning of these witnesses must be extremely limited. If you get in over your skis, I will shut you down."

I knew I would win that first motion. I thought the same about my next one. "My next motion *in limine* is pretty straightforward. My client had been in prison, and I made a motion to exclude any reference to his prison stint. I know that's kind of a 'goes without saying' type of motion, however, I want to make sure to lay the groundwork, in case we lose. I want to preserve my objection to any kind of reference to my client's prison stint."

Since I successfully argued that Beck's position in the Aryan Brotherhood was a no-fly zone, I would also make sure they couldn't reference his prison stint at all. At least, not to impeach him. If they made reference to his prison stint, the prosecutor could show Beck joined the AB gang in prison. That would wind up as a one-two punch for them – they not only could show my client was allegedly a white supremacist, but could also show that he had been in prison. It would've been a backdoor way of introducing his felony record. I killed two birds with one stone with my first motion *in limine*, so this motion *in limine* was just a chance to button things up.

"Again, I'm inclined to agree with the defendant's motion *in limine* on the topic of his prison sentence," Judge Grant said. "It's a well-known rule of evidence that you generally cannot bring in evidence of a felony conviction to impeach a witness, so I see no reason to deny defendants motion *in limine*. So the defendant's second motion is sustained as well." She looked meaningfully at me. "That said, having read the state's rebuttal to your motion, I understand that bringing in the defendant's prior felony record will be necessary to establish motive. Therefore, I will allow the state to bring in the defendant's felony record and prison stint for that reason alone. The state may inquire about the defendant's felony record but may not use it to impeach."

I nodded. I thought that was a fair ruling, but it didn't accomplish much for our side. The prosecutor could still bring in Beck's record, but not use it to impeach him. However, once the horse had left the barn, that was that. But I had to move on.

"Now, my third motion *in limine* is to have my client's confession suppressed," I said. "I have obtained a videotape of the confession. It clearly shows that my client asked for an attorney and the cops ignored him. They pretended they couldn't hear him ask for the attorney. They pressed on and he signed a confession within 1/2 hour after he asked for an attorney and was rebuffed. Moreover, the reason why he signed a confession was because the cops lied to him and told him that his little brother would be in trouble because he was dealing drugs. While I realize that the police are allowed to lie to a suspect in order to obtain a confession, they are not allowed to ignore a suspect's request for an attorney. Therefore the confession was fruit from the poisonous tree and needs to be suppressed."

"Counselor, is this true?" Judge Grant asked Alayna. "Did the cops in this case ignore the defendant's request for an attorney?" She appeared to be somewhat perturbed by this entire exchange. Of all the rookie mistakes a cop could make, ignoring a request for an attorney was one of the worst.

"Well," Alayna said with a clear of her throat. "The request for an attorney was ambiguous. I saw the videotape and Mr. Harrison simply said he wanted to speak with Fred Moore. He didn't say that Fred Moore was his attorney."

"With all due respect, Your Honor, that's a ridiculous argument," I said, secretly thinking it was a decent argument. "No, my client did not say the words 'my attorney,' but he gave a name. The cops should have asked him if he was referring to his attorney. Fred Moore is a well-known member of the defense bar and I think the cops know this. Or they should know this."

"And why didn't your client hire Fred Moore for his counsel?" Judge Grant wanted to know.

That was a complicated thing to make the judge understand. I didn't quite know how to explain to her that the only reason why he hired me was because I agreed to work for free because of Heather's situation. If he hired Fred Moore, he would've had to pay his full fee, and there was no way in hell he could've afforded that.

"My client didn't hire Mr. Moore because he couldn't afford his fee."

"And yet he can afford your fee?" Judge Grant asked in wonder. "What am I missing here?"

"Your Honor, I'm taking his case on a *pro bono* basis. So, yes, he can afford my fee."

Judge Grant looked like she didn't quite understand what was going on, but shook her head. "I'm not going to ask you why you would take a murder case on a *pro bono* basis. That's not my business." She looked over my motion *in limine* and appeared to contemplate it. "So, let's see. Now, tell me why your client just didn't tell the interrogating officers that he wanted an attorney? Why would he just throw out a name, instead of saying the words 'I want to speak with counsel?'" She peered at me from behind her glasses. "It seems to me that your client was deliberately trying to throw some ambiguity into the proceedings, because he wanted to sign a confession to get his little brother out of trouble and knew that if he would've come right out and said he wanted to speak with an attorney, the questioning would have to cease. He was trying to play things both ways. I must say that his whole plan was too clever by half."

The judge figured out Beck's game. I knew she would. It

was very easy to see what he was doing when he asked for Fred Moore, instead of saying the words "I want my attorney." Nevertheless, I thought I had at least a 50-50 chance of getting the confession thrown out.

The judge sighed. She looked over at Beck, who was standing next to me. She wagged her finger at him. "You think that you're so smart, Mr. Harrison. I know what you were doing with the policemen who were interrogating you. I'm inclined to overrule your motion *in limine* on the confession, just because your little game pisses me off. However, because you threw out a name, and that name was of a well-known member of the defense bar, combined with the fact that the police interrogators lied, I will sustain your motion to have your confession suppressed. I don't want to reward bad behavior, which this definitely was, but, in the end, the police who interrogated you didn't have clean hands, either. In fact, of all the parties involved, their hands were the most unclean. And, as it turns out, your little brother was not even in trouble, so you didn't gain anything by confessing. So I guess it's a wash, in a way." She banged her gavel. "Defense counsel's motion *in limine* to have his confession suppressed is sustained."

I nodded, knowing we were winning the first battles already. That was important to me, to win these early battles, because I wanted to put the prosecutor on her heels. And she deserved it. Once she found out the nature of my client's relationship with the victim, she should've dropped the hate crime designation right then and there. But she didn't. So now she was being made a fool of. And I couldn't have been more happy about that.

I was finding that, even though Beck was not my favorite client in the entire world, I was getting my trial mojo back. Whenever I had a client I wasn't fond of, I still gave it my all, because I enjoyed the game. The competition. The chance to best the other opponent. That was a flaw of mine, and I knew it. I knew there would be at least one or two clients I would go balls to the wall defending, knowing they were guilty. Knowing they would probably go out and commit more crimes once they were acquitted. But that wasn't my concern – my concern was winning the game. I was required to give every one of my clients zealous advocacy, and that was what I did. Win, lose or draw, I would always go down swinging.

"Okay," Judge Grant said to the two of us. "Unless there's more motions for me to entertain, I think it's time to get the show on the road. Let's pick a jury. I'll bring in the potential jurors, the two of you will work your magic, and hopefully we can have a jury impaneled by lunch time. Do you guys think that's a possibility?"

"Sure," I said. "I'm sure that's a doable timeframe."

Judge Grant nodded her head. "Okay then, I'll start calling everybody in."

The jury came in batches of 50. This was something I usually wanted Harper to do when she second-chaired me. She was almost an empath when it came to reading people, in trying to find out what their true natures were. That was because Harper was so sensitive to what other people were feeling. She was a master at picking up on tics, facial expressions, and general body language to decide if someone was telling the truth or not.

I had found that almost everybody, when asked, would say out loud that they could judge the case on its merits. No matter what kind of experience they had in their lives, they always said that they would not prejudge the case. Harper and I both knew, as did every attorney, that this wasn't true. Even if the juror thought he or she could be an unbiased observer, this simply wasn't true most of the time. They simply gave the answer they thought was socially acceptable – they would not be prejudiced against our client, whomever the client happened to be.

Harper was a master at deciding when people's unconscious biases would dictate how they looked at the case. If their unconscious bias helped us, she made sure to get that person on the jury. If the opposite was the case, she made sure to use her peremptory challenge on that person.

Alayna started the questioning of the potential jurors. She asked the usual questions about whether anybody knew any of us, including the defendant, and if anybody's relatives were in law enforcement. She gave a brief statement about what the case was about and asked each person if they could judge the case on its merits. Her list of questions were perfunctory, but they did the job.

Then Harper got up and asked her questions. Her *voir dire* questions were always slightly left of center, because she was looking for something very specific from her people. In her case, she wanted to weed out people who might be unusually sympathetic to transgendered people. Someone who closely identified with the transgendered person might want to convict our client based on that reason alone. Especially if they had experienced some kind of prejudice themselves in their life, related to their sexuality. Harper didn't want those people on the jury. So she had questions about whether anybody in the jury had a close relative, friend, or lover who was transgendered or gay. Several people raised their hands, including two different people who were transgendered themselves.

One was a 6-foot tall transgendered female. She was in full makeup and wore big earrings and a long dress worn with tennis shoes. She walked with a cane. When she opened her mouth, it was clear she was pre-op, at best, but most likely had never fully transitioned into a female.

The woman, whose name was Carmen, talked about how she was treated throughout her life. She talked about the bullying, the name-calling, and all the times she had felt threatened by people who hated her for who she was. I saw Harper had tears in her eyes, as Carmen told her story, but I also knew Carmen wouldn't be on the jury panel.

The other one was a transgendered male by the name of Christian. He explained that this was his given name, because when he was a female, he was also named Christian. "Well, that's not entirely true, it was actually Christiana. It was simple enough just to drop the final A, though." He, too, told stories about how he had been treated throughout his life. He had a slightly better story than Carmen, however – his parents were very accepting of his identity, and they never forced him to be somebody else. "I just think that's so important," he said. "Parents just don't know what kind of damage they do to their children when they try to force them to be someone they're not. And when the parents don't force them, society does." He shook his head. "But I can judge this case on its merits, absolutely."

Those were the only transgendered people, but quite a few others had people in their lives struggling with some kind of sexuality issue. This was a double-edged sword for us, considering our client was apparently either gay or bisexual and the victim was transgendered. We had every designation of the LGBT group, aside from the L.

When it came time to pick a jury, I was surprised to see that Harper was advocating for Carmen. "I hope you know what you're doing," I said.

"I do. I just have a feeling about her." That was all she said about that.

That was one thing about Harper - if she had a feeling, I didn't question it. I thought for sure that Carmen would be one of her first peremptory strikes, but she knew something I didn't. On some level, she knew something.

BY NOON, we had a jury selected, and it was time to get the show on the road.

The game was about to begin.

Chapter Thirty

ALAYNA GAVE her opening statements first. "Ladies and gentlemen of the jury, thank you very much for being here, and performing your civic duty. I appreciate every one of you." She walked over to the jury, and paced back and forth in front of them, and looked each one in the eye. Alayna was trying to connect with every person there. She was trying to communicate with everybody individually. She had a knack for that, I had to admit.

She was quiet for a few minutes. She narrowed her eyes. Nodded her head. Finally, she began with her statement. "I'd like to tell you the story of a young woman by the name of Adele Whittier. She wasn't always known by that name. In fact, up until a couple of years ago, she was known by her birth name – William Page. But, for the sake of this court case, I will simply refer to her as Ms. Whittier."

I knew that my motion *in limine* being sustained was tying the hands of Alayna. I knew she wanted to tell the jury her theory about how my client killed Adele out of hatred of himself, which manifested into loathing of Adele. But she couldn't go there. So she was going to have to discuss the circumstantial evidence, which was much less powerful.

"Ms. Whittier, and the defendant, Mr. Beck Harrison, were friends." She shook her head. I knew she was having trouble. The facts in this case were suddenly not on her side. She was in a struggle to show motive on my client's part. Originally, of course, the motive that they were going for was that my client was prejudiced against transgendered people in general. That my client killed Adele because he didn't know she was transgendered, then, when they went somewhere to have sex, he found out, freaked out, and killed her. That was their original theory.

Then, once it came to light the true relationship between Beck and Adele, the motive switched to the self-loathing thing. While I knew that Alayna would do her best to try to show the self-loathing thing by getting witnesses on the stand, who allegedly could say that Beck told them how he felt, I knew that would be baloney. Beck was not the kind to confide in his friends that he hated himself for being gay. That much I knew about him. I felt pretty confident I could knock her witnesses over with a feather. Other than that, she had nothing. She would have to throw spaghetti against the wall and hope it stuck. I felt fairly confident in knowing I had a better argument.

She cleared her throat. "They were friends but they had a fight. On the night of June 5 of this year, they had a fight. A fight that ended up with Ms. Whittier dead." She bowed her head. "You will hear evidence that Ms. Whittier and Mr. Harrison left the Zoo Bar together at around midnight on the morning of June 6. The bartender that night can testify that they were together all night and left together.

The Hate Crime

You will hear testimony that this was the last time Ms. Whittier was seen alive." She paced back and forth, looking at every juror. "Let that sink in. Mr. Harrison was the last person to see Ms. Whittier alive. That morning, her body was found by the dumpster in the alleyway next to the defendant's apartment. She had been strangled, and her body was left for the rats to eat. She was thrown away like so much trash. In fact, her body probably would've been thrown into the trash, except the regular dumpster was full. So she was left by the dumpster as if she was a couch to be thrown away."

"You'll hear evidence that the defendant and Ms. Whittier had a complicated relationship, to say the least. You'll hear evidence from friends of Mr. Harrison, who had no idea that Mr. Harrison was gay. However, these friends will testify how hard it was for a man like Mr. Harrison to be gay. These friends will testify that because Mr. Harrison had deep-seated dark feelings about the way he felt about men, he was prone to lash out at people."

I knew that at that moment, Alayna was kicking herself for not lining up an expert who could testify what self-loathing does to a person. I knew, as well as anybody, that when you hate something about yourself, you might lash out at the people who display the trait you hate. If you struggle with addiction, and hate that part about yourself, you're going to lash out at other druggies. If you grew up poor, and you're ashamed of that, and you get out of poverty, you might have a loathing for poor people. And if you were secretly gay, and you really hated that fact, you would be more likely to lash out at gay people. I knew that if Alayna had tried, she probably could have found a good psychologist who could testify that some people who hated that they were gay, especially if they had anti-gay authoritarian parents, could end up being homophobic. But she didn't try. She was just going to have to let the jury draw their own conclusions.

I knew the truth. I knew that, while Beck struggled somewhat with his homosexuality, it wasn't too debilitating for him. He didn't appear to me to have any kind of animosity towards gays or transgendered folks. I knew this murder had nothing do with any of that. I was just going have to show that.

She continued on. "You'll hear evidence that just before Ms. Whittier and Mr. Harrison went to the Zoo Bar that night, they had words in the car. The evidence is that Mr. Harrison and Ms. Whittier had a conflict regarding some illegal things Ms. Whittier was into. Mr. Harrison, as a parolee who spent 5 years in prison for a robbery, had no desire to go back to prison and wanted no part of that life. Ms. Whittier, however, did not want to go straight, for her current drug activities were just too lucrative. You'll hear evidence about a conversation about that, which gives Mr. Harrison another reason to kill Ms. Whittier. Ironically, he killed her because he didn't want her bringing him down."

I thought that was probably the prosecutor's weakest argument. Beck didn't want to go to prison, so he murdered somebody? That made no sense at all, especially since, if the prosecutor's argument was true, he didn't even try to hide the murder. According to the prosecutor, he just left her body by his apartment dumpster. Wouldn't that alert the authorities to the fact that he was involved in this? That is, if the prosecutor's theory was true. At this point, I knew they were grasping at straws.

She was coming up on the close of her opening argument. She paced back and forth, back and forth, back and forth. "Once you hear the evidence against Mr. Harrison, you will return a verdict of guilty. I ask for this verdict of guilty in advance. Thank you very much, ladies and gentlemen of the jury. Your service is appreciated."

It was my turn. And I hoped to rip the prosecutor's theory to shreds.

Chapter Thirty-One

IT WAS time to begin my case. "Ladies and gentlemen of the jury, I don't know about you, but I think the prosecutor's opening statement was a little bit, shall we say, short on substance? There's a reason for this, and I think you all know what that reason is. My client didn't do it. He had no motive to do it. The prosecutor tells you my client was struggling with his homosexuality, and his feelings for Adele Whittier's former male persona, William Page. I can tell you that nothing can be further from the truth. My client is very confident in his sexuality. He has no problem with transgendered people, or gay people, or any members of the LGBT community. You'll hear evidence from Mr. Harrison himself that he had no problem with the fact that Adele Whittier was transgendered. And it's true that Mr. Harrison did have a romantic relationship with Mr. Page. But there was nothing contentious about the relationship. There was no reason that Mr. Harrison would ever want to murder her."

"The prosecutor has also introduced a crazy theory that Ms. Whittier was killed because she was involved with drug

The Hate Crime

dealing and that my client, Mr. Harrison, killed her because he didn't want her to bring him down. The prosecutor herself admitted that my client has served time in prison and doesn't want to go back. So, if you follow the prosecutor's argument to its logical conclusion, my client killed somebody in order to stay out of prison." I shook my head in wonder, and couldn't help but smile a little. The argument was just so stupid. "Let that sink in for a second. My client has no desire to go back to prison, so he killed somebody. And he didn't even try to cover it up, if you believe the prosecutor's argument. No, he apparently, according to the prosecutor, killed Ms. Whittier and left her body by a dumpster by his apartment complex, all because he has no desire to go back to prison." I shook my head again, rolled my eyes, and looked every juror in the eye.

"Now, if my client was so calculating that he would kill somebody because he didn't want her to bring him down and cause him to end up back in prison, don't you think he would try to cover up her murder just a little bit? I mean, seriously. The prosecutor would have you believe that my client planned out this murder, yet he did nothing whatsoever to cover his tracks. Do you believe that? No. I don't believe that either."

"Now, on the other hand, while my client had no discernible motive to murder Ms. Whittier in cold blood, there were several people who *did* have motive to do so. The first person I'm going to present to you is Larry Rodriguez. Mr. Rodriguez had motive to kill Ms. Whittier because Mr. Rodriguez paid a lot of money and took a lot of time to transform my client from Mr. Page into Ms. Whittier. He paid for Mr. Page's plastic surgery, which was hundreds of thousand of dollars, because his entire face was transformed to make it look completely different. Not to mention the fact that Mr. Page had to take expensive hormone injections so he could grow breasts and hips and obtain a more womanly figure. Moreover, Mr. Rodriguez hired somebody to steal the identity of Adele Whittier, who was an actual woman who lived and died in Boston, Massachusetts. In the end, Mr. Rodriguez spent close to a half a million dollars to transform Mr. Page into Ms. Whittier."

I paced the floor, right in front of the jury box. "Now why would Mr. Rodriguez spend so much money to transform Mr. Page into Ms. Whittier? Well, Mr. Page was an indispensable member of the Sharpelli crime family who sold these pilfered drugs on the black market. The Sharpelli crime family is headed by Vincent Sharpelli and Mr. Page worked for this organization for five years. He knew the inner workings of the organization and ended up stealing $200,000 from Mr. Sharpelli. Mr. Page's immediate superior's name was Jordan Kennedy."

"So, here's what happened with this. Mr. Page stole this money from the Sharpelli crime family, and knew he wouldn't be long for this world unless he did something drastic. And so he did. Mr. Page partnered with Mr. Rodriguez, who had the money to transform him into a woman, and he stole the identity of an actual living person in Boston, Massachusetts - Adele Whittier, who was a nurse with excellent access to powerful drugs. This cost Mr. Rodriguez a lot of money, but it was worth it to hire somebody who knew so much about a powerful crime family like the Sharpellis. That was why Mr. Rodriguez spent all that money on Mr. Page."

"And how did Mr. Page repay Mr. Rodriguez for his generosity? I'll tell you how he repaid him. Once he became a woman, he decided that he didn't want to be involved in a life of crime anymore. The real Adele Whittier had nursing

The Hate Crime

credentials, a BA in nursing, and a Masters Degree as well. Mr. Page was a very intelligent man, so he was able to study up enough about nursing protocols that he was able to fool the staff at Truman Medical Center. William Page, in becoming Adele Whittier, actually realized one of his dreams – to lead a life that did not involve crime. At least not the kind of crime that Mr. Rodriguez was asking of her. And Ms. Whittier therefore left Mr. Rodriguez holding the bag. Not to mention holding the half-million dollars that he invested in her. It doesn't take a rocket scientist to understand how angry this must have left Mr. Rodriguez."

"Especially when you consider the fact that Adele Whittier was actually still involved in underground activity, but it was more subtle than the activity that Mr. Rodriguez wanted from her. Mr. Rodriguez wanted information about the Sharpelli crime family. He wanted to know all the inner workings of it, but he also wanted Ms. Whittier to be a drug mule for him."

"Ms. Whittier found that to be too dangerous, however. She found another illegal way to make money when she became a nurse, and that was stealing prescription drugs for yet another drug dealer in town named Charlie Williams. Mr. Williams partnered with Ms. Whittier to distribute prescription drugs, such as OxyContin and Percocet, on the black market. She and Mr. Williams worked hand-in-hand for two years. However, at one point, about six months ago, Ms. Whittier informed Mr. Williams she could no longer steal drugs for him to distribute. She explained to him that she knew her superiors were catching onto what she was doing and didn't want to end up going to prison. Especially because this entire scheme was Mr. Williams' idea in the first place."

"So, here you have two people who had reason to kill

Ms. Whittier. We have Larry Rodriguez, who spent a lot of money on transforming Mr. Page into Ms. Whittier, only to have her not only not give him what he needed, which was secrets about the Sharpelli family, but also refused to work for him. The second person who had clear motive to kill Ms. Whittier was Charlie Williams. Mr. Williams had reason to kill Ms. Whittier, because he had a deal with her to distribute prescription drugs, and she not only told him she would have to stop doing that, but he also suspected she had enough evidence to finger him to save her own skin if her employers called the authorities on her."

"So you'll hear testimony from Mr. Rodriguez and Mr. Williams. You'll hear evidence that each one of these men had a reason to kill Ms. Whittier. Each one of these men had a motive that was far above any kind of motive my client would've had to kill her."

"And what about the fact that Ms. Whittier's body was found so close to Mr. Harrison's apartment? Well, ladies and gentlemen, the fact her body was found close to his apartment does not make it more likely that my client killed her. On the contrary, the fact that her body was found so close to his apartment makes it *less* likely he killed her. Think about it – if he killed her, don't you think he would try to do something to cover that fact up? The fact that her body was found so close to his apartment screams a set up to me. And, as it happens, each one of these men also had a reason to frame my client."

"Mr. Rodriguez had a reason to frame my client because my client used to work for him a long time ago. My client knew about Mr. Rodriguez's activities, and Mr. Rodriguez wanted to shut him up. So he framed him for murder, which would make him go away to prison, which would, in turn, serve the purpose of silencing him. Mr.

The Hate Crime

Williams also had a reason to frame my client, because Mr. Williams had a problem with a woman by the name of Heather Morrison. My client has information about Heather Morrison, information that could possibly implicate Ms. Morrison in a crime. Mr. Williams' motive was simple - he knew that if my client got convicted for murder, he would turn on Ms. Morrison to save his own skin. This was Mr. Williams' end game, because he and Ms. Morrison used to be lovers, but things ended acrimoniously. Mr. Williams paid Ms. Morrison's bond, and her attorney's fees, when she was accused of murdering her mother several years back. You will hear evidence about these transactions."

"So you see, ladies and gentlemen of the jury, there were people who had reason to want to see Ms. Whittier dead. The same people also wanted to see my client behind bars. They wanted to have both of them out of the way. These people would have much more motive to have killed Adele Whittier than my client did. And, after you hear the evidence, you will agree that my client had less motive to kill Ms. Whittier than did Mr. Williams and Mr. Rodriguez. Once you hear the evidence, you will have no choice but to vote to acquit my client. I ask you for a verdict of not guilty. Thank you very much."

Chapter Thirty-Two

WE FINISHED OUR OPENING STATEMENTS, and the judge announced a 10-minute break. The jury filed out, and I sat down next to Beck. He looked nervous, but not overly so. "So what do you think?" I asked him.

Beck shrugged his shoulders. "I don't know, dog. I think you did an okay job in defending me. I don't know though. It seems like this can go either way."

"Of course it can. Of course the case can go either way. But I think we'll win this." I often said this to my clients, even when I wasn't confident. And, truth be told, I wasn't entirely confident now. I had some pretty good suspects on my list, but that didn't mean I could break them down and show the jury they had motive to have done this. "If we lose this case, are you still going to the authorities about Heather to try to get a lighter sentence?"

"Sure, dog. I'll do anything to make sure I'm not in the joint for the rest of my life." He closed his eyes. "I'll do anything."

I knew that would be the case. I knew the prosecutors

The Hate Crime

would shorten his sentence in exchange for information about Heather, even though Heather's case was unrelated.

I also knew Beck was more worried than he let on. If nothing else, it would be humiliating for him to have his sex life hashed out in front of the court. He was very secretive about that, obviously. He didn't want to tell me about it at all and I was his attorney. To have that fact splashed in front the world would be embarrassing for him, to say the very least.

He crossed his arms in front of him and shook his head. With closed eyes, he said "I hope you know what you're doing, dog. You're going to be dragging my name through the mud. It better be worth it. If I lose this case, I ain't going to prison being known as some kind of namby-pamby faggot. It's bad enough my homies gonna know it after today. But whatever. You're the lawyer, I'm the client. I'm just the dumb shit who managed to get his ass into such a situation. You're the guy who'll get me out of it. So my life is in your hands. But you know what's gonna happen if I go down. If I go down, I'm bringing a bunch of people down with me. That's all you need to know."

Chapter Thirty-Three

THE JURY CAME BACK IN, everybody took their seat, the judge came back, and it was time to get started. "Okay, counselor," Judge Grant said to Alayna, "Call your first witness."

I knew there were not many witnesses Alayna could call. She could call in the officers who arrested Beck, but there was only so much they could say. They certainly could not say that he confessed to them. That horse left the barn when they failed to give him an attorney when he asked for one. Granted, his request for an attorney was ambiguous, but I won the argument, and that was all that mattered.

Other than that, I knew Alayna would call in Quince Newton, the bartender from that night. And she would also call in two of Beck's friends from the outside – Cameron Jackson and Pete Taylor. Ostensibly, those two guys were going to testify to the fact that Beck was having problems with his sexuality, but I thought the real reason for calling them was because she wanted to psyche Beck out. She knew I would call him to the stand and she wanted to rattle him.

The Hate Crime

As I looked at Beck, I realized that was probably a good strategy on her part. Beck didn't want people knowing the gay side of him. He certainly didn't want his friends to know about it, but it was safe to say they probably would know about it after the trial. They might even know it at the moment. Not that Beck knew if they did or not – those two guys had stopped talking to him several months ago.

Other than that, she would call in the medical examiner, and she was going to display the obligatory blowup pictures of the victim. None of which proved anything. I was going to object to the pictures being displayed because they weren't helpful to the jury. They never were. What was proved just by showing them pictures of Adele's body splayed out on the ground next to a dumpster? The fact she died? It certainly wasn't helpful in allowing the jury to determine who killed her. And that was the only reason why we were having a trial. To find out who killed Adele Whittier.

The first two witnesses that Alayna called were the officers on the scene and the medical examiner. It went just like I knew it would. She just asked the officers questions about finding Adele's body next to the dumpster by Beck's apartment, and she questioned the officers who brought Beck in and interrogated him. She couldn't go very far with that, however. She tried to skirt the line to imply to the jury that Beck had confessed, but I saw Judge Grant giving her the evil eye, so she shut those questions down pretty quick. As for the medical examiner, that was perfunctory and anticlimatic. The medical examiner simply stated that Adele had been killed by strangulation.

I leaned back in my chair, waiting for the witnesses who I thought might do some damage to us. Emphasis on the word "might," because I didn't think the people she was calling were really going to do much.

After she called the officers and the medical examiner, the first witness she called to the stand was Quince Newton. He was a bartender at the Zoo Bar, and would testify that he saw Beck and Adele leave the bar together. His testimony was also a wash, as far as I was concerned. So he saw them leave the bar together – so what? What did that prove? I could have just stipulated that Beck and Adele left the bar together. That was a fact and I wasn't going to try to deny it. No point. So, when Quince was done with his testimony, I didn't have any questions for him.

Nevertheless, Alayna managed to make his testimony more dramatic than what it really was. "So," she asked Quince. "You saw them leaving the bar together. Did you ever see Ms. Whittier in the bar after that night?"

"No. Obviously. She was killed that night, right?"

Alayna went over to the jury after that question. "I would like the jury to know that Mr. Newton was the last person to see Ms. Whittier alive." She told the jury that as dramatically as possible. I rolled my eyes. *Drama queen.*

Then came the two friends of Beck, Cameron Jackson and Pete Taylor. Cameron was first.

"Mr. Jackson, could you please state your name for the record?"

"Cameron Jackson." Cameron was somebody who resembled my client, in a way. He was extremely muscular, and, like my client, he had a lot of tattoos. Unlike my client, at the moment, Cameron was wearing a short sleeve shirt that showed off both his muscles and his tattoos. Like my client, his head was shaved bald. He had tanned skin and brown eyes. I looked at some of his tattoos and realized this guy was probably also a member of the Aryan Brotherhood.

"Mr. Jackson, did you speak with the defendant on the night of June 5 of this year?"

"Yeah. I did."

"And were you with the defendant, Mr. Harris, and the victim in this case, Ms. Whittier, on that evening?" Alayna asked.

"I was."

"What was your impression about the relationship between Mr. Harrison and Ms. Whittier?"

I got to my feet. "Objection. This question clearly calls for speculation."

"With all due respect your honor, I'm simply asking for Mr. Jackson's overall impression of the relationship between Ms. Whittier and Mr. Harrison."

The prosecutor was right about that. But I wanted to throw her slightly off her game. I gave her a free ride on the officers and the medical examiner, and it was time to mix it up a bit.

"Overruled. You may proceed, counselor."

Cameron looked confused, although I knew he was no stranger to court appearances. I checked on his record and found that he'd been in and out of the joint more than Beck. "Beck and Adele, they were dating."

I looked over at Beck, who was shaking his head. He explained to me that the guys apparently didn't know that Adele was not biologically a woman. Nevertheless, Beck had insisted to me that he was not dating Adele at the time she was killed. I was therefore confused about why Cameron was saying these things.

"You are aware that Ms. Whittier was transgendered?"

Cameron looked stunned and then gave Beck a look of disgust. "Hell, no. Beck, he don't play that."

"When you say that he doesn't play that, what does that mean?"

"That means he don't play that. He don't get with dudes."

"Is that what Beck told you?"

"Yeah, that's what he told me. He don't get with dudes. And he certainly ain't getting with a dude who's not quite a dude."

I suddenly knew where the prosecutor was going with this and it was very clever. She was clearly going to try to show guilt by association. That, because Beck's best friend was apparently homophobic, at least judging by the look of disgust currently on his face, the prosecutor would show Beck probably was homophobic as well. That, combined with the fact that Beck actually had a relationship with William/Adele was clearly how the prosecutor would try to show that Beck was very conflicted about his feelings. However, I wouldn't let her get away with it. If that was her plan, I would put a stop to it. On cross-examination, I knew just what to ask this guy.

"Is it safe to say that if Mr. Harrison came out to you and the other friends that you and Mr. Harrison hang out with, it wouldn't be accepted?"

"Oh, hell no. Sorry, ma'am, but that ain't happening with any of my homies. I would probably beat the crap out of him if I found out he was messing with dudes." Then he looked at Alayna quizzically. It was as if it just dawned on him what she was driving at. "Wait, are you saying Adele wasn't a woman?" He shook his head. "Man, if she wasn't a woman, she sure fooled me."

The Hate Crime

"Yes, Mr. Jackson, that's exactly what I'm saying to you. Ms. Whittier was biologically a male."

Cameron looked as if he was very confused and disgusted at the same time. Then he started shaking his head. "You're serious? My homey Beck was dating a woman who wasn't a woman?"

"Apparently so. If you tell me that Mr. Harrison and Ms. Whittier were dating, then the answer to your question is yes, Mr. Harrison was dating a woman who was biologically a man."

I had no idea why Beck didn't tell his friends about what was going to be said in court today. Beck should've known this scenario could occur and he probably should've come clean to Cameron long before he could be blindsided in court for maximum effect. In fact, I had strongly advised him to do just that – tell his friends that the woman he was dating, although whether or not he was actually dating Adele was still a matter of dispute, was biologically a man.

Cameron was still on the stand but was shaking his head. I wondered what he was thinking. The look on his face told me that he probably would stop hanging out with Beck after this. He kept looking at Beck with extremely dirty looks. "I'm sorry, ma'am, but I feel like I need to get sick. I mean, you're trying to tell me that my homey, the guy I grew up with, the guy I've always been tight with, is a homo? I'm sorry, I have to have a minute with that."

Even though Cameron told Alayna he needed a minute to process the fact that the man he thought he knew was, as he put it, a "homo," Alayna wouldn't give him that minute. "Now, I'd like to take you back to the evening of June 5. You were with Ms. Whittier and Mr. Harrison earlier that evening, isn't that right?"

Cameron sat silently for a few minutes. It looked like he was still trying to recover from being told that Beck was dating a transgendered person. He just stared at the wall and it was clear he hadn't heard her question.

"Mr. Harrison," Judge Grant said. "Please answer the question."

"I'm sorry, what was the question again?"

"The question was whether or not you were with Ms. Whittier and Mr. Harrison earlier in the evening of June 5 of this year?"

"Uh, yeah. I was."

"What was the nature of the relationship that evening between Mr. Harrison and Ms. Whittier?"

"I don't know, what do you mean?"

"Were they friendly with one another that night, or was there tension between the two of them that night?"

"Oh yeah, they were fighting. It wasn't nothing special. Beck was just pissed that he felt Adele wasn't being very quiet about her criminal activities. He kind of felt she would end up going down and taking him down with her."

"And what do you mean by that? What do you mean that he was concerned she would bring him down with her?"

"Just what I said, man. Listen, Beck's out on parole. He don't need his girlfriend going around being all open about her drug dealing ways. Beck, he had been to prison and had no desire to go back. He said once was enough."

"And why did he feel Adele's activities would impact him?"

"He felt that way because Adele kept on pushing him to help her. But you know, Beck ain't doing that. No way is Beck helping her out. Adele, she be working for Charlie Williams. Beck, he be working for one of Charlie's rivals,

Jordan Kennedy. Jordan Kennedy finds out Beck's working for somebody else and Beck ain't long for this world. So no, he ain't gonna help Adele out."

Cameron was referring to the fact that my client occasionally did clean-up work for Jordan's boss, Vincent Sharpelli. I already knew that, so I wasn't too put-off by Cameron's testimony about that.

"So you're saying Adele wanted Beck to help her but he wouldn't do it, and that was a source of tension between the two of them?"

"Yeah. They were always fighting about it. You know, Beck knows lots of people, and Adele wanted to open up her distribution channels. Adele knew Beck knew a lot more people than she did. She was getting tired of selling to only Charlie all the time. Charlie was kind of a jerk to her, to be honest with you."

I could have objected to that line of questioning, as Cameron was definitely getting beyond the scope of what Alayna was asking him. At the same time, however, what he was saying about Charlie was going to bolster what evidence I would bring into the court later on about him. So I decided to let it go.

Alayna recognized that what Cameron was saying would help me later on, so she decided to move on and try to get him on a different track. "Is it safe to say that Mr. Harrison and Ms. Whittier had words that night?"

I stood up. "Objection, Your Honor. Counselor is leading the witness." I sat back down.

"Sustained."

"What was the overall tenor of the conversation the night of June 5?"

"You mean what did they say to each other?"

"I don't want to know what Ms. Whittier said to Mr.

Harrison, but I do want to know what Mr. Harrison said to Ms. Whittier that evening."

Cameron shrugged. "I don't know. I think it was the same old, same old. I think he was mad because she kept bugging him to help her distribute pharmaceuticals, but I don't know why she wanted him so bad for that. I heard the cops were gonna arrest her for doing what she was doing. I think Beck knew that too and he didn't want to get involved with a sinking ship."

"I have nothing further for this witness."

"Mr. Harrington, your witness," Judge Grant said.

I approached Cameron. I would have to rehabilitate Beck on the gay thing. I didn't think Alayna showed much damage as far as the fact that Cameron apparently was discombobulated about Beck's relationship with Adele. He was. So what? What did that prove? As for the rest of the questioning, I would try to flesh out why he thought Charlie was kind of a jerk, and what kind of relationship he knew that Charlie had with Adele. That would be the most important thing to me.

"Mr. Jackson, you found out for the first time today that your friend, Mr. Harrison, was dating a transgendered woman. Is that right? You didn't know that before this proceeding?"

He shook his head. "No, man. I had no clue."

"Is it safe to say that Mr. Harrison's relationship with Ms. Whittier was a shock to you?"

"Yeah. I had no idea."

That, of course, contradicted what Alayna had promised to the jury in her opening arguments. She had promised them she would elicit on the stand testimony that indicated Beck had told his friends he was struggling with his sexuality. Clearly, this witness couldn't testify to something like that if he had no clue Beck was gay before this.

"Is it safe to say that Beck never confided in you about having sexual feelings about men?"

"Yeah, that's safe to say. To say the least." He shook his head and looked down at the stand. "No, Beck never told me nothing about being into dudes. If he'd told me about that, I would've told him he was sick."

I wondered how this testimony was setting with the jury. On the one hand, this testimony was establishing that Beck never told him about any kind of deep, dark feelings he had about men. That directly contradicted Alayna's opening statement where she promised to elicit testimony about Beck's confession about these feelings. But on the other hand, this guy was clearly hostile towards gays, so if the jury was thinking Beck held the same views as this guy, that would bolster the prosecutor's argument about Beck killing Adele because of animosity born out of his frustration regarding his own dark sexual feelings for her.

I decided this was a potential landmine, so I knew it was time to move on. I was more excited, anyhow, about asking this guy about Adele's relationship with Charlie. It seemed like he knew something about that and it sounded like Adele's relationship with Charlie was contentious, to say the least. That was safer ground for me, so I decided to attack that point.

"Now, you testified on direct that Charlie was treating Adele with a lack of respect. Is that correct?"

"Yeah, I think that's right. Charlie was an asshole, I hope I can say that in open court, because that's how I feel. He was getting pissed at Adele because he wanted Adele to find new buyers for his stuff. He was always threatening her, telling her she better get more aggressive in finding buyers.

That's why she wanted Beck to help her out. She knew he can find lots of buyers on the street, so they were always fighting about that. I think Beck knew it was only a matter of time before Adele got pinched. It's one thing dealing with regular drug dealers on the street, but it's another dealing with somebody stealing from a hospital. Cops be taking that shit seriously. You know, the opioid addiction that has been in the news lately. It was safe to say Adele would go down hard. And Charlie would've cut her loose like a stinking fish."

"And so why, exactly, did you think Charlie was disrespectful to Adele?"

At that, Alayna stood up. "Objection, Your Honor. This cross-examination is clearly moving beyond the scope of the direct."

"Actually," I said, "The state opened the door to this very line of questioning. If you can recall, on direct, the witness said Charlie was a jerk to Adele. So, this line of questioning is actually within the scope of the state's direct examination."

Judge Grant shook her head. She turned to the court reporter. "Could you please read back the testimony of this witness that would indicate this witness stated this Charlie was a jerk?"

The court reporter read back that exact statement, and Judge Grant looked at Alayna. "Ms. Wilder, while I would agree ordinarily that this line of questioning would be beyond the scope of the direct examination, your witness did state on the stand that Charlie was a jerk to Ms. Whittier. I know it's always a problem when your witnesses blurt out things you don't want them to, but live by the sword, die by the sword. I'll allow this testimony about Charlie. By the way, what is Charlie's last name?"

She addressed that question to Cameron.

"Williams," Cameron said into the microphone. "His name is Charlie Williams. He be a drug dealer in town and Adele worked for him. She be stealing drugs from the hospital for Charlie to sell."

"Counselor, you may proceed."

I was secretly thrilled how this was shaping up. I wasn't expecting to question Cameron about Charlie and Adele. And if it weren't for the fact that he just blurted out about how Charlie treated Adele, on direct examination, I wouldn't have been able to go there. I was going to elicit testimony from this witness that would reinforce the testimony I would get later on from Charlie himself.

"On what information do you base your observations that Charlie was, as you say, a jerk to Adele?"

"Charlie, he's always pressuring Adele, more and more, and, let me tell you, he was super pissed when Adele tells him she's not gonna steal drugs for him no more. I was there. I was there in the room when Adele tells him she's not stealing drugs for him no more. He got so pissed about that, he beat her ass."

This testimony was shaping up to be better than I had thought it would be. I had a feeling Charlie was the one who killed her anyway. Cameron's testimony reinforced this in my mind. He was just building the blocks and the foundation I needed to show that Charlie might have done this.

"So, Charlie was very angry at Adele when she told him she wouldn't be stealing drugs for him anymore. Do you know why he would have been so angry about that?"

Alayna was on her feet again. "I would like to renew my objection, and would also like to object to the speculation that Mr. Harrington is trying to get from this witness. He's basically asking the witness to read the mind of this Charlie Williams."

"I can ask a different question, one that is more specific on the facts, if need be."

"Please do, counselor. I'll allow limited questions regarding how this witness would know that Mr. Williams was so angry with Ms. Whittier. Emphasis on the word *limited*."

I nodded. That was reasonable. "Thank you, Your Honor." I was going to have to be careful not to elicit hearsay, yet try to get his impression as to why Charlie was so mad.

"Charlie be having problems in controlling his turf. He's not making the kind of money he was before and Adele had the good stuff. You know, lots of people be scared of the street drugs, but they be thinking the pharmaceuticals are all pure and pristine. Lots of people know dealers be putting rat poison into your heroin, and you never know what you gonna to get on the street, but the same people know that this 'Hillbilly Heroin' don't have the same problems." *Hillbilly Heroin* was the street name for OxyContin.

"So you said Charlie had problems controlling his turf. What did you mean by that?"

"I mean that Charlie was hoping to get a new clientele, you know, the people who got money. The people who live in those big houses on Ward Parkway and Mission Hills, the people who could keep him in business. He be trying to work the street, but he be having a war with some of the other dealers on the street. Those dealers, they all be fighting amongst themselves for the scraps. Charlie wanted out of that, so he wanted to be selling the legit stuff like OxyContin and Percocet to these richie-riches. He only had

The Hate Crime

Adele working that line, so yeah, when she told him that gravy train was getting gone, he got really pissed."

Cameron knew much more about Adele's dealings with Charlie than I ever would've guessed. That surprised me. I didn't know he knew so much. I didn't think Beck knew that either – if he did, he would've told me that Cameron would be a gold mine.

Then again, it was weird that Charlie would be so willing to kill his golden goose. It still gave me fruitful avenues for my direct examination of Charlie, which would be happening soon.

"I have nothing further for this witness."

"Ms. Wilder, do you have any further questions for this witness?" Judge Grant asked Alayna.

"No, Your Honor." I was sure she was kicking herself for how this witness went. She didn't get anything out of him that hurt us, while opening the door to testimony that clearly hurt her side.

I thought Alayna learned a lesson with Cameron, so I doubted she would still call Beck's other friend, Pete.

Indeed, Alayna chose to rest after Cameron's testimony. I didn't blame her. She did enough to show that Beck possibly killed Adele, just by showing that Adele's body was found in the alleyway by his apartment, next to a dumpster, and that he and Adele left together from the Zoo Bar that night. It was circumstantial evidence, but it was still powerful, so I knew that if I didn't bring it, we probably would lose. I simply had to show that somebody else was involved in this murder.

I knew I had my work cut out for me.

AFTER THE PROSECUTION RESTED, it was time to take a break and go home. By that time, it was already 4 o'clock, and the judge just let everybody go home early. "We're going to recess for the day," Judge Grant told the jury. "The court shall reconvene tomorrow morning at 9 AM."

I was excited about presenting my case. Yet, I could not foresee how everything would break. And I really couldn't foresee the piece of information that possibly would break everything wide-open.

Chapter Thirty-Four

I MET with Tom that night, as well as Harper. Tom had texted me while I was in trial, asking me to meet him. He'd come across some new information that could possibly be important.

As the jury left, I turned to Harper, and showed her the text that Tom sent to me. "What do you think this means?"

"I don't know, but it sounds enticing. To say the very least. I wonder what kind of information he'll give us?"

"We'll soon find out."

WE MET Tom at my office. One of the reasons why we didn't go to our usual bar was because of Harper. She was still struggling with her sobriety. She confessed to me that it was something she white-knuckled every day of her life, and during periods of stress, which trials inevitably were, she really felt like drinking. Because of that, I decided it was best that we met at my office. Plus, that was where everything was for the trial. Harper and I did our usual trial preparation, spreading out all the witness statements and key pieces of evidence in our conference room.

"What's going on?" I asked Tom when he arrived that evening.

"Did you happen to put David Harrison on your witness list?"

"Of course I did." I tried to be thorough with my witness lists. That meant I put on the list anybody who I could conceivably think to call during the course of the trial. That meant, of course, that I put Beck's father on that list. "Why do you ask?"

"Because I found out some information about him that I think you need to know. His prison cellmate, John Marelli, is not his cellmate anymore. In fact, he just got out of prison himself. He's on parole."

My heart started to race. I had a feeling about this. Early on, I wanted to look at the father more carefully, but didn't do it. I was too focused on looking at Larry Rodriguez, Jordan Kennedy and Charlie Williams. They all seem to be looking good to me as far as alternative suspects. Truth be told, I didn't want to bother with subpoenaing David Harrison for court. I felt he didn't have a reason to kill Adele, plus he was in prison, so how would he have killed her? Granted, he could've easily gotten one of his men to do that, yet I couldn't see a connection between him and Adele, so I didn't consider him.

"Well, you better issue a subpoena to the Cameron prison and get David Harrison into court tomorrow. John Marelli contacted me. He told me he needed to talk to me because he knew I was doing investigations for Beck. I'm guessing that John somehow was following the Adele case because he told me he had important information about the case."

"What's the information you're talking about?" The more Tom spoke, the more intrigued I became. I was mentally kicking myself for not thinking about David as a possible suspect. In hindsight, it seemed so obvious that David might be behind all of it.

"This is what John told me. He said David was getting extremely agitated and angry because he was hearing his son was possibly a homosexual. You have to understand one thing about David Harrison. He's a hateful person and his hate extends far and wide. He's not just hateful towards people who are brown, black, or Jewish, but he's also extremely hateful towards people who are gay and transgendered. I'm surprised that Beck never told you about this, but David Harrison not just killed Tyrell Washington, the coworker whose murder sent him to prison for the rest of his life, but he also killed a gay man named Sean Maddow. From what I understand, this John Marelli told me that David killed Sean Maddow simply because Sean was gay. Again, Sean was a coworker, and I guess David saw Sean out at a bar one night, kissing and dancing with another man, followed him out to the parking lot, kidnapped him, and killed him."

"Was that murder ever solved?"

"No, it wasn't. Apparently, he had a cleaner who got rid of the body."

Cleaner. My heart started to race. "Who was the cleaner?"

"Now, don't jump to conclusions. Consider the source, this is a felon telling me these things, but I just thought you should have a heads-up about all of it. Let me continue on with the story. I'll answer that question in a bit. But I need to tell you the rest of the story. I don't want you to get too bogged down in the weeds."

I felt impatient, but I knew Tom had to tell me in his own way. I couldn't rush him. "Go on. Tell me the rest of the story."

He took a deep breath. "Here's what else Sean told me. I'm not sure who told him about this, but David found out about his son being gay or bisexual. At any rate, David now knows Beck had a romantic relationship with a man. And he found out this man, William, became Adele, and found out his son had a romantic relationship with her as well."

I suddenly knew where this was going. But could I prove it? I would have to issue an emergency subpoena for David to testify the next day. I had a feeling my entire trial strategy would go out the window. But that was okay, because I had a feeling this lead would be the best one of all. "Go on. Tell me the rest of the story."

"Well, you might know what happened once David found out his son was dating a transgendered woman. Not to mention that Beck was dating that transgendered woman when she was a man. He became enraged. He contacted his men on the outside and told them he wanted his son to be close to him in Cameron Prison because he wanted to quote keep an eye on him unquote. He told anybody who would listen that he would make sure his son was where he could see him. He told John that if it was the last thing he did, he would make sure his son would end up behind bars because he would make a man out of him yet."

"Who did he get to do it?"

Somehow, I knew the answer to that question because I knew who Beck worked for on the outside. I remembered that Heather told me that Beck was Vincent Sharpelli's cleaner. I thought it would probably be poetic justice, on the part of the sadistic father, to hire Vincent Sharpelli, and Vince was the kind of mercenary who would do something like that to one of his contract employees. Which I assumed Beck was. From what I understood, Beck didn't work for Vincent Sharpelli on a regular basis but did occasional jobs when he needed to.

I looked over at Harper, who was already on the phone with our process server, subpoenaing David. Apparently, while Tom was talking to me, she was busy getting a subpoena ready.

"I just spoke with Scott Kelly," Harper said. Scott Kelly was our process server. "He's going to be here in five minutes to get the subpoena. He's going to take it to the prison tonight and we can expect to see David in court tomorrow morning."

"So Vincent Sharpelli was hired to kill Adele. Now I have to ask you this question. Who was the cleaner who got rid of Sean Maddow's body?" I braced myself for the inevitable answer, because I knew who it was. And I would have to talk with him about it.

"It was your client, Beck Harrison."

Chapter Thirty-Five

"THANK you for digging all this up." I would have to talk to Beck about the change in strategy. I also wanted to know why he would've protected his father when his father killed a gay man simply for dancing and kissing another man in a bar. It didn't surprise me that David Harrison would do something like that. What somewhat surprised me was that Beck apparently was in on this murder. If not in on it, he was involved in covering it up.

"Looks like I'm going to have to visit Beck tonight and tell him what's going on. I don't know how he'll take it. Something tells me he won't be upset about it. I wouldn't be surprised if he knew about this all along and was perfectly willing to throw Larry Rodriguez and Charlie Williams under the bus."

Perhaps I needed to not jump to conclusions. Maybe Beck didn't know his father was behind it. I thought there was an outside chance that Beck was as in the dark as we were up until now. I wanted to believe that.

The Hate Crime

"Come on, Harper, let's go over to where Beck's staying."

Beck went to stay with his sister Charity after he made bail. He was staying with her was because she was the only person he knew who didn't have a felony record.

Harper and I took one car over to Charity's apartment complex. We got to her apartment and knocked on her door.

"Yo, dog." Beck seemed like he was in a good mood. He and Charity were sitting in the living room, watching reruns of *America's Dumbest Criminals*, laughing and drinking beer. "Come on in. Me and Charity, we're just shooting the shit. I figure this might be one of the last times I can hang with her like this. No offense, dog, you did a good job in court and all today, but you have to admit things ain't looking good."

I looked over at Charity. I wanted to ask her to leave, since there was the possibility I would have to invoke attorney-client privilege on some of the topics I would be bringing up with Beck. Especially when I would have to ask him about cleaning for his own father. "Charity, I hate to ask you to do this, I know it's your own apartment, but I need to speak with Beck in private. I hope you don't mind."

She looked at Beck and at me. She had a question in her eyes, but she obediently went into the bedroom to leave us alone to talk.

Beck looked at us suspiciously. "What's going on here?"

"I'll tell you what's going on here. The first thing I want to ask you is what do you know about the murder of Sean Maddow?"

Harper did some quick research on the issue on the way over to see Beck. She found out that Sean Maddow went missing around five years ago, right before Beck went to prison for robbery. His body was never recovered. From what Harper gathered from her research, at the time Sean Maddow went missing, it was kind of a big story. Sean was just a regular guy. He was a waiter and was working at the same restaurant David Harrison worked at as a short-order cook. He was also going to school at UMKC, majoring in liberal arts, while living at home. He was only 19. The story was front-page news for a couple of days, but it soon faded off the front page.

I thought about Sean Maddow's family and how they probably were still, five years later, thinking about their son and wondering what happened to him. In my mind's eye, I saw his mother sitting in his bedroom, maybe looking at old pictures of him from when he was a boy, maybe smelling his clothes and hugging them to her chest while she sat down on his bed and thought about her missing son. I thought about his father, who maybe stoically came home every day after work to sit down in his easy chair and drink his problems away. I imagined their marriage was strained. Maybe Sean had a brother or a sister who thought about their brother every single day of their lives. Probably his bedroom was the same as when he left it.

I thought about how Sean Maddow's family never got closure on Sean's death and Beck was why they never got that closure. His family never knew what happened to him. Nobody ever knew what happened to him - he just disappeared one night. And the reason why he just disappeared one night was because of my client. That thought made me sick and it made me not want to go into court the next day and defend him.

There was a part of me that wanted to tank his case. If I tanked his case, the real killer wouldn't go free. The real killer, the actual killer, was already behind bars. I could go

The Hate Crime

into court tomorrow and announce to the judge that I would rest and my conscience would be completely clear. I could go to the jury, and, in my closing arguments, advise the jury to hang my client, and I would sleep like a baby.

I looked at his arrogant face and wanted to smash it in. I wanted to pummel that smug face with my fists. However, my professionalism won out in the end. And I still had to think of Heather. Heather was terrified that I would lose Beck's case. She knew that if I did, it would be all she wrote for her.

Beck looked like he didn't know what I was talking about. "Sean Maddow. Sean Maddow. Where have I heard that name before?"

I took a deep breath. And then another. I had to calm down before I told Beck what was going on. "Don't snow me. You know goddamn good and well who Sean Maddow is."

Beck assumed a defensive posture. "Yo, dog, I don't know what you're talking about."

I looked over at Harper. "You talk to him. I can't right now." At that, I went to Charity's sliding glass door that opened onto her balcony and sat down on a chair. I slammed the sliding door shut behind me. I knew Harper could take control of the situation. She didn't have the same kind of temper I did. She always felt sorry for her people too. She probably was feeling sorry for Beck right now. Let her be the good cop, I thought. One of us had to be.

About a half-hour later, Harper came out on the balcony, and sat next to me. "I told him what's happening. He's not happy about it."

"Of course, he's not happy about it. He just figured that we would go along and throw innocent people under the bus and leave his father alone. You can just tell him this –

either we tell the jury the truth about his father, and we bring in his father to break him down so that he'll tell the truth, or I'm going to rest tomorrow. I won't put one goddamn witness on that stand. No way will I drag people into some kind of dog and pony show, making the jury think this innocent person or that innocent person did it, when I know the truth. So does our client."

Harper was quiet for a few minutes. "For what it's worth, when I told Beck what we found out about his dad, he didn't seem surprised, but he also didn't appear that he knew this beforehand. He told me it sounded like something his father would do but didn't know it happened. I don't know whether to believe him or not. At any rate, I talked him into going along with this strategy. He figures it won't hurt his father any, because, after all, he's LWOP as it is."

"I have no doubt that he's okay with bringing his father into this, because, as you say, it won't be a big deal for his father to get convicted for this. It's just one more murder he'll be serving time for. To that guy, this is nothing. That's not why I'm angry, however. I'm angry because of what happened to that poor kid, Sean Maddow, and how Beck helped his bastard father cover up that murder. I'm angry for the father and mother of Sean Maddow, both of whom probably have never gotten over their son going missing so many years ago. I'm angry because if Sean Maddow's body had been found, his family would have peace. What do you think the chances are that our client even knows where Sean Maddow's body is anymore? After all, he also got rid of Reverend Scott. As Heather said, Beck's one of the best cleaners in the business. Reverend Scott will never be found because our client is such a good cleaner and you can be damned sure that Sean Maddow will never be found either.

The Hate Crime

That means his family will never get closure. That's why I'm angry."

Harper took a deep breath. "Go in there and talk to him about how mad you are about this whole situation. The two of you obviously need to clear the air."

That was the truth. I couldn't have this kind of animosity towards Beck going into the final part of his trial. "I –" I stood up, and sat back down. "Damn it. That boy has such an asshat for a father. Why would he do something like that to cover up what his bastard father did? That just makes me sick. That just –"

Harper was looking at me with big eyes. "Damien, you might be too close to this. After what happened between you and your father, I think what happened here is bringing all that up for you. Maybe you need to take a break. Maybe I need to finish the trial tomorrow." She put her hand on my shoulder. "You have to have some distance."

"That's not what's going on here. I'm just pissed because –" I took a deep breath. "You're probably right, Harper. You probably should finish the trial tomorrow. Not just because I think you're right that I can't be objective about this, but I also think that being examined by a woman on the stand will set David off. And that's what we need. But you're right, I don't think I can be objective on this. For obvious reasons."

"Go in there and talk to Beck. I think you'll be pleasantly surprised by his demeanor tonight."

I opened up the door and saw Beck standing in the living room. His head was down and he looked ashamed. He didn't look like the cocky jerk I saw earlier in the evening, drinking a beer with his sister and watching dumb criminals get arrested on TV. "You wanted to talk to me?" He didn't refer to me as "dog" and he didn't use street language. At this point, he just seemed like a bewildered twenty-something kid who was ashamed of his father yet strangely wanting to still please him.

"Sit down."

He sat down on the couch. He looked at his hands, which were clasped between his legs. His head was down. He finally looked up at me, and I could see anguish in his eyes. I could feel my defenses slowly melt away. Like Harper, I actually felt sorry for the kid.

"Beck, I know what you did with Sean Maddow. What I would like to know is why you did it?"

He still was looking at his hands with his head down. He finally shook his head. "My dad wasn't the easiest dad. He never was around when I was growing up, and when he was, he was beating on me. I never understood what I did wrong. All I wanted, all my life, was for him to see me as somebody he didn't hate. All I've done in my life have been things I thought would make my dad not despise me. I joined the AB because my dad was also in the same prison and I knew he would be proud of me if I joined the AB. I got these tattoos so he could see I'm serious about the AB creed. I went through all that pain to get these tattoos so he could see me as a son he could respect. I joined the AB because I thought it would bring me closer to him. That's why I cleaned up Sean Maddow. I so wanted him to see me as his son and not as somebody he despised. It didn't work. Of course. But I thought I should try."

I found myself feeling strangely paternal towards this poor kid. I never thought I would look at him and feel that way, but I did. And I suddenly realized, for the first time, that I wanted to win the case for him. Not just because I wanted the victory. Not just because Heather's freedom was on the line. But, rather, I wanted to win the case because I

The Hate Crime

wanted to keep him out of prison. My attitude towards him had changed once I saw what was behind his defenses.

"Beck," I began. "Do you know where Sean Maddow is?" I knew the answer to the question. I doubted very seriously that Beck knew. Even if he knew, I had a feeling Sean Maddow's remains didn't exist anymore. I didn't know what Beck did to get rid of these bodies, but I imagined he probably disposed of them thoroughly.

So thoroughly that their bodies were just completely gone.

He shook his head. "No. I dissolved it in acid. He's completely gone."

"Can you go to the police and tell them what happened? Can you do that? There's a grieving family out there who lost their 19-year-old son and will be forever hoping for him to come home. They're probably still waiting by the phone for that call, praying for the best, but fearing the worst. We just don't know what kind of twilight that is. How tormenting it can be to not know. Could you please go to the authorities and tell them that Sean Maddow was killed by your father? Can you do that? You don't even have to tell them that you disposed of the body. I just think those poor people need some peace."

Beck nodded. "Yeah. I've had this on my mind for all these years. Don't get me wrong, I clean up messes for Vinnie. But the messes I usually clean up are bad dudes. Guys that nobody's gonna miss. But that Sean, that's always been something eating away at me. You're right. I'm sure Sean has a family who loves him. So yeah, I'll tell the cops my dad did it."

"Harper's going to be taking over the trial tomorrow. I think it's best, after what happened with my father, but also I think Harper being a woman will set your dad off. And that's what we want. We want him to show his true colors to the jury. If she does it right, it should be an open and shut case."

"You didn't mention my dad in your opening statement. Will that be a problem?"

"No. The opening statement is more of a courtesy thing. In fact, I didn't even have to make an opening statement. All that matters is that your father is on the witness list I gave to the prosecutor. The prosecutor, therefore, had notice that your father would possibly be called to the stand. That's all that matters. The prosecutors have to have some kind of notice about my witnesses because they have to have a chance to depose them or otherwise prepare for them."

I was glad I was so thorough in my witness preparation that I put the father on there. I should've thought about him in the first place. I didn't know why I didn't. It was just a blind spot. Maybe it was a blind spot because of my own father – I had to put up with my criminal father and didn't want anybody else to go through that. I didn't know. It was probably some kind of a psychological block I had.

Beck took a deep breath and let it out. Then he made a little joke. "I guess the good news is that my dad's already a lifer. One more murder on his record ain't gonna do a thing."

I smiled. "True. Very true."

Chapter Thirty-Six

THE NEXT DAY, Harper and I got to the courthouse early. She wanted to make sure that David was transported from the prison in a timely manner. That's what kind of concerned me. If the prison couldn't transport him right away, I would have to put on my other witnesses, just to buy some time. And, at this point, I didn't want to do that. Granted, the other alternative suspects weren't exactly choir boys. They were bad guys. However, they weren't good for this case, so I didn't want to drag them into court and make the jury think they were. I didn't want the authorities looking at them for this murder.

We got to the court room and Harper went to find the guards who were responsible for transporting David to the courthouse. She came back up a half-hour later, and was smiling. "David's here. He's waiting in the witness room with the guards. I think it's safe to say that he has no idea why he's here. Or maybe he does. How could he not know?"

"How, indeed? But I've found that humans have a

remarkable ability to not see things they don't want to see. I have a feeling he probably genuinely has no idea he's about to get hammered on the stand. By a woman, at that." I had to smile at that one. "I just can't wait to see the look on his face when you start bringing him down."

At some point, the judge came out to the bench. This was before the jury was in the courtroom. She looked at me. And then she looked at Alayna, who had just arrived herself. "Well, counselor, is there anything I need to know before you start Mr. Harrison's defense?"

"Yes. There is. Besides my client, I'm going to only have one witness on the stand, and it's not any of the witnesses I mentioned in my opening statement. However, it is a witness on my list, so I ask the court to give deference on this and allow me to call him."

"Ah, counselor, you're going to disappoint your jury. They're looking forward to seeing certain people on that stand. But, yes, as long as this witness you'll be calling to the stand was disclosed to the prosecutor's office, I see no reason why you shouldn't be able to call him. And he's going to be your only witness, besides your client?" She smiled. "Sounds like we're going to be done early. Thank God."

At 9 o'clock on the dot, the jury filed in. It was almost time to start our case.

The judge addressed the jury. "Ladies and gentlemen, the defense will begin this case today." She looked at me. "Counselor, call your first witness."

At that, Harper stood up. "The defense calls David Harrison."

I turned around and saw David Harrison come through the door. He was accompanied by a guard. He was dressed in an ill-fitting suit that was probably given to him on the fly. He walked with a stoop in his shoulders. He had a full head

The Hate Crime

of silver hair. His eyes were steely blue, and his mouth was turned down in a frown. He looked like he probably had a permanent scowl on his face. He was slightly overweight, mainly in his stomach, although his legs were quite thin.

He was sworn in and Harper approached him. He looked her up and down. "Little Miss," he said. "What are you doing here? You're not going to be asking me questions, are you?" He shook his head. "I can never understand why you ladies want to do jobs like this."

I was quite sure he was questioning Harper because he felt Harper belonged at home, in a kitchen somewhere, making dinner for her man and children. In David's world, that's where women belonged. They certainly didn't belong in a courtroom. Not in his world.

Harper took a deep breath. "Could you please state your name for the record?"

David leaned into the microphone. "David Earl Harrison."

"Mr. Harrison, you are the father of the defendant, Beck Harrison, right?"

"So they tell me. I don't know. I've never taken a paternity test, but his old lady says I'm his dad. That's what his birth certificate says, so I guess, yeah, I'm his dad."

This was getting off to a stellar start.

"Mr. Harrison, are you currently serving time in prison?"

"Yeah. I am. For murder one. What of it?"

"Mr. Harrison, what is your relationship like between you and your son?"

He leaned back in his chair and crossed his arms in front of his chest. "I ain't got no relationship with my son. Why do you ask that question?"

Harper knew her work was cut out for her. But I knew

she would rise to the occasion. "So you say you have no relationship with your own son, correct?"

"That's what I just said. I got no relationship with him."

"So when you say you have no relationship with him, does that mean that if he were to have a homosexual relationship with somebody, or date a transgendered woman, you would be okay with that?"

He visibly fidgeted in his seat. He made a fist, and then released it. He took a deep breath. Then he spoke. His voice was dripping with tension. "Hell, fucking no. I'll say that right here in front of God and everybody. I don't even care if this lady judge holds me in contempt. That boy, I don't hardly know him, but he carries my name. He carries my name, so he better fucking live up to that name. And by live up to that name, I mean that he ain't going to be messing around with no man, and he certainly ain't going to mess around with no woman with a man's parts."

I looked at the judge. I knew she would have to hold him in contempt for using foul language in the courtroom. But she chose just to warn him. Which I was grateful for, because if she held him in contempt, and had him taken away, that would mean my star witness would be gone. I knew why David cursed like that on the stand. He literally had nothing to lose. So the judge held him in contempt, what would that mean to him? Absolutely nothing. Less than nothing. Even better, it would get him off the stand, and that's what he would want.

"Mr. Harrison," Judge Grant said to him. "If you use another profanity in this courtroom, I will hold you in contempt of court."

That was the wrong thing to say to him. "I'll say whatever I want, and I won't have some lady judge telling me I can't say this or that."

Harper looked back at me and I shook my head. The judge was put into a bad situation here. She knew that if she held him in contempt, and he was taken into custody, it would only be giving into what he wanted out of the situation. He would be fined, but who cared? He was serving life in prison. He wouldn't pay that fine.

She looked at Harper and Alayna. "Let's take a short recess. Mr. Harrison, please remain seated. Ladies and gentlemen of the jury, you may take a 10-minute break. Ms. Ross, Mr. Harrington, and Ms. Wilder, I need to see all of you in my chambers."

We followed her back to her chambers.

She didn't beat around the bush. "Ms. Ross, you put me into a really bad situation with this witness. I can't have him on the stand dropping F bombs. He doesn't show respect for this court and he doesn't show respect for the jury. I'm inclined to have him taken into custody, but I know that would do no good. It also wouldn't do any good to have him fined. So what am I supposed to do here? You didn't prepare him for the stand, did you?" Judge Grant was really steamed. She was looking at Harper accusingly. "Well?"

Harper looked embarrassed. "I'm so sorry, Your Honor, but this witness would be hostile for me. I didn't prepare him for the stand, because I need to blindside him with my questions. And, with all due respect, I don't think that preparing him for the stand would've done any good."

"What are you going to get out of this witness?" Judge Grant demanded from Harper.

"I have reason to believe that he is the actual murderer of Adele Whittier. I have this on good authority. Namely, his cellmate came to my investigator, who told me that Mr. Harrison confessed to killing Ms. Whittier. His motive for killing her is because he found out that his son was seeing her and he knew she was transgendered. He framed his son because he wanted his son to be behind bars so he could keep a close watch on him. So, again with all due respect, I need this witness on the stand. Without him, I don't have a case. Well, that's not necessarily true – I could try to put on my other witnesses, but they didn't do it. Mr. Harrison did it. David Harrison, that is."

Judge Grant shook her head. "Well, you've put me in a real pickle. You put a witness on the stand with nothing to lose, and he's just going to come out and say whatever he's going to say. And I guess we just have to take that. Oh, I'll fine him, and I'll scold him, none of which will do any damned good. But if he's your case, I guess we have to forge ahead and put up with his disrespecting this court. I hate to do that, but I'm sure the people on the jury have heard it all before. It's not like Mr. Harrison is offending any virgin ears. I don't like it, but it is what it is."

Harper looked embarrassed, but she knew there wasn't much she could really do.

All of us went back into the courtroom. David was still on the stand, with the guard by his side. He looked at Harper and Judge Grant, giving them both the evil eye. He looked at me and smiled and nodded. I was quite sure he liked me just because I was white and male. He probably felt like I was on his team for that reason alone.

I smiled as I realized something - the murder of Adele actually was a hate crime after all. It just wasn't a hate crime committed by my client.

The jury came back in.

"I would like to apologize to the ladies and gentlemen of the jury for the behavior of this witness," Judge Grant said. "Unfortunately, this witness is indispensable, and, while I will do my best to hold him in contempt for his rude

The Hate Crime

behavior and his profanity, my hands are basically tied." She turned to David. "Mr. Harrison, I would like to remind you that you're still under oath."

Harper took a deep breath and approached him again. "Mr. Harrison, before the recess, we were talking about your relationship with your son. I remind you that your testimony was that your son, because he carries your name, isn't going to shame that name by having a romantic relationship with a man or a transgendered female. Is that an accurate description of your testimony?"

He crossed his arms in front of him and just glared at Harper. He didn't say a word.

"Mr. Harrison, please answer the question," Judge Grant said to him.

"I'll fucking answer the questions I want to answer. And I don't want to answer that one."

Judge Grant banged her gavel on her bench. "I'm holding you in contempt, and I'm fining you $10,000."

"Ooooohhh, I'm scared. Lady, I'm serving life in prison, do you really fucking think I care if you fine me $10,00 or $1 million? The answer to that is no. I don't give a shit what you do to me. Unless I win the fucking lottery behind bars, I ain't paying that fine no-how. Go ahead, fine me all you want."

I looked nervously at Judge Grant, wondering how much more of this she could take before she just blew her stack and had him taken away. But she knew, as well as we knew, that doing that would be playing right into his hands. He didn't want to be on that stand. He didn't want to be answering questions. To have him taken away would be giving him exactly what he wanted. That meant that Judge Grant would keep him on that stand for that reason alone.

Harper continued. "You may not have answered the

question, but I can tell you that was your earlier testimony. You did say that because my client, Mr. Harrison, bore your name, he wouldn't shame you by having homosexual relationships, or having a relationship with a transgendered female."

"Yeah, what of it? Yeah, that's how I feel. Any son of mine ain't gonna be no faggot." He looked right at Beck. "Do you understand that, son? You ain't gonna get with no men. And you really ain't gonna get with no lady with men's plumbing. That's just sick. An abomination. What's wrong with these people? They're trying to mess up what God made them. If you're born a lady, you better goddamn well stay a lady. If you're born a man, you better goddamn well stay a man. The less sick freaks like that in the world, the better, but, son, you ain't going to be getting with them. Do you hear me, son? You're not to be messing with those freaks of nature."

This was going very well. However, I looked over at Beck, and he was shaking. He was near tears. He looked like a small boy desperate to please his father, but there was no pleasing him, and the father was a hateful bastard. Hateful, murderous, bastard.

Somehow, Harper was unruffled by this man. Judge Grant, by that time, was resigned. She fined him $10,000. She might as well have fined him $1 million. It didn't make any difference. So she was going to ride it out.

Harper would steer him to where she wanted to go. It would be extremely easy to do. "Mr. Harrison, would you like your son to be behind bars with you? After all, if he's behind bars with you, you can ensure Beck doesn't soil the good family name by dating a man or a transgendered person. Isn't that right?"

Judge Grant looked at Harper. "Ms. Ross, do you need to treat this witness as hostile?"

"Yes, Your Honor. I would like permission to treat him as hostile."

At that, Judge Grant smiled. "In this case, it's rather fitting that you would treat him as hostile. So please proceed." Judge Grant got her sense of humor back, which was a good thing.

"Please answer the question," Harper said.

He crossed his arms in front of him. "Yes. I would like my son to be where I can see him. If he's out here on the street, messing around with females who ain't females, or men, then I can't have that. If he's behind bars, I'm straightening his ass out. I'm making him a man if he's behind bars with me."

"Then is it safe to say that you would do something to make sure Beck went to prison? Something like having a transgendered female killed and ensuring her body is dumped close to where your son lives? That would be two birds one stone for you. Your son goes to prison and the transgendered female he's seeing is dead. That would be the best-case scenario for you, wouldn't it?"

He crossed his arms in front of him. It finally dawned on him what was going on. And, just like that, he apparently decided not to talk anymore. After all, he did all this to ensure his son went to prison. If he confessed on the stand, that wouldn't happen. So there was no way he would confess to it.

No matter. The damage was done. Harper managed to get him to admit on the stand that he wanted his son behind bars. She also managed to elicit every hateful thought the man had on gays and transgendered people.

He just stared at her. "I'm done. I ain't answering no

more questions. You can make me sit here all week, and I won't open my mouth again. So don't even try it."

Harper didn't care. Her work was done. "I have nothing further for this witness."

"Thank God," Judge Grant said. When she said that, everybody in the jury laughed. "Ms. Wilder, do you have any questions for this witness?"

"No, Your Honor." Alayna knew that it was pointless to ask him any questions. After all, he announced to the court that he wouldn't answer any more questions. Alayna knew that if she asked any questions, it wouldn't do any good.

"The witness is excused." Judge Grant looked like no four words she had ever spoken have ever made her happier. And that was probably the case. "Ms. Ross, call your next witness."

Harper called Beck to the stand. She simply wanted to establish that Beck didn't do it. She also wanted to ask him questions about his relationship with William Page and Adele Whittier. It was important for her to establish this, because it made David Harrison's reason for killing Adele that much more stark. Beck was ashamed to be giving this testimony, but he knew it was necessary, and it was probably also cathartic for him. Indeed, after he got off the stand, he seemed relieved.

Alayna did not bother with cross-examining Beck.

After that, Judge Grant asked Harper to call her next witness.

"The defense rests."

"Okay. We'll take another short recess, and everybody come back in 15 minutes, and then the defense and the prosecution will give their closing statements."

The jury left. Judge Grant looked at Harper, me, and Alayna. "Eye yi yi," she said after the jury left. "In all my years on the bench, I've never had to put up with that kind of disrespect."

"I know. And thank you very much for your patience." Harper was mortified.

"You know what, it's okay," Judge Grant said. "There wasn't anything any of us could have done with that. If I would've held him in contempt, and had him taken away, he would have loved that. And I'm all about making sure guys like him don't get what they want. Plus you needed to make your case. But, Ms. Ross, I hope you never do that to me again." Judge Grant popped a Tums into her mouth and shook her head.

Chapter Thirty-Seven

THE JURY CAME BACK IN, and Alayna gave her perfunctory closing statement. I could tell she wasn't into it. She was phoning it in, but I didn't blame her for that. She knew as well as we did what the deal was.

"Ladies and gentlemen of the jury. Again, thank you for your service. You heard evidence that Mr. Harrison and Ms. Whittier were together on the evening of June 5th of this year. You heard evidence that Mr. Harrison and Miss Whittier had words on that evening. Specifically, Mr. Harrison told Ms. Whittier that he would no longer help her distribute prescription drugs. Ms. Whittier was upset by this and she told him so. Mr. Harrison rightfully did not want Ms. Whittier to be dragging him down, and he knew she would be because she would've kept pressing him to help her distribute drugs. You also heard evidence that Mr. Harrison and Ms. Whittier were together at the Zoo Bar on the night of June 5 of this year. You also heard evidence that nobody ever saw Miss Whittier alive after that night. You heard evidence that Ms. Whittier's body was dumped in the alleyway next to Mr. Harrison's apartment. The evidence clearly points to Mr. Harrison murdering Ms. Whittier in the early morning hours of June 6. For this reason, I ask for a finding of guilty. Thank you very much."

It was time for Harper to give the closing statement. It was only fitting she give the closing statement, considering the fact she was the one who shut this case down with her examination of David Harrison.

She approached the jury, and looked at each juror in the eye. "Ladies and gentlemen of the jury, I think you know what happened here. You saw David Harrison. He all but admitted that he killed Adele Whittier, with the purpose of framing his son, because he wanted him to join him behind bars. He needed to make sure he kept an eye on my client because he was shaming him by becoming romantically involved with men and transgendered people. Well, that's not necessarily true. Mr. Harrison was only involved with one man and one transgendered person – and that person was William Page, who became Adele Whittier. Mr. David Harrison clearly found out that his son was dishonoring him by getting involved with a person that he, Mr. David Harrison, found to be sick. He, Mr. David Harrison, is evidently a very hateful man. He especially is hateful against transgendered people."

"So, here's what happened. Mr. David Harrison found out his son, Beck Harrison, was romantically involved with a man and was later on involved with that same man, who was transformed into a woman. Mr. David Harrison found that out and knew that he would have to do something about it. So, from behind bars, he arranged for Ms. Whittier to be murdered and his son framed for it. Granted, his testimony did not establish that, because he was not a cooperative witness. But that's what happened. Mr. David Harrison killed Adele Whittier in order to frame his son, so his son could join him in prison."

"I ask for a finding of not guilty. Thank you very much."

At that, the judge gave the jury instructions about murder one. It was all anti-climatic, however, because everybody knew what would happen.

50 minutes later, the jury was back.

"Has a jury reached a verdict?" Judge Grant asked them.

"We have, Your Honor," the jury foreman said.

"Would the defendant please rise?" Judge Grant said to Beck.

Beck stood up. He stood up proud. He was proud of himself. I was proud of him, too.

"On the count of murder in the first degree, what is the finding of the jury?"

"We find the defendant not guilty."

"Very well. The defendant is free to go."

Beck turned to me and shook my hand. "Thanks. Thank you for taking my case and believing in me. And having patience with me. I haven't been the easiest client, I know that."

I put my hand on his shoulder. "You've been fine. Now, you know what you need to do about Sean Maddow." I lowered my voice, because I didn't want anybody to hear me. "Remember, you don't have to tell them about your involvement. But they deserve to know."

He nodded his head. "I'm gonna do the right thing. I'm getting out of that racket, anyhow. I only did a few jobs for the AB. You know, they'd be pissed at me if I just turned my back on them completely. But, I don't want to do it anymore. They might kill me, but I guess that's just the chance I'll have to take. Because, I realized one thing – I don't want nothing to do with the man on that stand. And that means I'm going to completely turn my back on the AB. There's just no cause to hate like that. No cause at all."

I knew he would be as good as his word. I worried about him, however. He couldn't just leave the AB. He was pretty much stuck with them. He was right – once he renounced them, they might kill him. And that would actually make me very upset. I was starting to be very fond of the kid. He was wayward, mixed up, and, up until recently, too much wanting to please his awful father. But, underneath it all, he wasn't a bad kid at all.

Not at all.

I GOT a new case that Monday morning. It was Silas Porter, one of the wealthiest men in the world. He was accused of killing his socialite wife. He was a billionaire, and could afford the highest-priced attorneys on the globe.

Yet, he wanted me, and only me. Why that was, remained to be seen.

Next in the Kansas City Legal Thrillers series

vinci-books.com/secretslies

A twisted billionaire stands accused of murdering his wife in a sex dungeon inferno.

Silas Porter, a wealthy man with dark secrets, is accused of killing his wife in a sex dungeon inferno. Desperate for the truth, he turns to attorney Damien to unravel the mystery. As Damien investigates, he discovers a family history riddled with mental illness, obsession and tragedy, including the possibility that Silas himself may have set a deadly fire as a child.

Turn the page for a free preview…

Secrets and Lies: Chapter One

I GOT into the office and saw a man sitting on the couch. He was an elegant man - dressed in a high-dollar suit and red silk tie, with wing-tipped leather shoes buffed to a high-gloss shine. He had a head of dark wavy hair and light eyes, like those of Benedict Cumberbatch. He was sitting with his legs crossed, one over the other, and, when I walked in, he glanced at me, but did not smile.

Nor did he get up.

I had no idea why he was sitting there.

I looked over at Pearl quizzically. She knew my expressions and could read what I wanted without my saying a word. She cleared her throat. "Silas Porter," she said, motioning to the man on the couch. "He, uh, didn't have an appointment."

I looked over at the man, who was now staring at me. With those penetrating, super-light eyes and an expression that belied exactly nothing, I felt just a little creeped out. I looked down at my arm and saw the hairs standing on end. In prison, I met guys that gave me the creeps like this one did. They were usually the psychos, the guys who had no conscience and could kill you with a smile on their face. I tended to steer clear of guys like the ones I knew in prison, although I sometimes took them on as clients, as I loved a challenge. Still, I was just a little bit pissed, because the guy had just barged on in the office without an appointment. I had things to do that afternoon. Didn't this guy know how busy attorneys are? Maybe he just didn't care.

"Hello, Mr. Harrington," he said, finally speaking in a booming voice. "I'm very sorry I came to see you without calling ahead."

"Uh, it's okay," I lied. "I have a deposition in an hour, and court appearances after that, so I have a few minutes to talk to you." As I looked at him, I couldn't help but feel there was just something so familiar about his face. I couldn't quite place it. As I stared at him, a vague kernel entered my mind. There was something in the news about Silas Porter. It was something I'd glanced at in the morning before I began my day. I seemed to remember reading something about how he had been arrested for murdering his wife, Ava. The story, however, was hazy, nebulous.

"Mr. Porter," I said to him. "I hope you don't mind, but I need to take a few minutes. I'll call you in when I'm ready to see you." I had no idea why I didn't just throw the guy out of the office, but I had to admit, I knew he probably had the money to pay a big fee and I had kids to feed at home.

I could see in those light eyes a hint of disapproval. It seemed he wanted to speak with me right at that very second, even though I wasn't ready for him at all. He stared at me briefly and put his finger to his cheek. And then he nodded ever-so-slightly. "As you wish," he said curtly.

What the hell? He's going to give me attitude, even

though he was the one inconveniencing me, not the other way around? Also, I couldn't shake the cold feeling I felt being in this guy's presence. I shook my head as I walked towards my office. I got in to the door of my suite, sat down and brought out my newspaper. I scanned it, and it wasn't long before I found the story I was looking for – apparently that elegant man who just addressed me so formally had, to put it mildly, a freaky side to him. At least, according to this paper, he did. The story in the paper was about how Silas apparently killed his wife, but, according to him, he didn't mean to do it.

As I read the article in the newspaper, I decided I probably didn't want to have a thing to do with this guy. Not only because the article portrayed him as abusive to his wife, but also because this case was on the front page, and that meant media attention I just didn't want.

Silas was apparently a billionaire by the age of 32. He had founded a tech firm out in the Silicon Valley five years ago, and it just went public, which made him one of Silicon Valley's newest billionaires. He and his wife, Ava, who apparently came from old money, and was a multimillionaire in her own right, were in Kansas City for a tech conference at the time of Ava's death. Ava's family was from this area, so Silas and Ava apparently maintained a home in the Hallbrook area, a tony area in Leawood, Kansas, where sports stars, CEOs, and other wealthy individuals lived.

I read on and found out a guest house behind the couple's main house apparently burned to the ground with Ava inside. The conflagration was so sudden and violent that Ava's body was burned to the point that there was nothing left of her except for her two hands.

I shuddered as I thought about the possibility that Ava burned to death inside that house. I couldn't think of

The Hate Crime

anything more agonizing than that. I closed my eyes and pictured the searing pain she must have felt as the flames hit her and I shuddered. At the same time, I wondered why Silas would've been charged with murdering her. It sounded like the fire that trapped Ava was accidental.

As I read on, I got the answer to that question. Apparently at the time of the fire, Ava was chained to a wall, and the police found accelerant at the scene, so Silas was also being charged with arson.

Ava was apparently helpless, unable to avoid the flames because she had no means of escaping. After reading this, I immediately prejudged the case. I wouldn't take this guy. No way, no how. Not for all the money in the world. And he had all the money in the world, so he really didn't need me to represent him.

I summoned him into my office and he sat down across from me. True to form, he just stared at me. Waiting for me to speak with him.

"Mr. Porter," I began. "I thank you for coming in here, although I'm not quite sure why you came in here without making an appointment first, but that's neither here nor there. But I'm afraid this is not a case I'm going to want. Now, I would refer you to some other criminal defense attorneys in the area, people I know, but I'm quite sure you have at your disposal access to the most expensive hired guns in the city. I don't think you'll need my referrals."

Silas sat across from me, still not say anything. Then, after a few minutes, he finally spoke. "Mr. Harrington," he began. "I understand you probably have your own views of the case. After all, the media tends to be very one-sided in these things. And, my wife, Ava, her family is very well-to-do. Very old money in the area. They've never liked me. They don't like anybody who's new money. And they're convinced I murdered her in cold blood. They're controlling the story. Of course, I'm changing that today. My publicist is getting in touch with the newspaper and my side of the story will dominate the headlines from now on."

"Well then, I guess you'll be just fine. You'll get some kind of high-dollar lawyer on the case, your publicist will control the narrative, and everything will turn out great." I wondered how his stock was doing. After all, when something like this happens to the CEO of a major multinational corporation, the stock prices usually plunge. If that was the case, the guy probably lost millions of dollars overnight. Of course, losing millions of dollars overnight pales in comparison to losing your freedom and your livelihood, which was what this guy was facing.

"Mr. Harrington," he said. "I don't think you understand. I'm determined I'm going to hire you as my attorney. You are right about one thing – I have access to any lawyer I want. This is the kind of case that can make a career. That said, I have access to lawyers who already have a stellar career. Attorneys who have tried cases much more high-profile than this one. But I want you. Only you."

That was weird. I had no clue why he wanted to hire me so desperately. I had some high-profile cases of my own in the past but they were all local. I'd never been involved with something this high-profile. I certainly was not a hired-gun celebrity attorney in any way, shape or form, which was what this guy probably should've hired. I wasn't a nobody, but I certainly wasn't a somebody either.

It was my turn to stare. "I'm not sure I understand. I'm telling you I don't want the case. Full stop. I've got enough on my plate and I don't want to get involved in something that'll lead to me being hounded by the pap. I'm not quite sure why that message isn't getting through."

The Hate Crime

"I think you will want this case once you hear my side of the story. And please hear me out. That's all I ask of you. An hour of your time, and I think you'll want this case."

"As I said earlier when you first came into the office, I have a deposition in an hour. So –"

"Then I shall return this evening. At what time do you have free in the late afternoon or early evening?"

I sighed. I had to admit to being intrigued on why this guy was so adamant to hire me. And maybe I shouldn't prejudge it so much. I could listen to his story and kick him out the door. I owed him that much.

"I don't like taking clients in the evening because I have two kids at home who need me to feed them and get on them about doing homework and that sort of thing. So…" I sighed. I didn't want this guy. But at the same time, I had to find out why he wanted me so badly, and I had to admit the prospect of being able to charge $500 an hour, and get it with no problem, was a bonus for sure. I hated that I had to be a hired gun who took cases I didn't really want, but at the same time, the kids' private school was not cheap, and both of them wanted to go to Harvard. I knew they both were smart enough to do just that, so I had to put as much money away as possible. My multi-million dollar settlement a few years back would only go so far in today's world.

"So what time can I come back?" he asked me coolly.

I regarded him, not wanting for him to come back at all, yet also feeling something pulling me into this case against my better judgment.

"Come back at 4 o'clock. I can only give you an hour though. After that, I have to head home." I actually had planned on heading home even earlier than 4 o'clock that day, but I supposed I could make some time out for this guy. "I have to warn you though, I'm leaning against taking your case. I just don't want to deal with the publicity, for one thing, but also, I've read the newspaper article about you, and I just don't like to sign up misogynists." I was raised by a woman who attracted nothing but violent misogynists, so I, as a rule, wanted nothing to do with misogynistic men when they showed up in my office wanting me to represent them.

"I assure you I am not a misogynist. No matter what the paper says about me, I assure you I'm not a misogynist. I respect women very much. I will tell you upfront, however, I am into the lifestyle. The alternative lifestyle."

"By lifestyle, I assume you mean you're into BDSM, right?"

"Yes, you are correct about that. I wanted to tell you this right up front because that's a part of my story. I would never intentionally kill my wife. I loved her very much. She and I had a very passionate relationship but it was also based upon mutual respect." When he said that, he had a sad look in his eye, and I almost believed him. It was the first time I'd seen some kind of emotion in his eyes and that encouraged me a bit.

"Okay. I'll see you in a few hours. In the meantime, I have to get prepared for my deposition, so I'm sorry, but I really have to get going."

"Of course. I understand. You have a life and it was rude to drop in on you like this. So thank you for at least being willing to hear my story. I'll see you soon."

At that, he left. And I felt I could breathe. I shook my head, wondering what the hell I was doing. This guy freaked me out, more than anybody had in a long time. And yet I was considering taking him on as a client. What was my problem?

I didn't know what my problem was. I only knew I was

The Hate Crime

somehow getting involved with a situation I didn't want to get involved with. And yet I had a feeling that when all was said and done, he would be my client.

I just hoped I didn't live to regret that. Although I knew I would.

Secrets and Lies: Chapter Two

I GOT BACK from my deposition, and found that Silas was waiting for me once again. This time, he didn't stare at me, but, rather, he actually smiled a little bit. I swallowed hard. "Mr. Porter, come into my office, and I need to get your side of the story."

"Of course." He followed me into my office, and we both sat down while I closed the door behind him.

I got a yellow pad of paper and a pen and started to write. "Okay, here's what I read in the paper. I read your wife was chained to a wall when a fire swept through your dungeon. As I understand it, from reading the newspaper, your dungeon is a structure you have behind your swimming pool. It was formerly used as servant's quarters, from what you told the police, but you currently are using it as your dungeon. Is that correct?"

He nodded. "Yes, that is correct."

"The way she died is partly why I don't want to take this case. I just can't imagine being in her position. Being helpless and not able to do anything and seeing a fire sweep through. I'm sure she died in agony." I had Public Defender cases where I represented drug dealers accused of burning people to death. Those were some of the worst cases I'd ever encountered. Of course, those were also cases I ended up pleading out. I had a feeling I would have to try this case, assuming I took it. Which meant I would get into all the painful details of what happened.

"I assure you my wife did not burn to death. She was dead before the fire swept through the dungeon."

"What do you mean?" If she was dead before the fire got to her, that would be better facts for me. Marginally better, but better nonetheless. "Are you telling me something else killed her besides the fire?"

"Yes, that's what I'm telling you. There was a preliminary autopsy done on the body. However, since my wife's body was severely burned, as she ended up just ashes and bones, there wasn't much that could be ascertained about how she died. You'll find out all of this when you get the file. To tell you the truth, I don't know how my wife died. I have no idea."

I sighed. "Okay, please explain what you mean. Are you saying that –"

"I'm telling you my wife and I were being intimate, and, I will admit, we typically do things that skirt the line of what is safe and what's not. I can also tell you we never crossed that line and never came close to it. For instance, we were involved with body bag bondage. Are you aware of that term?"

"I am." I had a little bit of knowledge about BDSM because I'd once taken a case where a child was in the house when his mother and her boyfriend were involved in the practice. The child's actual father was suing for custody, because he didn't want his son exposed to that in the home.

I had to do as much research as possible on the lifestyle for that case so I felt reasonably informed.

I knew body bag bondage involved putting one's partner into a body bag and suffocating them to the point that they would almost pass out. This act apparently gives the participants some kind of a high. Apparently, whenever you restricted your air in that way, you get lightheaded, which induces mild euphoria. Men often strangled themselves with a belt while they masturbated, and this practice was called auto-erotic asphyxiation. Sometimes they ended up accidentally killing themselves when they did that. Allegedly, the famous actor David Carradine, of *Kung Fu* fame, and Michael Hutchence, the lead singer of INXS, died that way.

"Well, if you're familiar with the concept of body bag bondage, then you know about the level my wife and I went to when we would play. In this case, I had her chained to a wall. That was something we did often. And we were intimate that way." He paused. "She asked me to put a plastic bag over her head, which I often do. I know how long I can do that before it gets dangerous. I timed it perfectly, the way I always have, but, when I took the plastic bag off her head, she was dead."

I made notes as he spoke. "So this was something you two did habitually and it was never a problem before?"

"Right. So I didn't know how she died. I am trained in CPR of course. That was mandatory for both Ava and me - we both had to know how to revive one another if the time came. So I unchained her and was going to perform CPR, but then I saw she completely stopped breathing and I found no pulse. She was dead. I had no idea how. But I wanted to try to revive her anyway, so I went to get the key to the lock for her handcuff. The fire suddenly came out of nowhere and swept through our dungeon. It was a conflagration. I had no idea how it got to be so much of a wildfire in such a short period of time. I don't know where it came from."

"That's the reason why you were charged with her murder - it sounds like there was some kind of accelerant in the fire. Is that what happened?"

He nodded silently. I could see pain in his expression, and the fact he had emotion behind those light eyes made me feel slightly more comfortable with him.

"Yes. That's why I was charged with her murder. Yes, when the investigators came to the house, they found an accelerant. I was barely able to get out of the dungeon myself. I was barely able to outrun the fire. It was that swift. I'm lucky to be alive. But yes, the investigators decided my dungeon burned down because of arson. Because Ava was chained to a wall at the time, they just assumed I burned down my own dungeon while entrapping her because I wanted to kill her. That her parents were pushing the police to charge me with her murder did not help matters any. They've always hated me. They've never thought I was good enough for their daughter. They didn't even know about our lifestyle - they just didn't like me because I came from nothing. I think they wanted her to marry somebody whose last name was Vanderbilt or Carnegie or something along those lines. So when Ava died in such a way, they were pressuring the police to make an arrest. And that's how I got arrested."

I made a note about this. I would have to talk to Ava's parents and find out what the real story was. I needed to find out if it was true that they just didn't like him because he grew up poor. I knew he was telling the truth when he said he didn't grow up wealthy. I had read in the paper that his mother worked as a waitress and an office cleaner and his father worked at Walmart and as a cook. Of course, I wouldn't take him at his word that the only reason why Ava's parents hated him was because he wasn't "good enough" for her. It was entirely possible the newspaper article was true – Silas might've been a wife abuser. I would have to get to the bottom of that before I made a decision or judgment on this case.

For the moment, however, I would have to take him at his word. If he told me the only reason Ava's parents hated him was because he grew up poor, then I would just have to take that as gospel until I found out differently.

"Okay, so Ava's parents were pushing for you to be arrested for her murder."

"Yes. But it wasn't a murder. I still don't know how she died. I have no clue. We were doing our usual playing, and as far as I know, she wasn't even sick." He shook his head. "It was as if she had a heart attack, a massive heart attack, and died. However, she was only 32 years old. And, as far as I know, she did not have a heart problem."

"Are you sure about that? Are you sure she didn't have a heart problem?"

He shifted uncomfortably in his seat. "No, I'm not sure about that." He blinked a few times. "I do know my wife was seeing a doctor at the time she died, however, as far as I know, there was nothing wrong with her."

"What do you mean, as far as you know, there was nothing wrong with her?" I wondered how much Silas really knew about his wife. It was entirely possible she had a heart problem but didn't tell him about it. After all, if she enjoyed participating in bondage games with Silas, maybe she didn't want to tell him she had a heart issue - maybe she figured if she told him about her heart issue, he wouldn't play those games with her. That would be a reason for her to hide any kind of health issues from him.

"Exactly what I said. I don't believe she had any health issues. However, I'm not positive about that. I would always ask her if there were health issues I needed to know about and she always told me she was fine and healthy." He shook his head. "That said, I suspected maybe there was something wrong with her. I never saw any prescriptions around the house. But when I got back from Europe, I noticed she had lost a lot of weight and seemed very tired and fatigued. I guess it's possible she was suffering from some kind of heart issue, or some other kind of undisclosed health issue, and that's what killed her."

"But you never saw any prescriptions, correct?"

"That is correct."

I bounced my pen up and down on the page, as I thought about what he was telling me. "Did you travel with her?"

"I used to. I used to travel with her all the time. As you probably know, I travel quite a bit for my work. In fact, I was overseas in Europe for six months. I had just returned when this happened. From Europe that is. And she did not go with me."

"She didn't go with you? So I guess it's possible she was suffering from some kind of health issues and you might not have known about it because you were overseas."

"That is definitely a possibility." He clenched his jaw. Tapped his fingers on the desk. "I suppose you could get her medical records, and find out if there was anything wrong with her. There must've been something. There had to have been some reason why she died the way she did. All I can tell you is she was dead before the fire swept in and I did not do anything to bring about her death."

I knew the prosecutors probably were aware that Silas and Ava were involved in BDSM. And, because of that, they probably reasonably thought maybe Ava died during some kind of hard-core playing, unless they just assumed Silas had set the fire in his own home to kill his wife.

"Now, let's get back to what the newspapers say about your relationship with Ava. It indicated you were abusive with her. Is that true?"

He straightened up in his chair and glared at me. "I told you that was not true. I told you that earlier. In no way, shape or form was I abusive to her. Some people don't understand alternative lifestyles – they think people involved in these lifestyles are abusive to one another. Or, especially, the man is abusive to the woman because the woman likes to be beaten, or whipped, or degraded. By the way, our relationship did not involve any of those things. I did not whip her, I did not beat her, and I did not degrade her. I did not humiliate her. We were more into bondage than anything else. The body bags, the chains, the feeling of latex. She enjoyed being confined. I sometimes put her into a small box, the size of a coffin. I would put her in there for a very set period of time. Just like I would put her into a body bag for a very set period of time. I knew my limitations and knew hers as well. And I've never come close to the point where I would have accidentally killed her. You have to trust me on this. So when she died, there was nothing I did that brought it about."

"You do know I'm going to be speaking with her friends, and her parents, and people who were aware of her situation with you. I need to know from you what kind of story I'm going to hear from them. What kind of words am I going to hear from her friends and family and people whom she held dear?"

"Her parents will tell you I was abusive to her. That's what they told the newspaper. But you have to understand, they have their own agenda. They want to see me fry. They're convinced I murdered my wife and did it in cold blood. There are a variety of reasons why they are so convinced about that. So, fair warning, that's the kind of story you'll get from them. As for her friends, I don't know what kind of story they'll give you. I don't know what Ava told them about her relationship with me. I don't think they believed I was abusive to her, however. They have no reason to believe that."

"But her parents have a reason to believe that? Why would they have reason to believe that but her friends don't?"

"Because they have an agenda." He rolled his eyes. He tapped his fingers on the desk and took a deep breath. "She had bruises."

I made a note of this. "She had bruises? But you told me you didn't beat her. So why would she have bruises?"

"I didn't beat her. And that's the truth. However, other people beat her."

"What's that supposed to mean?"

Silas made a steeple with his hands. "I allowed my wife to stray. She had very singular desires and fantasies, and I couldn't fulfill them. I had a problem with beating and whipping her, but she needed that in her life, so I allowed her to see people who would do that for her. And she allowed me to see other people as well."

Grab your copy...
vinci-books.com/secretslies

About the Author

Rachel Sinclair was a criminal defense attorney for eleven years, so she doesn't scare easily. She graduated from the University of Missouri-Kansas City School of Law in 1998, and worked for the Public Defender's Office for several years before striking out on her own. She currently lives in San Diego, California, with her boyfriend, Joey, and her two fur babies, Annie and Toby. In her spare time, she likes to read, bicycle all over town, Boogie Board at the beach, and watch trashy television.

www.ingramcontent.com/pod-product-compliance
Lightning Source LLC
LaVergne TN
LVHW030241250326
834688LV00047B/1748